Blood on the Roses

Bonus: *Equinox,* a short story by Robert Hays

Robert Hays

Thomas-Jacob Publishing, LLC
USA

Blood on the Roses

Bonus: *Equinox*, a short story by Robert Hays

Copyright 2011 Robert Hays

Published by Thomas-Jacob Publishing, LLC
ThomasJacobPublishing@gmail.com

ISBN-13: 978-0-9963884-6-7

ISBN-10: 0-9963884-6-X

Library of Congress Control Number: 2016912062
Thomas-Jacob Publishing, LLC, Deltona, Florida

First printing Prairiescape Books February 2014

Second printing Thomas-Jacob Publishing, LLC July 2015

Third printing Thomas-Jacob Publishing, LLC August 2016

Printed in the United States of America

Dedication

This book is dedicated to the most beautiful person ever produced by the American South, Mary Corley Hays of Columbia, South Carolina.

One will rarely err if extreme actions be ascribed to vanity, ordinary actions to habit, and mean actions to fear.

–Friedrich Wilhelm Nietzsche

Blood on the Roses

by

Robert Hays

Chapter 1

The Tennessee Bend Motel squatted on a level ribbon of land carved into the side of a steep Appalachian ridge like a thin slice pared from a luscious apple. All around it, the trees were well into their September colors, leaves on the tall oaks and hickories ranging from muted browns to brilliant reds and oranges mixed with scattered splotches of lingering summer green. There was a busy highway in front, but it was at the bottom of the slope, some hundred yards distant. It carried traffic heading north from Knoxville and south from Kingsport and was an everyday path for the constant comings and goings of locals.

The ample grounds of the Tennessee Bend posed a stark contrast to its surroundings, lacking any sign of formal landscaping. Shortleaf pine and black oak trees appeared to have been planted haphazardly to provide shade for chosen areas of the parking lot, and the only touch of elegance was a rose garden that stretched across the crown of the incline, along the edge of parking spaces adjacent to the front row of motel rooms. The summer roses that welcomed visitors still were vibrant and from inside the lobby, looking down the slope toward the east, the garden made an appealing foreground in a picture-postcard view of Cherokee Lake.

Although only a narrow neck of the lake was visible, the scene was a stunning sample of the region's ubiquitous natural beauty. The Bays Mountains and the foothills of the Great Smokies lay in the distance beyond the lake to the east, while to the west the forested hills rising behind the motel gave way in turn to the razor-spined, peakless pleats of the scenic Clinch Mountains, which stretched northward toward the Cumberlands.

Rachel Feigen was tired when she checked into the Tennessee Bend, after the long drive from Baltimore, and unsure where to begin. She already had a deep emotional attachment to this assignment and had come to face it with a sense of dread. This one did not hold much prospect for a pleasant outcome.

Not that Feigen was accustomed to happy endings. She had just spent a grueling three weeks piecing together a story on the effects of the Supreme Court's *Brown v. Board of Education* ruling, and was left discouraged if not downright despondent by what she'd found. In the several months since the court struck down "separate but equal" as a legal basis for racial segregation in the schools, little had been done to implement the court's decree. This was not what she had hoped to find.

Her disappointment in the outcome of the investigation pleased Bill Skyles, her editor at the Associated Press. Skyles demanded absolute impartiality when his reporters' work went to print, but he wanted them to understand and feel the impact of their stories.

Skyles was sufficiently impressed with Feigen's performance on the story to hand her a new assignment that he called the most important one he had. He said it could be her biggest challenge since joining the AP national reporting team and she had dug into the story just deep enough to see that he was right.

Feigen had barely managed to get three days off. Skyles wanted her to get onto the story immediately. She was eager to tackle this new project, but she had an accumulation of personal things to attend to and she wanted at least one day when she could sleep in and have nothing to do. Reluctantly, Skyles gave in.

Friday was the first of her precious days of freedom. She slept late, took a long, luxurious shower, and had breakfast at lunchtime. Then she called her father in New York. As usual, Judge Max Feigen skipped the pleasantries and got straight to the point.

"Your series on school integration was very perceptive," he told her. "I'm proud of you, Rachel. But not surprised. I always knew you'd make a good journalist."

"I owe it all to you, Daddy. We grew up thinking the *New York Times* was the gospel and journalists were the last best hope for the world—after the law, of course. You never finished your first cup of coffee until you'd read every word of the front section of the *Times*."

Her father chuckled. "I still do pretty much the same thing, but it takes me quite a while longer. My eyes aren't as good as they used to be. That's one of the prices of old age, I'm afraid."

"You can't imagine how hard it is for me to associate old age with you," she told him. "To me, you're still the stern, uncompromising judge who must have scared the hell out of bad guys when you wore your robes and then turned into a loveable old softy when you got home to Morrie and me."

"That was the happiest time of my life, Rachel, but we have to live in the present. It seems as if I've been retired forever. Your mother and I just rattle around in this big old empty house."

There was a clear note of melancholy in his voice. It had been one of her biggest worries that after all the years during which he had put in endless hours keeping up with the law, insisting there was no margin for error in his determination to hand out justice in his courtroom, her father would find retirement difficult. He had told her once that retirement was nothing less than a fast track to senility and he didn't look forward to it.

"But now you have time to read all those books you never could get to before," she said, hoping to give him at least a modest shot of encouragement.

"Yes, of course. And I do more reading than these old eyes are up to. But bring me up to date on you. What kind of story are you off on now? Something in-depth like the school integration story?"

"That's exactly why I called. Have you heard anything about a missing man from Baltimore named Guy Saillot?"

"I don't think so. Who is he?"

"Nobody who's very important, as far as I can tell. But his family is."

"And so what's your story?"

"He's been missing for more than two weeks. He left Baltimore to visit a friend at the University of Tennessee, as I understand it, but he never showed up there. His family is prominent here and the *Sun* has run a couple of stories on it, but the authorities don't seem to be pushing it very hard. Anyway, my editor is sending me to look for him."

"His name sounds French."

"Yes. His father's a big shot with the Franco-American Transatlantic Company's Baltimore office."

"The University of Tennessee, that's in Knoxville?"

"Yes."

Now there was concern in his voice. "There's a lot going on in the South these days, Rachel. This isn't going to be dangerous, is it?"

"I don't see how it could be," she answered, trying her best to sound confident. "But I'll call you every few days and let you know what's happening. Okay?"

"You be sure and do that, angel. And please take good care of yourself."

Feigen felt guilty for not having told her father what she already knew about the Guy Saillot case. But she still held out some slight hope that she was mistaken in her first impressions of Anton Schuler, the FBI agent in charge. There was no way she could have said much without getting into what Schuler had told her, and being as perceptive as he was her father would have picked up on her doubts in an instant.

She also had deliberately avoided mentioning another big thing coming up in her life, one that was much more pleasant. It had been a mantra of the Feigen family for as long as anyone could remember that pride in personal possessions, no matter what they were, was selfish. She would have been embarrassed to let him know that she was as excited as a little girl at a birthday party because she was about to get her first new car.

Feigen had set her heart on one of the new 1955 Chevrolets the instant she saw the line introduced in a *Life* magazine advertisement. Her old Plymouth was just about done for and Skyles had recommended she see Mike Sodeman, a salesman he said wouldn't talk down to her just because she was a woman. Mike turned out to be an agreeable young man and, true to Skyles's promise, he began at the outset to talk about things like horsepower and V-8 engines and transmissions and not about colors and upholstery fabrics. He helped make her purchase easier than she expected and the car would be ready for her to pick up first thing in the morning.

For now, though, she needed to push aside all thoughts of the new car and her father and Feigen family mantras and whatever, and force herself to refocus on the Guy Saillot story. This meant going back over her notes and looking for any detail she might have missed. Agent Anton Schuler had irritated her to the level that she felt lucky to have any information at all.

It had been clear from the minute she walked into his office that Agent Schuler was not especially concerned about finding this particular missing person. "The FBI has a lot of important things to do," he told her flatly, "and I'll give it to you straight. Looking for a queer little Frenchman who probably found a boyfriend and decided to hide out for a while and have fun isn't real high on our list."

His attitude had taken Feigen by surprise. It took her a moment to recover and get back on track with the questions she wanted to ask, now even more important.

"Who was he visiting in Knoxville?"

"We have not released that information," Agent Schuler said matter-of-factly. "It wouldn't do you any good, anyway. He says Frenchie never got there."

"He called him 'Frenchie'?"

"He may have called him 'Darling' for all I know. The point is, we have checked him out and his story holds up. He is not involved."

Feigen's patience was at an end. "If Guy Saillot weren't homosexual, would you just assume he had found a girlfriend and was shacked up somewhere, not worth your time to look for? That's a pathetic way to operate, Mister Schuler. I'd expect more from the FBI."

With that, she had stormed out of his office.

It took only a few minutes for her to go over her skimpy notes. Guy Saillot was twenty years old. He was a slight man, barely five feet, four inches tall and weighing only about a hundred and thirty pounds. He had a sallow complexion, green eyes, and black hair. Nothing on what he might have been wearing, nothing about his habits—except his sexuality. The FBI was not even sure how long the young Frenchman had been missing.

Feigen had no intention of working on her free time, and she had two more days off before she left for Tennessee. But she could not get Guy Saillot out of her mind. When she couldn't stand it any longer she picked up the phone and dialed the number of the Saillot home for probably the twentieth time. This time there was an answer.

"This is the Saillot residence. Hello."

Surprised finally to hear someone on the other end of the line, Feigen fumbled for words. "I'm sorry," she said, "may I ask who I'm speaking with?"

"This is Marie Saillot."

"Miss Saillot, or missus, my name is Rachel Feigen. I work for the Associated Press and I'm doing a story about Guy. Are you a member of the family?"

There was a lengthy pause. "I'm Guy's mother," the woman said then. "How can I help you, Miss Feigen?"

Feigen was nearly breathless with anticipation. "Missus Saillot, would it be possible for me to come and talk with you? Anything you can tell me about Guy might help us find him. Anything at all. I've talked with the police and the FBI, and my editor is sending me to Tennessee to see if I can track down something they may be missing. I truly apologize for intruding on your privacy, but you could be very helpful to us if I could have just a few minutes of your time."

After another pause, but this time a shorter one, Guy Saillot's mother consented. Could Feigen come by her house tomorrow afternoon? And please don't bring a photographer.

Feigen skipped dinner and made a list of questions for tomorrow. There was so much she didn't know. Marie Saillot obviously was her best hope, yet she felt guilty for invading a mother's private grief. Surely to have a son missing, a son who apparently had never been in the least bit of trouble, would be as difficult as anything a mother could face. The uncertainty must be terrible. On the one hand Feigen was eager to learn more about Guy Saillot, the person, but on the other she dreaded looking into the eyes of Marie.

She hardly slept that night. She had interviewed people faced with tragedy before, and it always left her with a hurt inside that sometimes lasted for days. This one might be the worst.

In the morning she got up early, eager for her meeting with Marie Saillot and mildly excited about picking up her new car. She had a quick breakfast, then got into her old Plymouth for the last time and drove to Coastal Chevrolet, a highly advertised suburban dealership where it looked like there were dozens of new automobiles on a spacious lot bounded by red and white pennants on tall poles. She was determined to keep her composure and act as if this was all routine and not her first time, but this might be difficult.

Mike Sodeman hurried out to meet her, welcomed her with a big smile, and said her car was waiting. They went directly to the gleaming BelAir hardtop faux convertible Mike had ordered for her.

On her first visit to the dealer, Feigen had looked at a car like this except that it was two-toned. It had a cream-colored top and red bottom and she told Mike she wanted one just like it except all cream. She'd paid no attention to the interior. When her car came it was bright red inside and she had been very much put out with herself for such a foolish oversight. But now she liked it. Others might find it gaudy, but she preferred to think of it as a flamboyant expression of her good taste.

Mike handed her the keys. In a final gesture of good salesmanship, he had tuned the car radio to her favorite station and the metallic notes of Perez Prado's melodic and cheerful instrumental, "Cherry Pink and Apple Blossom White," drifted from the speaker. Feigen managed to stay calm until she drove off the lot, back onto the highway. Then she pumped her fist in the air and shouted, "Yes, Rachel, it's *yours!*" So much for the Feigen mantra.

When it came time for her to meet Marie Saillot she still was in high spirits, although it was no longer because of the new car. She was at last going to learn more about Guy. Not merely Guy Saillot the missing person, but Guy Saillot the individual human being—this mother's son. She was barely aware that she was driving a new Chevrolet as she set out for her appointment.

Chapter 2

Guy's father was supposed to be a prosperous man. Feigen was surprised at the modest neighborhood where the Saillot family home was located. But the lawn was well kept and there was a lovely, though tiny, formal garden at one side of the house. Marie Saillot met her at the door. She was a small woman, fair-skinned nearly to the point of paleness, with long ebony hair and beautiful emerald-green eyes that cried out the unspoken hurting of a mother's deepest fears. She looked as if she had not slept for a month.

"I am Guy's mother," she said. Feigen introduced herself and expressed her sympathy.

The Saillot home was tastefully furnished and immaculate. There were oil paintings comparable to the work of the French masters on the walls and exotic rugs on the floors. And fresh cut flowers in lovely vases.

Feigen got straight to the point of her visit. What could Marie tell her about her missing son?

Marie Saillot's voice was shaky as she began. "Guy is a gentle soul who would never hurt anyone. I can't understand how anybody would ever want to hurt him. He has lots of friends here, you know, and I was surprised that he wanted to go to Tennessee in the first place. But it was supposed to be for only three or four days and now it's been more than two weeks."

"Was he in good spirits when he left?"

"Guy is always in good spirits. He is such a happy person and he's interested in almost everything. I remember him saying once, when he was about fifteen, that he didn't really want to grow up because he had no idea what he wanted to do when he was an adult. That wasn't a negative thing, Miss Feigen. He wanted to do it all."

"And he's in college?"

"Yes, at the University of Maryland. Except that he had taken a semester off to try and decide exactly where he was heading before he accumulated too many credits that might be wasted. He started as a music major and now he thinks maybe he wants to go into business. I know that may sound wishy-washy to anyone who doesn't know him, but that's Guy. He is good at everything he's ever tried. He got interested in business last summer when he worked in his father's company."

Marie Saillot seemed to be getting more at ease as she talked.

Feigen asked her, though she already knew, "What kind of business is Mister Saillot in?"

"It's the shipping business. The Franco-American Transatlantic Company, a French company you probably wouldn't know about. He's in charge of the American division. They have offices down at the port."

"How long have you lived in Baltimore?"

"Almost ten years. We came here shortly after the war. Guy—I didn't tell you, but he's our only child—Guy has spent his growing up years here in Baltimore. Right from the beginning he had lots of friends. They couldn't pronounce his name and he told them to call him 'Gee Sailboat.' We still try to visit La Havre at least once a year, but Guy considers Baltimore home."

"He does speak French, though?"

"Yes, of course he does. He speaks and writes beautifully in both French and English."

"Missus Saillot," Feigen said, "I'm very grateful for everything you've told me. I only have a few more questions. Do you know who he was supposed to visit in Knoxville?"

Marie Saillot nodded. "Yes. A friend of his named Mark Kinder. Mark's actually from Maryland somewhere, and Guy knew him in school. I think Mark went to Tennessee for graduate study, but I can't be certain about that."

"Have you talked to him? Mark Kinder, I mean."

"Yes, I called him the first thing. He said Guy never got there."

"And you believe him—no reason to question what he says?"

"I'm sure he's telling the truth."

"Can you describe Guy's car for me?"

"He drives a Ford. A two-tone green sedan."

Feigen hesitated. This was the kind of question that she always hated to ask, especially of a mother. But she had to do it. "Missus Saillot, does Guy have any bad habits that might get him into trouble—does he ever drink heavily, or gamble, or anything like that?"

"No. We always have wine with dinner, but Guy hardly ever drinks his. He doesn't drink alcohol, or even smoke. But . . ." Now it was Marie Saillot who was hesitant. "Maybe you know this already, but Guy is homosexual."

"Yes, I knew," Feigen said. "Is he open about it?"

"He accepts it for what it is. But he doesn't behave in a way that should lead to trouble. Do you think that might have something to do with all this?"

Feigen shook her head. "I certainly hope not. I'm truly sorry to have to put you through this, Missus Saillot. I know how painful it must be for you. It's just that anything you can tell me might help us find Guy. I know that you have talked with the FBI—Agent Schuler? Is there anything you can think of that he didn't ask about or you didn't think of that might be helpful? Anything at all?"

Tears welled up in Marie Saillot's eyes. "They just don't know my son," she said softly. "He is so good to everyone. He wants to understand the world and make it better. If you read his journal—"

"Excuse me," Feigen interrupted. "Guy keeps a journal? Do you know where it might be?"

"Oh, yes. He has it with him. He always has it with him. And he always carries a pen and a little notebook to write things down when he thinks of something or sees something interesting. He would never have left home without his journal."

"And you never heard from him at all after he left for Knoxville?"

"Oh, yes, I did. He sent a postcard. He said the country down there was beautiful and he was enjoying his trip."

"Did Agent Schuler take that postcard?"

"No. The agent didn't see it. He didn't ask me the question you just did."

"Missus Saillot, this could be very important. Could I please see the card?"

Marie Saillot excused herself and was gone from the room for a few minutes. When she returned, she handed Feigen a picture post-card that carried a handwritten note, "This is where I stayed tonight. I will be in Knoxville tomorrow. Love to all, Guy."

On the front of the card was a picture of the Tennessee Bend Motel. A caption included no post office address but located the en-terprise at "Half way between Kingsport and Knoxville on U.S. Route 11W, at the gateway to Cherokee Lake."

"It's postmarked August twenty-seventh."

"Yes. That's two days after he left."

Feigen carefully copied the information from the postcard in her reporter's notebook.

"Missus Saillot," she said then, "as soon as I leave here I want you to call Agent Schuler at the FBI and tell him about this. It's very important. Will you do that?"

"Yes."

Feigen thanked her profusely, expressed her sympathy again, and promised to be in touch. As she drove back to her apartment, she felt somewhat more optimistic about the prospects for finding Guy Saillot. She was eager to get started. Taking another day off sud-denly looked like a waste of time. That night she packed, and early Sunday morning she left for Tennessee.

Chapter 3

The Tennessee Bend Motel was owned and managed by Barney Vidone, a short but husky man with broad shoulders and coal-black hair and wide-set dark eyes who loved east Tennessee and had never considered living anywhere else. He often complained that Tennessee in 1955 was not the Tennessee he used to know, that the wartime industry had brought in too many people who came from outside the South—somewhat ironic in that his own Southern roots did not run deep.

Barney Vidone was a worrier. He worried about the rising costs of running his business, of course, but there were other things as well. Social issues like America's declining moral standards, the lack of civility among today's youth, and what to do for all the men who had come home from the war in Korea with broken bodies and troubled minds. He had seen combat himself and always held men in uniform in high esteem.

But his biggest concern these days was his fear of what might happen to the South now that the government said colored children and white children would have to go to school together. To Barney Vidone, how the South ran its schools was no affair of outsiders.

Although he was proud of his establishment, Barney held no illusions as to the Tennessee Bend's rating among first class places to stay. He freely confessed to fellow beer drinkers at Big John's Place that it was getting somewhat shabby and needed at least superficial sprucing up and said someday he would bring all the rooms up to the same high standard as Room 10. He had boasted often enough that

Room 10 was a masterpiece of his own unique design and craftsmanship, but never hinted at the dark and ugly secret hidden within its walls.

If pressed for a timetable, Barney explained that it was hard to justify spending money for improvements that were merely cosmetic. On many nights all thirty-six of his single-room units were filled. His place was handily located for deer hunters in season and Cherokee Lake fishermen and travelers from the northeast on their way to or from certain parts of the South.

Hunters and fishermen who reserved rooms at the Tennessee Bend generally considered their accommodations adequate, but travelers often found things to complain about. Unhappy guests were referred to Effie Catlin. Effie was a woman with graying hair and kind hazel eyes that made her look like everyone's favorite aunt. She listened patiently to all grievances and said she was sorry. That was as far as Barney allowed her to go; refunds were out of the question.

Barney Vidone liked having people under his control. Once, after he'd had a few beers at Big John's, he compared himself to the overseer on an antebellum plantation. "I have good workers who don't really need many direct orders," he bragged, "but they sure know who's the boss and they're not about to give me any trouble."

No one mentioned the number of workers Barney had. With housekeeping duties contracted to a firm that brought its cleaning women to the motel every afternoon on a bus, Effie Catlin and a handyman named George were his only employees. Effie had been a fixture at the Tennessee Bend from the day it opened for business. The former owner recommended her to Barney and he was happy to keep her on; she knew a lot more about running the place than he did. This was a decision he'd never regretted.

Effie's competence was balanced by the hard fact that George couldn't handle much beyond simple chores. He spent most of his time taking care of the grounds, and just now he was on hands and knees, pulling grass and weeds in the rose garden. He straightened up and smiled, as if some sixth sense told him the boss was watching, then quickly went back to work once it was clear that Barney did not need him for something else.

Barney stood in the motel parking lot with Bishop Collins and Harlan MacElroy. He nudged Bishop with his elbow and nodded toward his handyman. "Look at George up there," he said. "He works like a slave and never gives me any trouble."

"Yeah, well, just be sure you don't pay him too much," Bishop replied. "We don't want them boys to start thinking they're worth more than they are."

"You needn't worry about George," Barney assured him. "He knows his place."

Barney's connection with George went back a good many years. George was one of his playmates when he was little, when the Vidone family was poor white trash and lived a long way back in the woods and his father competed with black men for work at the sawmill and wherever else a low-paying job might pop up. His father was a hard worker with a young wife and five children—Barney was in the middle—but never found a steady job. They might have gone hungry at times except that the plentiful rabbits and squirrels made for easy hunting and an occasional deer and now and then even a 'possum showed up on the Vidone kitchen table.

Barney felt good about giving George a job. It seemed obvious to him that his handyman would have a hard time finding work anywhere else. He paid George less than the minimum wage, but let him live free in a comfortable room at the motel so he'd be available at all hours.

"I expect he'd work for me for nothing," Barney said rather loudly, to make sure the point got across to Bishop and Harlan. Their opinions mattered to him and he wanted them to be impressed with George's loyalty.

Effie complained that Barney spent too much time with Bishop and Harlan. The pair stopped by several times a month and drank Effie's coffee and told stories Barney had heard before. She said they were a bad influence and she wished they would stay away. Barney liked them. Bishop and Harlan tended to view the world about the same way he did, and even though the trio's discussions were wide ranging and often got into areas that none of them knew anything about, there was very little likelihood of a serious disagreement.

Barney assumed that Effie was watching at this very minute, from inside the front office. He could almost feel her disapproving eyes on him and his two friends as they talked. He didn't think she was able to read lips, not from that distance anyway, but she seemed to have a knack for sensing what was going on. Woman's intuition, probably.

Just to make sure, Barney kept his back turned to the office. This was a serious conversation and he did not particularly appreciate Effie's surveillance.

Bishop Collins—Bishop was his given name, not a title—usually did most of the talking. Bishop was a pudgy man with a round, pallid face and gray eyes so pale they might have been colorless. He had large, beefy hands and kept his head cleanly shaved to hide the fact that he was as bald as an egg except for slight fringes of red hair just above his ears.

Barney Vidone didn't pay much attention to appearances. He considered Bishop Collins one of the smartest men he'd ever met.

Harlan MacElroy, on the other hand, never was likely to gain much recognition for his intellectual capacity. He was a handsome man, a couple of inches over six feet tall and muscular, with a nice face enhanced by his ruddy outdoors complexion. It was a standing joke among people who knew him that he was a perfect example of nature's balance. "The Lord gave Harlan his good looks to make up for his lack of smarts," they'd say, and usually throw in a few good stories to back up their keen perception.

Barney and Bishop Collins were religious men. Harlan rarely had been inside a church and never had given much thought to whether there was a supreme being or not.

Bishop was a mainstay in the Appalachian Church of the Living God, where his fellow members gave him most of the credit for a successful fundraising drive that put money in the bank for a new auditorium. Groundbreaking was scheduled in a few months and there was a move afoot to get a fancy bronze plaque engraved with Bishop's name displayed prominently above the front door.

Although he hadn't mentioned it to anyone, as soon as the new building was done Bishop planned to lead a movement to get rid of the pastor and bring in a new man whose theology was closer to his own. Pastor Tim believed that Christians should preach to Jews the same as they did to other non-Christians and seek to convert them to Christianity. This was a view that Bishop found thoroughly distasteful.

Barney Vidone didn't go to church anymore, but he still tried to live up to the teachings of Preacher Jonathan Ward. Although his father and mother had been staunch Catholics in the strict Italian tradition, there was no Catholic church anywhere near after they moved to Tennessee and with no priest to answer to they soon lost all interest in religion. Young Barney started going to meetings at the Walnut Ridge Primitive Baptist Church an hour's walk down in the valley and soon learned that his only hope of making it into heaven was to devote his life to doing God's work. And God's work, according to Preacher Ward, centered on preserving the white Christian way of life.

Barney looked up to Preacher Ward. At one time he considered becoming a preacher himself, but he doubted that he ever could be as effective a messenger for God as Preacher Ward was and there also was some question as to whether he actually had been called to the gospel. Preacher Ward said a man ought to hear the voice of God calling him, like he did the day God caused an accident at the sawmill in which his right arm was severed and his left arm mangled. In the end, Barney's lack of confidence on both questions caused him to give up the idea of following in Jonathan Ward's footsteps.

But he'd never forgotten Preacher Ward's passionate sermons. He gave Preacher Ward credit for setting his moral compass and he was concerned every day about working his way toward heaven.

Given all that he had done to carry out the fiery little preacher's teachings, he took comfort in the fact that he never had been a racist. There were plenty in the community who were, but he never had understood that point of view. He did not hate black men and he found many of the colored women to be quite attractive.

And the little nigger children were fun to watch—their happy songs and dances, the way their mothers dressed them up for church on Sunday, the way they stepped aside and made way for their elders, the way they ran and played and never acted like they cared that they didn't have bicycles and wagons and other things the white children had.

He seldom made a point of it anymore, but in the past Barney often had told how he played with the colored kids when he was little and got along with them just fine. He liked them and he was pretty sure they liked him. And unlike the nigger men and women, the little ones always knew their place.

In Barney's view, the world was filled with all kinds of human trash. Niggers and Jews were at the top of the list, of course, but there were lots of immoral white folks, too. If a white man did things against God's natural law he was just as vile as any colored man or

Jew. And although Barney was rarely as eager as Bishop Collins and Harlan were for overt action, he was not one to look the other way when evil behavior took place right in front of his eyes. God would not forget such failures.

Barney had first come to know Bishop Collins when they both stood up against formation of a local chapter of the KKK. He knew the Klan had done good things, but he didn't always agree with their tactics. And Bishop was interested in keeping local control over action on local problems. He said Klansmen took orders from higher ups who didn't necessarily understand things the way men like him and Barney would.

"You and me could do a better job of keeping scum in its place around here, and we wouldn't have to wear no sheets over our heads," Bishop said. Barney bought into Bishop's way of thinking right on the spot.

There had been times when he questioned the earnestness of Bishop Collins's dedication, though. Sometimes it looked as though Bishop took pleasure in the meaner-spirited things which Barney himself detested. Harlan, on the other hand, simply went along to get along. No one ever had expected much of Harlan MacElroy.

Harlan, for his part, had no doubt that his life had taken a turn for the better since he started hanging around with Barney Vidone and Bishop Collins. People seemed to look up to Bishop Collins, and Barney was a prominent businessman whose Tennessee Bend Motel had been written up a year or so ago in a tourist brochure published by the State of Tennessee. He was proud to be associated with both men, but if he ever had to choose between them he felt a greater loyalty to Bishop Collins. He still wondered whether he'd done the right thing helping Barney that time without consulting Bishop. But Barney said don't tell anyone, and Harlan promised he wouldn't. Once he had given his word he was bound to keep it.

Harlan never had been much of a success at the things he considered important, except for one—shooting. He was proud of his marksmanship and would bet money there wasn't a better shot in the county. Bishop Collins had told people all over that "Harlan can nick a gnat's nuts at two hundred yards," which Harlan considered the highest compliment he'd ever had.

Other than shooting, Harlan didn't have much to brag about.

Scratching out a living as a hog farmer was hard work and there was never much of a reward for his labor. He appreciated Bishop giving him a job at the sawmill two or three days a month. He worked hard to make sure he earned the few dollars Bishop paid him, and he always tried to make sure that Bishop noticed how hard he worked.

Number one on the list of things Harlan wanted to be good at was making money, and number two was having people look up to him. He used to think that if he had money the being looked up to would come naturally, but his association with Bishop Collins had given him reason to reconsider this. Bishop had money, yes, but Harlan had seen how people looked up to Bishop because he was a leader, a man who got things done.

Harlan had been trying to figure out exactly what made Bishop Collins a leader. He believed that if he could imitate Bishop and become a leader himself, people would look up to him, too, even though they never had before. If he became a leader he could get things done the way Bishop did and if he could get things done he might make more money. He therefore lived in hope that his best days still were to come.

He didn't dwell on it much, but there hadn't been too many good days in Harlan's life. His mama died bringing him into the world and nobody ever knew who his daddy was. He was raised to the age of thirteen by Papa and Grandma Puckett, two people he would always remember as being among the vilest humans God ever put on this green earth.

He remembered Papa Puckett, his mama's great uncle as best he could sort things out, as a giant of a man who often was drunk by noon—and a man who hated kids. Papa resented being stuck with Harlan and never missed a chance to make this clear. Harlan could not remember Papa ever saying a kind or gentle word.

Grandma Puckett was even older than Papa, a frail spit of a woman who seemed to feel put upon every morning she woke up alive. Her only hope was to escape her hard, miserable life with Papa and go on home to be with her Lord.

Harlan did have at least a few good memories of Grandma. She would never let him go hungry. She would cut down Papa's old overalls so that Harlan could wear them without the legs dragging the ground and she'd tear off scraps from old newspapers to put in the bottom of his shoes when the soles wore completely through. She said he would need the clothes in case he ever decided to go to school.

Once a week, after she had washed all their clothes and sheets and towels and the like, Grandma would save the wash water and put Harlan in the tub for his bath. She'd take a rough washrag and a shaving off the bar of harsh laundry soap and scrub him good. This went on until he was old enough that his manhood began to show, and although Grandma always acted like she enjoyed what was on display, Harlan was embarrassed.

He took to hiding in the woods until she gave up and dumped the wash water. Sometimes, when he got to stinking too much, he would go down to the creek and bathe. Handfuls of sand took the place of soap.

Like Papa, Grandma always made clear that she never wanted Harlan and her life would be much easier without him. He could never tell if she really meant it.

Harlan recalled keenly the cool spring morning when Grandma Puckett finally got her wish and passed away. They said it was the consumption. Papa's response was a four-day drunk that ended up in a fall down a steep cliff. He left chunks of flesh, lots of blood, and even bits of his brain tissue splattered over several sharp limestone outcroppings that he bounced off of on his way down.

Harlan remembered all this very clearly, also. He recalled worrying that he was supposed to be sad over the loss of the only family he had, when all he felt was a great sense of relief. He was free.

Now, he was blessed with a wife and two beautiful little girls, and Harlan liked to think that Bishop Collins and Barney Vidone were almost like brothers.

Bishop Collins liked having Harlan MacElroy around. He'd be the first to admit that Harlan was not the brightest star in the universe, but Harlan was loyal. Loyalty meant a lot to Bishop. He had a great deal of confidence that both Harlan and Barney were devoted to the cause, but if push came to shove he had more faith in Harlan to do whatever needed to be done.

The cause, for Bishop, was clear-cut. It was to preserve white supremacy forever. This called for keeping colored people, Jews, Asians, and anybody else who was not pure Caucasian Christian in their place. And their place was separate from him and his kind, the further the better. It went without saying that he and Barney Vidone were on the same page when it came to concern about "outsiders."

Given his role as a father, a leading businessman, and a leader in the local Christian community, Bishop Collins felt strongly that he was the one to lead the critical battle against changes in the way of life he believed in. If there was anyone who exemplified this way of life more perfectly than he did, he had yet to find them.

Bishop considered himself fortunate to have been brought up right. His father ran a small grocery store and his mother worked as a scrub nurse at the hospital. He'd often heard his father complain about the niggers who ran up big grocery bills that were hard to collect, but even more often the ire had been aimed at the Jews who controlled the food warehouses and the distribution system and raked off most of the profit right from the top. All they had to do, Luther Collins said, was count the money and cook the books, while he spent twelve hours a day packing heavy cases of canned goods around, stocking the shelves, sweeping floors, and dealing with customers who were never satisfied.

Bishop Collins and his three younger brothers had led good lives. They all went to school as long as they wanted to, could go hunting almost any time, and enjoyed the affection of both their parents and the two remaining grandparents. The Collins family never missed church on Sunday and stayed together as a tight-knit unit until Bishop was drafted early in the war. Two of his brothers still lived in east Tennessee and they all went together at least one Sunday afternoon a month to visit Mama and Papa. His brothers counted on Bishop to tell them when.

Although Bishop did not look down on Harlan and Barney for their lack of education—Barney had almost finished high school, which was pretty good given his hardscrabble upbringing—he was proud that he had been to college. Not that he actually had learned much in his single semester at the University of Tennessee. He never fit in there, and he was happy when his mother called him home to take over the store after his father fell down the steps and broke a leg.

And he'd done well in business. He closed the store after a couple of mediocre years and took a job as manager of the sawmill he now owned. He was proud that he had been a good provider for his own little family, his wife Marguerite and a son and two daughters. He had one of the best sawmills in the area.

But like his friend Barney Vidone, Bishop had a great many concerns about what was happening to the South. The Supreme Court ruling in *Brown v. Board of Education* was just the beginning. And although he felt helpless to do much on the larger front, he was determined to see the white Christian way of life maintained at the local level.

"We've got us some work to do around here," he told Barney and Harlan. "Pretty soon I'm going to come up with a list. There ain't no place around here for nigger-lovers like Earl Warren, and trying to keep 'em out's like trying to stop the spread of kudzu vines. Somebody needs to be out there every day chopping 'em off at the roots."

"You got that right," Harlan said. "They'll just keep on spreading if somebody don't chop 'em off at the roots."

Barney Vidone unconsciously glanced back toward the motel office. He could feel Effie's eyes on the back of his head. "We can't wait for somebody else to do what needs to be done," he said. "Make up that list, Bishop, and we'll get us a schedule put together and have us some fun."

Their little parking lot discussion had been productive.

Chapter 4

Rachel Feigen arrived at the Tennessee Bend uncertain what to expect. The place looked respectable enough from the highway—in fact was rather attractive in its sheltered wooded setting. There was a rather plain sign that welcomed visitors to Cherokee Lake and encouraged them to enjoy an extended stay and she was struck by the beauty of the long rose garden across the front. There were few cars in the parking lot, but it was still early for travelers.

She drove up to the motel entrance and left her car in a space reserved for guests who were registering or checking out. The oppressive heat almost took her breath away when she stepped out of her car, even though she was in the shade of a clump of shortleaf pines. She had experienced the Southern summer during visits to Georgia and South Carolina while working on the school integration story, but hoped it might not be so hot in mid-September. And shouldn't it be cooler in the mountains?

Feigen had spent very little time in the South. Until the past summer, her Southern experience was limited to vacations in North Carolina, and even those were years in the past. Her mother loved Asheville and her father loved the Smoky Mountains—or any other part of the ancient Appalachian chain, for that matter. On three or four occasions when she was a child the family had spent a week in August at a luxurious Asheville resort. She did not remember its name, nor whether it had been hot there.

Half way to the door of the motel office, she halted and looked back. Bill Skyles had told her once that truck drivers walking away from their rigs never got more than a few feet before they turned back and checked to see if the big machines they were so proud of looked as good as they thought. She studied her new Chevrolet. It had picked up enough road dirt to diminish its shine ever so slightly, but it was still beautiful and yes, it really was hers. A Feigen or not, it was impossible not to feel a hint of pride.

The low afternoon sun reflected off the car's windshield and temporarily blinded her so that she lifted a hand to shade her eyes. She had a clear view of the wooded mountains to the west and stood for a moment and took in the beauty of her surroundings. East Tennessee was a much more appealing place than she had expected it to be.

So this is it, she mused, the place from which Guy Saillot seems to have vanished from the face of the earth. *Dear God let somebody around here know something!*

The front entrance to the motel was not appealing. There was a single door, the top half of which was frosted glass. The gray paint on the door frame had scrapes and scratches so that a lighter underlying yellow showed through and there were dirty smudges around the door handle. The lobby was shabbily furnished and showed its years of wear. There was a large natural-stone fireplace across the south wall which she supposed would be comforting if it ever got cold hereabouts but struck her as a glaring incongruity on hot days like this.

Two men sat on a faded orange and green sofa in front of the empty fireplace, caught up in conversation with a third man seated in a green upholstered chair. Coffee cups and a tray of cheese and crackers sat on a low table within easy reach. Although she had to walk near them, it seemed as if the men were fully engrossed in their own little world and completely oblivious to the fact that someone else had entered the room.

A woman whose nametag identified her as Effie Catlin greeted Feigen casually, though her demeanor was pleasant. "Welcome to the Tennessee Bend," Effie said, then looked behind Feigen as if expecting someone else and added, "Are you traveling alone?"

"Yes." Feigen's answer was as abrupt as she could make it. Whose in the hell business was it if she was traveling alone or with a three-ring circus? The question reflected an attitude she had experienced much too often when she traveled, even more frequently in

24

big-city hotels than in rural areas such as this. Hotel clerks in the city often gave her that smug look she assumed was reserved for call girls. She did not know what Effie Catlin might be thinking, and she didn't much care.

"I didn't mean that the way ladies take it sometimes," Effie said quickly. "I consider myself a professional woman, and I'm happy to see women out and about on the road. I was only wondering if you'd need help with your luggage."

Feigen smiled and Effie smiled back.

"No offense taken," Feigen said. "And yes, I am traveling alone, on business."

"What kind of business are you in?"

Feigen showed her a press card. "I'm a reporter for the Associated Press in Baltimore and I'm here because of this man." She slipped a photograph of Guy Saillot from a jacket pocket and held it up for the other woman to see. "Does he look familiar to you?"

Effie took the picture and held it at arm's length. "I'm sorry, my eyes aren't what they used to be," she said, "but no, he doesn't look familiar. Who is he?"

"He's a missing man from Baltimore whose last contact with his mother was a postcard from this motel. I thought you might remember him."

Effie Catlin looked at the picture again, and shook her head. "How long ago would it have been? I can check our registration files back for a couple of months," she said. "If it's longer than that there's not much I can do."

Feigen told her it would have been about two weeks earlier, sometime near the end of August. "Given that he was here as recent as that, I hoped he might look familiar."

"Honey, I just see so many different people in here every day. There'd have to be something really unusual about a face before I remember it that long. Especially if he only stayed a night or two. Now, some of the men who come on fishing trips to the lake and stay for a week, them I'm more likely to remember. And if he checked in late, I wouldn't have been here. The manager takes over after I leave, usually by six o'clock."

"I understand," Feigen said politely. "But if you don't mind, could you please check on the registrations for August twenty-fifth and the next five days?"

Effie nodded. "I sure can. What did you say his name was?"

"It's Guy Saillot. That's spelled 's-a-i-l-l-o-t.'"

"Not a common American name."

"He's French."

Effie turned to a filing cabinet behind her and pulled open the top drawer. She systematically went through a thick folder and, turning up nothing, shook her head. "Nobody by that name registered that whole week. And a name like that would jump out at me, too."

"And there's no place else the registration could have been filed?"

"No, ma'am. The manager personally makes sure every night's registrations go into that file. You know, just in case."

"I appreciate your help, anyway," Feigen said. "I need a place to stay, so I might as well register for a room if you have a vacancy."

"No problem. How long will you be staying with us?"

"I don't know. It depends on how long it takes me to do what I came for."

Effie called toward the three men seated in the lobby, "Barney, are the front-row rooms all ready?"

The man sitting in the green chair got up and came to them, then went behind the counter and stood beside Effie. He looked at Feigen intently. "Some are," he said. "Put her in Room Ten."

"She needs you to look at this picture," Effie told him. "This fellow's missing."

Effie pushed the photograph of Guy Saillot in front of him. The man glanced at it and shook his head. "Nope. That doesn't look like anybody I ever saw," he said. He turned and hurried back to his chair in the lobby and the two men he'd been talking with.

"That's Barney Vidone, the manager," Effie whispered. "He's too busy with his country cousins over there to take time for little things like missing persons, I guess."

Feigen giggled and whispered back, "I haven't heard 'country cousins' in a long time."

"That's Harlan and Bishop over there with him," Effie said, still whispering. "They come around all the time. I think they waste too much of Barney's time, but he's too nice not to make them feel welcome."

Effie pulled a motel registration form from a drawer and laid it on the counter. "Room Ten is our best room," she said, in a normal voice again. "I hope you enjoy your stay."

Feigen registered and took the key. She turned back toward the door and nearly ran head-on into a man who was standing close behind her, although she had not heard him approach. He was a middle-aged black man, slight of build, with unruly hair and piercing eyes. "Excuse me," she said, embarrassed by her own lack of awareness. "I'm sorry, I didn't know you were there."

"He can't hear you, honey," Effie said. "That's George, Barney's handyman. He's a good hard worker but he's deaf as a stump and so far as anybody knows he's never said a word in his life."

Feigen smiled weakly at the man, slipped by him, and quickly made her way out. She went to Room 10 and started to insert the key. The door was not locked. It swung inward easily at her touch and she went inside.

Except for a subtle stench of stale cigarette smoke which obviously had survived efforts to freshen the air with more agreeable aromas, the room was surprisingly nice. It was bright and cheery, with white walls that made it seem larger than it was, and it had good quality furnishings. It seemed to her that the room was more than adequate for a few nights' stay and a bargain at the modest price she'd paid. She had slept in a number of cheap motel rooms in recent weeks, traveling over a good part of the country working on the school integration story. None of them was as nice as this room in the Tennessee Bend.

Before she joined the Associated Press, cheap motels were as foreign to Rachel Feigen as castles on the Rhine. She was a city girl, her father was a prominent judge, and she was accustomed to better things. Nothing ostentatious, but all the comforts of a good home with parents who doted on her.

She looked the room over and found everything to be in order, then went back to her car and moved it to a parking space directly in front of the door to Room 10. She brought in an overnight bag and one suitcase and unpacked just enough to meet her immediate needs. Bill Skyles would be pleased. He constantly preached an old cliché that reporters must follow a story wherever it takes them, and this truly was where the Saillot story had brought her.

She needed to report in to Skyles, and after a quick bathroom break she picked up the room phone and called the AP office in Baltimore.

"What's up?" her editor asked, almost gruffly.

Feigen was relieved to hear his voice. There was something comforting in his usual direct, no-nonsense manner. "Greetings to you too, Bill," she laughed.

"Okay, good to hear from you. Where the hell are you, Feigen?"

"Room Ten, Tennessee Bend Motel. Right at the gateway to beautiful Cherokee Lake."

"Sounds like a vacation. You *are* on the job, right?"

"You got it, boss. This is the place Guy Saillot sent his mother the postcard from. He said he spent the night here, but so far I haven't found anyone who remembers him. Of course, I just got here."

Skyles's abrupt tone turned more gentle. "Is everything okay, Rachel?"

"So far, so good. I hope to find somebody Guy's picture looks familiar to. I'll get back to you the minute I get anything. And by the way, Cherokee Lake really is beautiful. If I had a few days off I might stay around here for a little longer. My accommodations are a lot better than I expected, too."

As she talked with Bill Skyles, Feigen studied herself in an oversized framed mirror mounted on the wall, facing the bed. Although vanity never had been one of her faults, she was well enough pleased with what she saw: an attractive person, looking a bit worn following the long drive from Baltimore, but a woman with a nicely featured face, a luxurious, flowing crown of chocolate-brown hair, and pretty brown eyes, There was the somewhat broad "Jewish nose" her brother used to tease her about, but what the hell—she was proud of her heritage, even though as far as she knew there hadn't been a practicing Orthodox Jew in the family for at least three generations.

"Take as much time as you need," her editor said. "And Feigen, listen to me. Don't take any foolish risks. You're more than likely to run into an authentic redneck or two down there."

"Nothing but nice so far," she told him. "But you know I always follow your advice. I'll be in touch."

It took very little to stir memories of her brother, Morrie, and observing her own image in the mirror had done just that. Morrie was her elder by barely two years and was stricken with polio at age fifteen and died just before his sixteenth birthday. He had been the apple of his father's eye and was destined for law school and a career as a jurist, precisely tracking Judge Max Feigen's footsteps.

Rachel wanted to please her father, too, and decided early on to become a reporter. Her father's respect for the *New York Times* was barely secondary to his respect for the law. He would be proud to have a reporter in the family.

She lay across the bed and considered her situation. It was almost hard to believe that she really was here in east Tennessee, that she really was investigating an important story, that she really was a reporter, that she really did work for the Associated Press. This was the kind of thing she had dreamed of ever since she first knew she wanted to be a journalist. She had a hunch that even at her relatively young age she'd already gained more satisfaction from her work than many people did in a lifetime.

The Associated Press had hired Feigen right after she finished a master's degree in journalism at Columbia University, this following her studies in history and political science at NYU. She worked in New York City for two years, assigned to a court beat, and reported on some of the biggest trials of the day. Then the AP sent her to Baltimore and she would always be thankful. Bill Skyles was the best editor she could ever hope for. He taught her something new almost every day and he had drilled into her the importance of being persistent and being skeptical without being cynical. And most of all, being accurate.

Feigen's thoughts came full circle. She'd always wanted to make Morrie proud of her and it was one of her great regrets that he would never be witness to her success. He was her hero and she still missed him dearly.

Chapter 5

It was a struggle for Rachel Feigen to put aside the past and realign her thinking with the present. She needed to take stock, but it was too late to do any more poking around today. She decided the best use she could make of her time would be to study the phone book and try to get a sense of this place—see what restaurants there were where Guy Saillot might have eaten, look for other places he could have visited, make a list of stops she could make tomorrow and show Guy's picture around and hope to find at least one person who remembered seeing him. Just one. Surely that would be enough to stir Agent Schuler's interest and maybe get the FBI back in the game.

Feigen had skipped lunch on the road and was terribly hungry, but she took a few minutes in the bathroom to clean up and refresh her makeup and change into a clean blouse. It was still hot when she left her room on the way to the motel desk to ask Effie Catlin where to eat. When she got there Effie was gone.

The short, heavy man, Barney Vidone, was behind the counter. He had changed from the informal clothes she'd seen him in earlier and now wore a jacket and tie and had a rather large nametag that identified him as the Tennessee Bend's manager.

"Yes, ma'am?" Barney queried as she approached the desk. "Is everything okay?"

"Everything's fine," she answered. "I just wondered if maybe you could suggest someplace nearby where I could get dinner." The manager studied her with an intensity that made her uncomfortable.

But maybe she was imagining things. As Bill Skyles would admonish, be skeptical but not cynical.

"Yes, ma'am," Barney said. "If I were you I'd go right down the road to Big John's Place. It may not be up to the standards of a fine Baltimore restaurant, but Big John puts out some good groceries. They serve good beer, too. 'Bout a quarter-mile, on the right."

"How do you know I'm from Baltimore?"

"I'm the manager, ma'am. I look over all the registrations. It says right there on the form, you're Rachel Feigen from Baltimore, Maryland. I'm supposed to know who our guests are, in case something unusual happens."

"Has something unusual ever happened?"

"No, ma'am. This place is always quiet," Barney Vidone replied.

"I'm glad to hear that," she said, and smiled. "I should sleep well, then. Thank you for the information. I'll try Big John's Place."

"Like I said, 'bout a quarter-mile down the road. On the right."

Feigen found the motel manager almost comical. Was he trying to impress her with his competence and his level of responsibility? Did he really go over every registration after Effie Catlin had checked people in and know his guests by name and where they came from? This seemed farfetched. But if he didn't, how come he knew all about her?

But she was being foolish. *What do I know about how a motel manager does his job?* This one had been reasonably polite and efficient, and what more did she ask?

Precisely as Barney Vidone had told her, Big John's Place was only a few hundred yards down the highway from the Tennessee Bend, on the right. And like the motel, it was not what she expected. Perhaps it didn't qualify as a five-star restaurant, but it looked better than average. The bar was separated from the dining room by a wide entrance hallway that had an authentic Italian tile floor and burgundy walls and elaborately carved dark oak trim. There was a hostess station and an agreeable seating area where an overflow crowd could wait in comfort. There was no crowd tonight.

Although Feigen couldn't see the bar, she heard no noise from that side of the building and assumed there were not many people there. Maybe it was too early. Hadn't the motel manager stressed the fact that Big John's Place served good beer?

The hostess introduced herself as Mandy and showed Feigen to the dining room. A thin pall of cigarette smoke hung over it like exhaust fumes over a busy Baltimore street in rush hour traffic, even though there were few diners there ahead of her. The dimly lit room was decorated in shades of dusty rose and lilac and was easily equal to the dining rooms of many of the better hotels and restaurants Feigen was accustomed to.

"There's a nice table for two over there toward the back," the hostess said. "Would that be okay?"

"Of course," Feigen told her. "And Mandy, may I ask you a question?"

"Sure."

"Have you been here for a while?"

"Yes, since eleven this morning."

Feigen laughed. "I didn't state that very well," she said. "I meant to ask if you had worked at this job for very long."

Mandy laughed, too. "Well, in that case the answer's the same," she said. "I've been here for almost four years and it seems even longer. Why?"

Feigen slipped the photograph of Guy Saillot from her jacket pocket and held it out to the other woman. "I wondered if this man might look familiar to you," she said softly. "He may have been around here a couple of weeks ago but now he seems to have disappeared."

Mandy took the picture and studied it closely. "You know, he does look familiar," she said. "Yes, I definitely remember his green eyes. Like emeralds, almost. I'm pretty sure he was here two or three times. Once with another guy. He was such a sweetie we talked about him after he left and hoped he'd be back again. Yes, I'm sure this is him. He sat right over there." She indicated a table nearby.

"Mandy, are you sure? This is very important."

"I'm sure. Can I ask who he is?"

"His name is Guy Saillot. He's from Baltimore and we think he was in this area before his family lost track of him."

"That's kind of a funny name. I don't know as we would have heard his name, but if I had I think I would remember that one."

"It's a French name," Feigen said. "A very nice family, and his mother is very worried. Look, let me give you my card. I'm staying up the road at the Tennessee Bend Motel for at least a couple of days. If you think of anything more, would you please give me a call?"

Mandy took her card, looked at it, and said, "Associated Press. This must be some big shot you're looking for."

Feigen shook her head. "No," she said, "he's just a nice young man whose family is very, very worried. Any information I get will end up in the hands of the proper authorities. And could I ask you one more thing?"

"Of course."

"What do you know about that man Barney who manages the motel up there? He struck me as a bit odd."

"I know enough about him to tell you to be careful," Mandy told her. "He's probably harmless, but he mixes with some bad company. You know, the kind you think may be out there doing things in the dark."

Feigen was hesitant. "I'm not sure I know what you mean."

"Look. Ugly things happen around here. Somebody's out of line, their house gets burned down in the dead of night. Things like that. Nobody ever gets caught."

"You just got my attention," Feigen said.

The hostess left her sitting alone in the back of the dining room. A young waitress who had been hovering nearby promptly took her order and soon brought to her table one of the best dinners she'd had in a long time—a rib eye steak with boiled potatoes and asparagus and a generous salad with a nice house dressing. But she could not enjoy the meal. Too many uncertainties surged through her head.

Her waitress was not friendly and when Feigen showed her Guy Saillot's picture she merely glanced at it and shook her head. Feigen knew she was lucky to have found Mandy, and she was afraid to push her luck trying for something more. She needed rest. She ate no more than half the dinner, left a tip that was too generous because she didn't want to bother to get change, and left Big John's Place eager to get back to the Tennessee Bend Motel and get to bed. She saw no sign of Mandy as she went out through the entrance hallway.

Back in her room, she called her father. "Daddy, I'm just checking in to let you know I got down here all right," she said.

Judge Max Feigen's relief was apparent in his voice. "Honey, I'm glad to hear from you. I'm going to worry about you down there."

"Oh, come on. I'm not in a foreign country, I'm in Tennessee. What is there to worry about?"

"Well, for one thing, that young Negro who was murdered in Mississippi. The boy from Chicago. There's a trial coming up and the story's beginning to get a lot of national attention. That might stir things up. Honey, I know there are good people down there, but there are crazies everywhere. Promise me you'll be careful."

"I'll be careful. I haven't run into any crazies yet. But then I just got here."

"Rachel, this is serious. I mean it. You be careful, and check in with us often. At least once a day. Will you do that?"

"Daddy, I'll check in every chance I get. And I will be careful. Are you and Mother doing okay?"

"On top of the world, as always."

Feigen laughed with him, and said she was tired and wanted to get ready for bed. "It was a long drive," she told him. She almost said, "even in my new Chevrolet," but caught herself just in time. The longer she waited to tell him about her new car, the less danger that it would sound like she was taking too much pride in material things.

She had barely put down the handset when the phone rang. Her father had forgot something he wanted to tell her, no doubt. She answered, "Hello, Daddy. Didn't we just talk?"

After a moment's silence, a quiet and somewhat hesitant woman's voice: "I beg your pardon. Is this Rachel?"

"I'm sorry," Feigen said. "I was just talking to my father and I thought he was calling back. Yes, this is Rachel."

"Rachel, this is Mandy. You remember, from Big John's? Look, I may be way off base here, but if I were you I'd try to get close to George, the poor fellow Barney hires to keep things cleaned up around the motel. They don't think he's smart enough to know what goes on around there, but I believe George is smarter than they think he is. I don't know how you can get to him, but try to let him know you're a friend."

FEIGEN GOT UP IN the morning still tired. She had had little sleep, even though the bed in Room 10 was very comfortable. She had spent much of the night awake, worrying. Guy Saillot's trail clearly led here and ended here, and she was uncertain whether she could go any further on her own. Or whether she should even try. She was a stranger here. She needed the help of friendly law enforcement, preferably local police who not only knew how to run an investigation but also knew their way around.

And while she was setting her own criteria, dare she hope that local police might show greater enthusiasm for the Saillot case than Agent Anton Schuler had displayed back in Baltimore? That would be a good step in the right direction.

In the middle of the night, when she couldn't sleep, Feigen had mentally catalogued her options. If she could get the local authorities more involved, she might be able to bring some pressure on Schuler. This should be her starting place. Also, she wanted very much to find others besides Mandy who remembered Guy Saillot, people who would bear witness to the fact that he had been here. This was one thing she could do on her own.

She also wondered about Barney Vidone. She was uncomfortable with him, though she had no reason to suspect him of wrongdoing. She supposed she might be overreacting to the way he'd looked at her. Not exactly a leer, but too close and personal in a way she could hardly put her finger on. Mandy's warning hadn't helped.

Perhaps this all stemmed from her irritation at the Tennessee Bend manager for his cavalier dismissal of Guy Saillot's photograph. He hadn't bothered to look at it, really, as if he didn't care about her missing person quest. But that was his prerogative, especially given that she carried no real authority, and she had no basis for complaint.

Looking ahead, Feigen had vowed to push harder when the new day came. Unless she soon turned up more than she had now she probably would have no reason to stay in east Tennessee much longer.

She dressed hurriedly. She wanted a quick breakfast and after that she'd go directly to the police station and give the authorities all the information she had on Guy Saillot. Even if the FBI had stirred them up—of which she was by no means confident—a little direct pressure wouldn't hurt. It also might help if she demonstrated her openness to sharing information. Maybe then they'd have less of a problem with her sticking around and asking her own questions. She felt hopeful as she closed the door to Room 10 behind her.

The sun already was high in the eastern sky, over the mountains, and the air was sultry. The blue waters of Cherokee Lake sparkled in the sunlight and Feigen was struck again by the natural splendor she saw in every direction. She felt as if she was surrounded by a world as pure and primitive as the Garden of Eden. She wished for an instant that she could forget everything else and head off into the mountains and find a prominence where she could sit in quiet solitude and let her worries melt away.

Someday perhaps she could. But not now. *You have work to do, Rachel. Get with it.* It was almost as if she could hear her father's stern voice—the one usually reserved for the courtroom.

George was tending rose bushes in the garden beyond the parking lot. If Mandy thought he might know something about Guy Saillot, Feigen needed to get into George's good graces, let him know she was a friend. She strolled over toward him and watched from the driveway, but George never looked up. There would be other chances. She turned back and walked quickly to the motel office. Effie Catlin sat at a desk behind the counter, filing the records of overnight room registrations. She looked up and smiled when Feigen entered.

"Good morning, Effie," Feigen said. "It looks like you spend a lot of time here."

"Good morning, Miss Feigen. You bet I spend a lot of time here. More than I do at home, it seems like. I'm sure my husband thinks so, but he won't complain."

"Do you have a family—besides your husband, I mean—any children?"

"Three married daughters and five grandchildren."

"Do they live nearby?"

"One lives over in Jellico, one in Lexington, Kentucky, and one in Asheville, North Carolina."

"So you don't get to see the grandchildren as often as you'd like."

"Jellico's not too far, but no, I don't see none of them all that much."

Feigen liked Effie Catlin, who impressed her as level-headed and sincere. She probably would have taken time to talk with Effie anyway, but she had deliberately tried to make conversation about personal things for a reason: She wanted to find out more about Barney Vidone. Effie probably knew him as well as anyone did.

"Can't you get more time off?" Feigen asked. "Your manager seems like a nice enough fellow."

"Barney? Oh, he's as nice a man as you could ask for." Effie's face seemed to light up at the mere mention of her boss. "I know I could get time off if I needed it. It's just that, I don't know, it's like him and George would never be able to take care of this place without me. Barney likes to pretend he does all the business part, but just between the two of us he'd be lost if I wasn't here to point him in the right direction."

"Story of our lives, right? We women, I mean."

"You got that right," Effie said with a big smile.

"Does he have a family?"

"He was married once but it didn't last long. No kids. The way Barney tells it, his wife just wasn't ready to settle down. He's got brothers and sisters that all live in Knoxville and Chattanooga, I think. He don't talk about them much."

"Did you know his wife?"

"No, I didn't. She was out of the picture a long time before I went to work for Barney."

"And now he lives by himself?"

"Right here on site, him and George both. They made three rooms into an apartment that Barney lives in and George lives in one of the regular units. This place used to have forty rooms open to occupants. But as far as Barney's concerned, I think he spends a lot of the night up here, in case somebody comes in late. He's got a television and refrigerator back there in his office, just like home."

Feigen was reluctant to push too far. Effie Catlin was accommodating, but no doubt there was a point at which she might feel that Feigen was trying to pry more information out of her than she wanted to give. And of course she didn't know Effie all that well, not nearly well enough to trust her completely. Effie might be loyal to her boss to the extent that she would cover for him if she sensed that Barney was in trouble.

Feigen pointedly turned the conversation in another direction. "Well, speaking of home, where's the best place to eat breakfast around here?"

"It's not a question of best if you want someplace close. Big John's is the only place. Well, there's the bus station, but you wouldn't want to eat there."

"Big John's is good enough for me. I'll probably see you later today."

"Stop by whenever you can. I don't get much woman talk in here."

As Feigen walked to her car, she watched for George. She still didn't know if she would be able to communicate with him, but she needed to gain his trust and she was ready to give it a try. As was the case with Effie, though, she would have to be cautious. George also might be a loyal friend to Barney Vidone, especially if he depended on Barney for a job. That was a hard hold to have on a man—particularly a man who had George's limitations.

Her concerns proved irrelevant. George was nowhere in sight. She hurried on, but paused and took the time to look over her new car for a moment before she got in and drove away from the Tennessee Bend.

She had to wait for two logging trucks to pass before getting on the highway. They were going the direction she wanted to go, and she followed them until she turned off at Big John's Place.

No one was at the hostess stand when she went inside and a sign directed patrons to seat themselves. She went back to the far side of the dining room and took a table near where she'd sat the night before. There were perhaps eight or ten other diners. Sunlight streamed in through the windows on the east.

This time she had a polite and attentive waitress who introduced herself as Kathy. The pleasant atmosphere magnified her appetite and, recalling her father's maxim that when traveling one should eat what the locals ate (she'd often teased him that his appreciation for good food was the main reason he couldn't have survived as an Orthodox Jew) she ordered eggs with grits and biscuits and sausage gravy. And coffee that turned out to be so strong she asked Kathy for water to dilute it with.

"Big John says if it don't dissolve the spoon, coffee's too weak," Kathy said with a giggle.

"So there really is a Big John?"

"There sure is. He's around here most of the time, but we ain't seen him yet this morning."

"Could I ask you about something else?"

"Sure. If I know, I'll be glad to tell you."

Feigen slipped the photo of Guy Saillot from her purse and held it up where Kathy could see it. "Does this man look familiar?" she asked.

Kathy took her time studying the picture. Then she shook her head. "Nope, it don't look like anybody I know," she said. "Who is it?"

"Oh, just a young man I thought might have been here recently. He's not been heard from for a while now and his mother's worried."

"Well I reckon she would be. But he don't look familiar to me."

"Is the police station close?" Feigen asked. "I need to check with the local authorities and see if they know anything."

Kathy shook her head. "We're not incorporated here so there's no police force," she said. "You'd want to go to the sheriff's office. That's just a couple of miles down the road, heading south. Go till you see a Shell gas station on one side of the highway and the bus station on the other. Turn in at the bus station and the sheriff's office is right behind it. It's right hard to miss."

Feigen thanked the waitress for the information and rushed through the rest of her breakfast. Ten minutes after she left Big John's Place she was in front of the sheriff's office. She walked in with Guy Saillot's picture in hand.

A stout, ruddy-faced man sat slouched on a stool behind a service counter that blocked her way just inside the door. She took a quick mental note of the nameplate that identified the on-duty desk sergeant as Andy Campbell. Sergeant Campbell studiously ignored her for as long as he could. When he eventually seemed to recognize that she intended to stand there until he acknowledged her presence, he mumbled a slurred, "Yeah, what'daya need?" in her direction without looking up.

Feigen put the photograph on the counter. "This man's missing," she said. "I'm trying to find him. Could I get some help from this department?"

"You some kind of fed, or what?" But he did stop pretending to be busy and looked at her.

"I'm a reporter for the Associated Press."

Feigen believed she saw a shadow of contempt in the desk sergeant's eyes. He leaned over and spit into something under the counter then looked up again with exaggerated slowness, his face grim and his jaw set. This time he spoke directly and firmly. "We don't have a lot of use for reporters around here. 'Specially women reporters that come all the way down from Mary Land."

Although taken aback by Sergeant Andy Campbell's barefaced display of insolence, Feigen was determined to maintain her composure. "Why does it matter that I'm a reporter?" she said calmly. "As I told you, this man is missing. I'm looking for him on behalf of his mother, and I need the help of this department. Isn't that what you're here for?" She instantly wished she could take back the last question. It was a challenge she hadn't intended.

It was too late. Sergeant Campbell's face reddened with anger. "Now look here," he growled, "I don't know's we need anybody coming in here and telling us what our job is. Certainly not a Jew reporter from Mary Land. So why don't you just get your ass back in that fancy new Chev'olet out there and hightail it back up north and mind your own damned business."

He turned his back to Feigen and made a deliberate show of spitting again into whatever was on the floor at his feet, wiped his mouth with a shirt sleeve, and walked to a desk at the back of the room and began to shuffle papers.

Feigen stood awkwardly for a moment before she went back to her car, slid behind the wheel, and slammed the door. She seethed with anger. She wanted to laugh at the absurd treatment she'd just been subjected to, but she was nearer to crying. She pulled down the sun visor in front of her face and studied herself in its makeup mirror. Was her Jewishness really that obvious? She'd experienced prejudice before, of course, but never in such blatant fashion. The sheriff's office desk sergeant suddenly made Anton Schuler, the Baltimore FBI agent, look pretty good.

Chapter 6

As much as she despised Agent Anton Schuler's homophobic attitude, Rachel Feigen at least understood it. She did not understand the total indifference she'd just run into in the sheriff's office. These people—or, more precisely, Sergeant Andy Campbell—offended the title of law officer. She had heard Bill Skyles complain often enough about "bad cops" who are a disgrace to the badge and now she had a great deal more sympathy for his point of view.

As soon as she got back to the Tennessee Bend Motel, she called Skyles to bring him up to date. This time, she had good news.

"Guy Saillot was here," she told her editor, with no concern for the excitement in her voice. "The hostess at a restaurant called Big John's remembers him well."

"That sounds like my kind of place. Did you eat there, yourself?" Skyles asked.

"I've been there twice. There aren't all that many places to eat around here."

"This is critical, Rachel. Does that hostess strike you as a reliable source of information? How sure would you say she is in her identification?"

"Bill, she talked about his green eyes. She remembered where he sat. She said he was a real sweetie and they talked about him after he left the place. Oh, and another thing, she said he was with another guy one time. I forgot to say, she said he was there more than once."

"You may have just come up with enough to stir the pot on this one. Right good day's work, Rachel. And now that you've seen the lay of the land, so to speak, what are your feelings in general?"

"In general, I can pretty much sum things up with a report on my visit to the local sheriff's office. They don't feel obligated even to give the time of day to a Jew reporter from Mary Land. They don't much like a Jew reporter—especially a *woman* Jew reporter—trying to tell them how to do their job, either."

Bill Skyles hesitated for an instant before he responded. "Rachel," he said finally, "I think we need to get you out of there. I shouldn't have sent you to a place like that."

"I'll be all right, boss. Just give me another couple of days, okay?"

"Okay, two more days—against my better judgment."

"And one more thing," she added. "Can you call that FBI man and tell him what I just told you? Maybe knowing there's a witness who remembers Guy Saillot being here will help light a fire under his sorry ass. He needs to get down here."

"That's as good as done," Skyles said. "The FBI should have had somebody in there getting the kind of stuff you are a long time ago."

After she'd hung up the phone, she sat for a moment on the end of the bed and studied herself in the large mirror on the wall. Damn it, Morrie, she thought, you were right about my big Jewish nose. *Funny that nobody ever identified me that way before!* Sergeant Campbell could have seen the Maryland plates on her car, but unless he had some secret source of information he had identified her as a Jew strictly from her appearance. She was quite sure she hadn't given him her name.

It hadn't taken Feigen long to conclude that there were not a lot of places in the area where there was any need to ask around. Big John's, the sheriff's office, the bus station, a filling station or two—she wasn't exactly in the heart of a metropolis. She tried to put herself in Guy Saillot's place.

Had Guy stopped at the Tennessee Bend Motel for any particular reason, or was it simply where he happened to be when he felt he was ready to find a place to sleep? Mandy said she'd seen him in Big John's more than once, and one time with another person. Could that have been somebody he knew, somebody he had arranged to meet? Or, in line with Agent Schuler's thinking, had Guy simply met a local boy that he found attractive?

But why did she have to think in these terms? If Guy weren't homosexual, would she be asking herself these same questions? There were as many possible explanations for where he had been and what he might have done as there would be for anyone else. She needed to start over.

Marie Saillot said her son drove a two-tone green Ford sedan. Someone might have seen it. And apparently, given her recent experience with Sergeant Campbell in the sheriff's office, Maryland license plates attracted a great deal of attention in east Tennessee. Hers certainly had. It was time for her to get back on the street—or, more accurately in this location, the highway.

Feigen had seen both the Shell gasoline station and the Greyhound bus station on her way to the sheriff's office. Damn, she thought, why didn't I stop when I was there? *Some detective I'd make!* But since the gas station looked to be the closest one where Guy Saillot might have bought fuel if he stayed at the Tennessee Bend, it was the next place she ought to go. And perhaps he had stopped at the bus station for lunch or something. If he'd been here for any length of time surely there were others besides Mandy who could have seen him. And might remember it.

After checking to make sure she'd locked the door to Room 10 behind her, she turned toward the motel office. George was deadheading a row of vigorous looking marigolds that lined the walkway fronting the rooms. He looked up, smiling. He stood waiting expectantly as she approached. Feigen wondered if he might have been watching for her, purposely choosing a job close to her room. But that probably was just her imagination—or perhaps nothing more than wishful thinking.

She returned his bright smile and said, "Good morning, George. It's a beautiful day." Maybe it was useless to speak to him, but surely he could not misread her smile.

George stood aside to let her pass. Feigen hesitated, hoping to prolong the contact. She leaned down and smelled the flowers, then stood up straight and sucked air into her lungs in an embellished fashion, closing her eyes and pretending to take in even more of the pungent fragrance of the marigolds. George's smile grew wider. She put a hand on his arm and looked straight into his eyes.

"Thank you, George," she said. "Your flowers are beautiful."

George tipped his hat and went back to work.

Effie Catlin was leaning over the counter in the motel office when Feigen entered, staring ahead, toward the highway and, beyond it, Cherokee Lake. Her expression was blank but brightened to greet her visitor. There seemed to be no one else around.

"All caught up on your work?" Feigen asked.

"Not that much to catch up on. Once I finish filing the registrations and counting the money, all I have to do is stand here and hope something happens. Can you think of a more boring job?"

"Well, as my mother would say, it keeps you off the street."

"I'll bet your mother never faced being on the street," Effie said. "You strike me as a high class lady, Miss Feigen. Like you come from a good family. Am I right?"

"We were comfortable. My mother did her best to teach us good manners and see that we had a chance in life, my brother and me."

"Where's your brother at now?"

"My brother passed away when he was fifteen—from infantile paralysis."

"Oh, Miss Feigen, I'm awful sorry. I know that's a painful thing to have to go through."

Feigen forced herself to put on a cheerful face. She would never get over the loss of Morrie and she still missed him dearly, but she had learned over time not to let herself dwell on it. "Yes," she said, "but I have many pleasant memories. And speaking of which, what do you like to do on your time off?" She also had learned over time that when someone brought up the topic of her brother it was easier if she changed the subject and let them off the hook.

"Oh, just about anything that lets me spend time with my family," Effie said. Then abruptly, "I'm sorry, that was thoughtless of me, when we were just now talking about your loss."

"No, no. Not at all. We all have to deal with the circumstances at hand—make the best of our lot in life. That's something else my mother always taught us. But one of the things that keeps me going just now is remembering how terrible it must be for Guy Saillot's poor parents—that's the missing young man I'm trying to track down. Can you even begin to think how hard it must be for them? Having a son just disappear without a trace?"

"Oh, it would be terrible. Do you have any hopes of finding him?"

"There's always hope, Effie," Feigen replied. "Yes. Always hope. But I need to get out now and show his picture around. I'd better get to work."

Three hours later, Feigen was less optimistic. She found no one at the Greyhound station or the Shell gas station who seemed to remember Guy Saillot. A waitress in the small coffee shop at the bus station expressed great concern and promised to ask around, but said from the beginning that the photo Feigen showed her did not look familiar. At the gas station, the manager and a mechanic made clear that they couldn't help and, further, didn't much care about her missing stranger.

"You say he's from Baltimore?" the mechanic inquired.

"Yes," she told him. "And he's been missing for quite a while."

"Maybe he'd ought to have stayed up North where he belongs," the mechanic said. Then he turned his back on Feigen and went back to work.

Discouraged, and too tired for dinner, she picked up coffee and donuts at the bus station and went back to the motel. It was nearly five o'clock when she got to Room 10 and the first thing she did was pick up the phone and call Bill Skyles before he left the office. Her intention was merely to report in, but she couldn't help but express her frustration. "If one person saw him," she said, "there has to be others. I don't know what to do other than to keep on talking with people and showing Guy's picture around. Am I missing something, Bill? What would you be doing if you were here?"

"The same thing you're doing, Rachel," her editor said. "There's nothing else you can do—or ought to do. Remember, you're a reporter, not the law."

"But the law's not doing anything!"

"That may change pretty soon. I think Agent Schuler's finally about ready to pull his head out of the sand and try to do something on this one."

"About time, wouldn't you say?"

"Don't look a gift horse in the mouth, Rachel. An FBI agent or two would shake things up pretty good around there. Make somebody nervous. And in the meantime, you be careful where you stick your nose. I don't want you stirring up the locals any more than you already have."

"Are you talking about my big Jewish nose? Just the sight of it seems to make some folks around here uncomfortable."

Bill Skyles chuckled, but it was an uneasy chuckle. "Just keep your head down," he said. "The AP can't afford to lose one of its best reporters."

Chapter 7

Marie Saillot woke with a start. She had been dreaming and in her dream there was a clear vision of Guy, the child, the darling little boy who used to love to sit on her lap and listen as she sang. In the dream she was singing and she heard her words as if the dream had been real, as if Guy were there, looking up into her face and smiling, and she loved to sing because it made him happy and that time long past might have been only yesterday. Wide awake now, she let the song run through her mind, over and over:

Au clair de la lune
Mon ami Pierrot
Prete-moi ta plume
Pour écrire un mot.
Ma chandelle est morte
Je n'ai plus de feu
Ouvre-moi ta porte
Pour l'amour de Dieu

Marie began to weep, softly at first and then in forceful sobs that caused her body to quiver. Either the sound or the movement, or the combination of the two, quickly woke her husband. Alain Saillot rolled over so that he faced her, then took her in his arms, wordlessly, and held her tightly against him. She knew that he would not ask the cause of her weeping, that he understood, that he held within himself the same pain, the worry, the fear that gripped her. He would not speak it aloud but he would comfort her and try to help ease her grief.

Simply having Guy away from home for any length of time was difficult for Marie. To have him missing was unbearable. In her mind, Guy was still a child—innocent and vulnerable, not wise in the ways of the world. And like any mother, she wanted to protect her son from harm.

Having Alain beside her always helped Marie face her troubles. She leaned on him too heavily, and sometimes she'd tried to keep it from him when she had a problem. He would scold her when he found out, insisting that supporting her and Guy was his main role in life. Not the physical support that came from his income—which was substantial—but the emotional and moral support that he believed was the most important obligation a husband and father had. And this was especially true if her problem concerned Guy.

"Both your blood and mine run in Guy's veins," Alain had told her once. "We produced him together, we nurtured him together when he was a baby, and we have done our best to raise him together so that he is an independent and happy young man."

This was true. Alain had been a good father, had done his part in rearing Guy. It was Alain who first suspected that their son was homosexual and it was Alain who had been most persuasive in assuring him that it didn't matter, that his parents loved him just the same and would always be there for him when life became too painful. Marie believed strongly that his father's support had been the principal factor in Guy's coming to accept himself for what he was and face an often hostile society openly and unafraid.

Not that it hadn't been difficult. For every high school friend who stood by him, there were others who wanted nothing to do with him once word got around. There were days when the hurt showed in his eyes, days when his mother wanted to destroy the bigots who insisted on judging this gentle and caring boy on the basis of his sexual preference instead of his character and his spirit and his brilliant mind.

"Don't be bitter, Marie," Alain would insist. "They are the ones who are incomplete as human beings, not Guy. We have to learn to forgive those we want to hate."

She knew her husband was right, of course. But sometimes it was too hard. If only she could have traded places with her son, could have made herself the target of the slings and arrows he surely must have faced every day, could have spared him the humiliation and anguish. When he was a child it had been simple to comfort his little hurts—holding him when he cried, kissing away the scratches and bruises, bringing light to his darkness and showing that his dragons were nothing more than shadows. That time was long past, though, and now a young man's distress inevitably became a helpless mother's agony.

Guy's learning curve had been steep. He went from being shy and backward, through a phase during which he was too open—"I'm as queer as a three-dollar bill," he told his classmates almost proudly—to a point at which he finally came to grips with and readily accepted his sexuality. While not attempting to hide it, he did not flaunt it. "Be who you are, and be the best person you can be," his father advised. Guy took that advice to heart and made every effort to live up to it.

Marie clung to her husband and cried herself out. When she had finished her emotional outpouring and had no more tears to shed, she finally spoke. "I'm sorry, Alain," she said. "It's so hard. He's such a sweet and innocent boy and there are so many people out there who would hurt him."

"I know, I know," Alain Saillot said. "I feel helpless because I don't know what to do. When he was little—"

"Do you think they're really doing all they can to find him?"

"We have to hope they are. Surely the FBI is doing their best."

"Should we call that agent in the morning and ask? He promised to keep us up to date, but we've not heard anything in what seems like forever."

"The woman reporter from the AP you talked to—do you know how to get in touch with her?"

"I have the name and phone number of her editor."

Her husband kissed her softly. "Marie," he said, "I'll call them both first thing in the morning. I think I've been afraid to, afraid I'd hear things I did not want to hear. We have to face the truth, though, and it's hard to believe that anything could be worse than knowing nothing."

"Guy's all we have, Alain. Can we get through this?"

Marie Saillot began to cry again, not softly now but in a sudden outburst of violent sobs. Her body shook and her crying became a wail, like that of a wild animal mother whose babies were being taken away, until her breath was spent and the sound settled into a low moan. She clung even more tightly to the man lying beside her. This man had been her anchor for thirty years, had shared every joy and every trial, had always given her the strength to go on. But this time, what could he do?

Alain once more said nothing until she'd cried herself out. He held her gently, stroking her hair and absorbing her grief into his bosom.

"I'm sorry," Marie said again. "I know you hurt as much as I do."

"I love Guy as much as any father ever loved his son," Alain Saillot said. "I'm so proud of him, the way he's lived his life. He had every right to be bitter about his circumstances and the way people act when they know. But I don't think he is."

"No, he's never shown bitterness. He has you to thank for that."

"I don't know. I always felt that I was of very little help."

"You were a real strength for him. And for me. Do you remember what a tiny baby he was? Such a fragile little thing. We were so afraid we were going to lose him."

"Yes. We're fortunate he lived, Marie. He came way too early."

"And it took us forever to have him."

"You called it hard work," her husband said. "Do you remember?"

"Joyous work, though. We did it with purpose."

"I didn't need a purpose, Marie. There's never been a time I didn't enjoy your body—then or now. You make me feel complete. I can't even think about going for long without you."

He drew her closer. She pressed her face hard against his chest, breathing in the familiar odor of his skin. She felt the pounding of his heart and the rush of air into and out of his lungs. This man was her anchor. "I need you now, Alain," she whispered.

His response was quick and passionate, gentle in the beginning then more forceful, driven by his own pain and frustration, his helplessness in the face of a son gone missing. They used each other. She drew from him and he from her, each coaxing and demanding, comingling limbs and bodies like vine and trellis until finally they reached fulfillment. And complete exhaustion. Their energy was gone, and with it some of the hurt. The fear and uncertainty would not go away but for now it was diminished.

Marie slept, restlessly, for the rest of the night. She awoke to the smell of fresh-brewed coffee.

Alain was up ahead of her. He'd made breakfast and was shaved and dressed for work. He greeted her silently, with a soft kiss, when she joined him in the kitchen.

"I'll need that reporter's number," he said. "I know how to reach the FBI man."

"Dare we hope for good news?"

"No. I don't think we do."

"But like you said last night, nothing could be worse than not knowing anything. Even if there's no positive news, wouldn't it be good just to know they're working to find him?"

"If they are."

"Of course they are," she said firmly. "The FBI surely has to be doing *something*. Don't you think they have somebody down in Tennessee working on the case?"

"I'll find out soon enough."

"And the reporter. If you can reach her, I know she'll tell you anything she knows. She cares about Guy. I could tell that from the look in her eyes. This is a lot more than just a story for her."

"Marie, I'll call them both right after nine o'clock. I'll let you know the minute I find out anything. Or nothing. Either way, I'll call you. I have to get on to the office now. La Havre will be calling. Will you be all right?"

"Yes. We have to stay strong." Marie Saillot hesitated, then said softly, "Thank you for last night. You keep me going."

Her husband kissed her lightly. "It works both ways," he said. Then he was out the door and Marie was left to face another day alone. He would call, of course. He always did, even when there was no reason. And today he would let her know about Agent Schuler and the young woman reporter, Rachel Feigen—whether he was able to reach them, whether there was any news, anything to give more hope.

Hope was growing more elusive. In the beginning, after they hadn't heard from Guy and had begun to fear that something was wrong, she'd stayed optimistic. Guy was traveling to new places and meeting new people. He was busy and excited. He simply had not found time to call home, to let them know where he was and what he was doing. No, this wasn't like Guy, but it had been only a few days, after all. Sometime today he would call. Or tonight. Or tomorrow for sure.

But that call never came.

She busied herself in the kitchen, trying to speed the passing of time until Alain called. The floor was clean and shiny but she mopped it and put on a new coat of wax. She took her fine china from the cabinet, one piece at a time, and washed it in the kitchen sink, submerging it in hot soapsuds and wiping gently with a soft dishcloth. The china had been in her family for two generations and was among the possessions she took most pride in; today it was unimportant, merely an instrument she used to dull her sense of time. She was on the final dinner plate when the phone rang at last.

She ran to the hallway where the old-fashioned telephone sat on its gilded little antique table and grabbed the handset from its cradle. Without bothering to speak a greeting, she choked out her query: "What did you find out?"

"Marie," her husband said, "we mustn't get our hopes up too much. But Agent Schuler said there is new evidence. That reporter— I wasn't able to reach her, by the way—that reporter found people who remembered seeing Guy and recognized his picture. The agent said this gave him sufficient grounds to authorize FBI activity down there. He will be headed that way himself sometime soon."

Marie Saillot heard her husband's words. She wanted to believe that the news he bore was good, that there were people who had seen Guy, who remembered him being among them. She wanted to believe that this meant her son was alive and well, somewhere in Tennessee, and it was only a matter of time until he turned up. Perhaps if she willed it hard enough she could accept all this in her heart. But in her mind she knew nothing had changed.

Chapter 8

Bill Skyles was a tall and sturdy Iowa farm boy with an unruly mop of blond hair and soft blue eyes. To him, journalism was more than a profession. It was a calling. As far back as junior high school he'd been certain that writing the news was what he was meant to do. The battlefield correspondents whose stories he read when the war came soon became his heroes, and he joined the Marines right out of high school. He saw first-hand the best and worst of humanity during a tour of duty in the Pacific, then used his veteran's benefits to study journalism at the University of Missouri.

His professors at Mizzou, for the most part experienced reporters themselves, drilled into him the Joseph Pulitzer dictum, "Accuracy, accuracy, accuracy." One of his favorite instructors used as a class theme the Shakespeare line, "An honest tale speeds best being plainly told." He left the university with little doubt that he'd had the best journalism training he could get.

A good education was not the only thing he gained at Missouri. He met Emily there. Emily was a pretty music student who proudly referred to herself as an "Ozark hillbilly." Emily was now his wife. Their baby daughter, Rhonda, was his pride and joy.

Skyles considered himself to be first and foremost a reporter. Sometimes he still wondered why he had given up his job with the *Des Moines Register* to work for the Associated Press. At the *Register*, he had covered city hall and the police beat and every day he had his share of good stories to write. And every day was a new day, with new stories to report. It had been the most satisfying work he ever could hope to do and he still missed it.

Des Moines didn't have a high crime rate, but the one thing he was least likely to forget from his days there was the year-long reign of terror imposed by a serial murderer dubbed "the mad hound killer" by the big city papers. The *Register* editors deplored this, and studiously avoided using the label, but a reporter on one of the Chicago papers had noticed that there was a pattern to the timing of the killings that almost paralleled the arrival of full moons. Skyles could still quote the sentence the reporter used to call attention to his discovery: "Like a mad hound aroused by the silver orb, the killer slinks out with the coming of a full moon and stalks his prey wherever he finds it."

Skyles, in his reports, had concentrated on telling the stories of the killer's victims. In time the murders took place over a broad area around Des Moines, and he recognized that the entire circulation area of the *Register* was significantly affected. People in the small towns and rural areas who never had worried about locking their doors before became obsessed with home security.

One of his most memorable pieces had been a feature on a car salesman who realized, after the murderer was apprehended, that he had sold the killer a used car after riding with him on a long drive in the country. The salesman claimed not to have had a good night's sleep since he found out how close he may have come to being a victim.

There had been a surge of relief all over Iowa—indeed, all over the Midwest—when the murderer finally was caught. Another *Register* reporter covered the trial.

At the AP, his stint as a reporter had lasted barely six months. They needed a regional editor in Baltimore and the pay raise was too good to turn down. But hardly a day passed that he didn't wish he was back on the street, gathering the facts and racing back to the newsroom to meet a pressing deadline, pounding out stories on a rickety old Royal typewriter.

Skyles sat at his desk in the AP office in Baltimore and tried to concentrate on a story that had just come over the wire. He was second-guessing himself again. He had felt good about Rachel Feigen's assignment at the outset; the Guy Saillot case was an important story and Feigen was the one he wanted to write it. She was a good reporter and she knew how to handle herself. But now he was mentally chastising himself for sending her to the South in these troubled times, a woman traveling alone on a hunt that might take her to dangerous places.

If Guy Saillot had been a victim of foul play, this meant there was somebody on the defensive. An old police detective in Des Moines used to say, "If there's foul play there's got to be foul players." It was the foul players who concerned Skyles now.

Although he still was a relatively young man, Bill Skyles had the self-assurance of a seasoned professional journalist who had faced hard decisions often enough and he accepted that as part of his job—enjoyed the challenge, actually. But making a decision usually meant choosing the best of two or more alternatives, and just now he wasn't sure he had a best alternative.

He had two choices and he didn't like either one.

He could renege on his word and call Feigen home immediately. That move would ease his own worries considerably. Or, he could stick with the two days he had promised and trust her to use her head and stay out of trouble. But there were all kinds of ways things might happen that were completely beyond her control. Trouble could be lurking at every corner, as the old cliché said, and there was no one there to watch Feigen's back.

Skyles picked up the phone and called the FBI office. Agent Anton Schuler was on the other end of the line in a matter of seconds.

"Can I ask you a quick question?" Skyles said.

"Of course, Bill. What is it?"

"Do you have any immediate plans to go to Tennessee—on the Saillot case, I mean. I'm worried about my reporter down there."

"Rachel Feigen, right?"

"Yes."

"I'll probably be heading down that way pretty soon. I need to talk to the Knoxville office. Since your gal came up with something we didn't have before, the case looks more promising."

"You mean the eyewitness?"

"Exactly," Agent Schuler said.

"If I tell you where you can reach Feigen will you check in on her as soon as you get down there? I have to tell you, I'm a little bit worried about her."

"I'd be checking in on her anyway, Bill. She's the one with the information."

Skyles gave the agent the information on Rachel Feigen's motel, complete with phone and room number. He felt a mild sense of relief as he hung up the phone. "Sometimes I wish I had stayed on the farm," he muttered, more to himself than to anyone else, although there were a half dozen other editors and reporters in the room. "There are times when journalism gets to be a heavy load."

One reason for Skyles's tension was the fact that Rachel Feigen reminded him of himself during those heady days on the streets of Des Moines. Although he wouldn't admit it if anyone asked, he lived vicariously through her work. Right now, he needed to let her know that Agent Anton Schuler was coming her way.

Skyles had a great deal of respect for Agent Schuler. This was not always the case when it came to law enforcement in general. He had known too many corrupt cops who were little more than armed bullies who liked to throw their weight around. It hadn't taken many of these to sour him on the police, generically speaking, and cause him almost inherently to feel sympathy for their targets. No other abuse of power offended him the way police abuse did. Police were there to serve, not to exploit or mistreat.

Intellectually, of course, he knew that there were a lot of good cops who put their lives on the line every day to protect the public. But emotionally, he'd seen just enough of the ugly side to leave him unfairly prejudiced against police officers and make it hard to be objective when working with them, at whatever level. He recognized his prejudice and struggled to be fair in what he reported. He was glad to be working with Agent Schuler—or rather, to have Rachel Feigen working with Agent Schuler.

Skyles called the Tennessee Bend Motel, but the pleasant-voiced woman who answered the phone told him Miss Feigen was not in her room and offered to take a message. He thanked her and said he would call again later.

He did not feel free to mention the FBI to someone else, and there was no point in leaving Feigen a message to call him back. She knew to call when she could, especially if she had anything solid to report. Rachel Feigen was not one who needed to be prodded.

But he would have liked to tell her that help was on the way, that her lead had been persuasive enough to get action out of Agent Schuler, that one or more Tennessee agents would be on the case, too, and that she might as well stay low for now and wait for the feds. All of which left him even more keenly aware that, on his orders, this reporter was still in harm's way. For the first time in years, Bill Skyles felt an emotion akin to panic. He had to do something.

He checked the work schedule. Ken Maddow was listed as managing editor on duty for the next five days. Ken was a good man, one of the best in the Baltimore office. Skyles had no reservations about leaving things in Ken's hands. It was too late to think about leaving today for Tennessee, but he decided to go home early and pack and first thing in the morning fill in Ken Maddow on everything he knew about the Guy Saillot case. And then hit the road. He would go straight to the Tennessee Bend Motel and make contact with Rachel Feigen as soon as he could find her.

On some days Anton Schuler hated his job. He'd learned years ago that police work of any stripe had its bad days and, for him, these most often came when he worked crimes so gruesome they made him want to give up on humanity. Less frequent but even worse were those days when he had to share tragic news with victims' family members. Contemplating the case of Guy Saillot, Schuler had a dreadful feeling that a day would come when he had to tell Alain and Marie Saillot their son was dead. He had no evidence to support this, but experience told him that cases like this one seldom turned out well and this one didn't look much different.

Not long after speaking with Bill Skyles, Agent Schuler placed his third call of the afternoon to the Tennessee Bend Motel. When he heard a now-familiar voice on the other end of the line he asked again for Rachel Feigen in Room 10.

"I'm sorry, sir, but Miss Feigen is still not in," the woman replied. "I know you've been trying to get her before. Do you want to leave a name and number, or is there a message I can take for her? I'm pretty sure she'll be back before long."

"Thank you, no," he said. "There wouldn't be much point. But you've been very helpful. Maybe I should get your name in case I finally give up and decide I do need to leave a message. You seem to know Miss Feigen when you see her."

"My name's Effie, sir, but you wouldn't need it. I'm the only woman who's likely to answer this phone. And I'm here every day."

Schuler summoned his most friendly tone of voice. "Thank you, Effie. You have been very helpful. I assume you're not on the job twenty-four hours a day, though. Who would I talk to if you happen to be gone?"

There was a pause, and Schuler sensed some reluctance to give him the information. But then she said, "Well, it would most likely be the manager hisself. He's here during the night. I work mostly days."

"I understand," Agent Schuler said. "Would you mind giving me his name?"

"His name is Barney. Barney Vidone."

Schuler thanked her again and hung up. He stood up from his desk and walked down the hall to a water fountain and took a long drink. He was a large man, big-chested and broad-shouldered, with long and powerful arms that might have given him the appearance of a circus strongman except that he was well dressed in a dark blue suit with a white shirt and gray tie. His black hair was cut close to the scalp.

As he walked back to his desk, Agent Schuler considered his next move. He needed to go over the Saillot file one more time, look-ing for anything he might have missed. First, there were Guy's par-ents. He liked the Saillots. Alain Saillot was a polite and considerate individual, and even though he held a high position with a powerful international corporation and was prominent in the Baltimore busi-ness community, he never had tried to throw his weight around and bring pressure on Schuler. Marie had come across as somewhat re-served, and probably shy, but she was driven by the formidable force of a mother's love. Both had behaved the way he might have ex-pected any concerned parent to behave.

Surely rearing Guy had not been all smooth sailing. Guy's homo-sexuality apparently had been a matter of common knowledge for some years—hardly the carefree days of youth most parents wanted for their children.

He had never met Guy, of course, and had to rely on Alain and Marie for insight into their son. The picture they painted was one of a well-adjusted young man who took life in stride and made the best of things he had no control over. Undoubtedly this included the preju-dice he faced virtually every day in a judgmental society that was not ready to accept him the way he was.

Schuler himself was uncomfortable with homosexuality, for per-sonal reasons he never had disclosed, although he tried not to openly denigrate queers the way some other agents did. At the same time, he sympathized with any victim of prejudice. He had experienced discrimination himself, not on the level he supposed Guy Saillot had, but discrimination nonetheless.

It had been nearly four decades since a Sunday afternoon in Stockton, California, when he stood and wept, trying to comprehend a crude hand-lettered sign nailed to a tree in his favorite neighborhood park: "No Germans allowed—loyal Americans welcome." He was seven years old and he knew the sign was meant for him. He still could see that sign in his mind's eye, still sense the hate, still feel the hurt. The little park had been his escape to a peaceful world, where he'd sit and wait to see if other kids showed up to play and be contented whether they did or not.

Even as a child, Anton Schuler had understood that he was both German and American. How could he deny his heritage? His grandmother still spoke mostly German in the home and often talked lovingly of her "homeland." His father still had a heavy accent. But Anton was American, born in America, proud to be American. It was not his fault that Germany had become America's enemy. His father said Kaiser Wilhelm was to blame.

Anti-German sentiment was rampant in Stockton, and Schuler never could forget the humiliation he felt sitting at the dinner table listening to his father's bitter complaints about the way he'd been scorned by people who had been friends and neighbors ever since he arrived in California. That was a dozen years past, before Anton and his little sister were born. And his father said the distrust in the eyes of coworkers at the bank was even worse. Every dinner table outburst ended with an expression of regret for ever leaving the Wisconsin farm where Anton's grandparents settled when they immigrated from Europe.

But in the long run, that early brush with discrimination had proved a good thing for Anton Schuler. He went on to earn a law degree from Stanford and had a good practice by the time World War II started. He was just old enough to escape the draft, but guilt carried over from childhood led him to enlist. He served on the intelligence staff of General George S. Patton Jr., under the tutelage of Patton's brilliant intelligence chief, Colonel Oscar Koch, and his aptitude for the field led to his interest in the FBI after the war and his eventual appointment as an agent.

The Guy Saillot case had fallen to Agent Schuler principally because it might involve kidnapping. This was a crime that intrigued him, especially the challenge of identifying the perpetrator once an act of kidnapping had been established. This typically came when the kidnapper made contact or there was evidence that someone may have had motivation. If Guy Saillot had in fact been taken against his will, Schuler had yet to put his finger on any possible motive. There had been no contact with either authorities or the missing man's parents, no ransom demands, no evidence of a grudge or competing interest with his father's business, nothing to point to a crime of jealousy or passion.

Poring over the case file and his field notes, Agent Schuler had no doubt that everything Alain and Marie Saillot told him was true. He believed Guy had left for Tennessee when they said he did, but never got to Knoxville. Guy's friend, Mark Kinder, had been checked out by agents from the Knoxville office and was not suspected of being involved with Guy's disappearance. The AP reporter, Rachel Feigen, had found someone who thought they'd seen Guy down in— wherever it was, somewhere on Cherokee Lake.

Schuler needed to know what Rachel Feigen knew. He needed to get an agent from Knoxville there, and he wanted to be there, too, and see "what was happening on the ground," as Colonel Koch would say. He needed to get down to Tennessee, and he needed to get there now.

In the penthouse office suite atop the Franco-American Transatlantic Building across town from FBI headquarters, Alain Saillot paced the floor restlessly. Guy was on his mind. He worried about his missing son night and day, at work and at home, and it had become almost impossible for him to focus on his responsibilities to the company. He did what he had to do, as if by rote, but spent most of his time agonizing over this thing he had no control over.

Saillot felt guilty about this; Franco-American had been good to him. Where else could a poor boy from Paris with only a limited formal education have done so well?

Guy's path would be smoother. He had vowed at the birth of his son that Guy would have as much college as he wanted and was capable of as well as every cultural advantage they could manage, advantages like the chance to travel, to be surrounded by music and art—all those things his father had missed. And he had been true to his word. From the time Guy was old enough to crawl, he'd had the best of everything.

He and Marie had worried about moving Guy to America. Although Guy spoke perfect English, he'd known nothing but the French culture and Baltimore would be much different. A ten-year-old was vulnerable and there would be dramatic change on many fronts—new school, new friends, new home, new city, to say nothing of losing those he would be leaving behind.

They needn't have worried. Guy took to his new American home with ease. He made friends easily and liked his new school. If he missed La Havre at all, it hardly showed.

And then came the day they learned that Guy was homosexual. Both his father and his mother were stunned by the news. Neither had strong feelings about homosexuality itself—they'd never had reason to give it much thought—but they knew intuitively that it would complicate their son's life. Must it not lead to unhappiness for this child they adored, this child for whom they would sacrifice everything? They had much to learn, and it had taken a great deal of time and effort for them to come to grips with the situation and accept Guy as he was and agonize less over what the future might bring. Nothing would lessen their love for this son.

Saillot paused before a wide, floor-to-ceiling window and gazed at the inner harbor below. A sleek yacht moved slowly toward the wharf at one of the more distant marinas. The marina closest to his building sheltered a few large vessels and several smaller ones, sitting like ducks on a pond, motionless on the placid water. Two of the larger yachts belonged to the company but from this high vantage point he could not tell which ones. Personal use of the yachts was one of the perks of his job, although it was one he never had taken advantage of.

The Saillot family's modest sailboat was tied up at a buoy near the end of a floating dock a bit farther out in the harbor. Since he had been old enough to take on the responsibility, Guy had taken immense pride in maintaining the craft. He also had become a skilled sailor, and time on the water with his son had been Alain Saillot's favorite time. The boat looked abandoned now, and for all practical purposes it was; it had not been touched since Guy left for Tennessee.

Alain Saillot was a small, wiry man, but usually carried himself in a way that made him look dynamic and forceful—like a little giant, as Marie used to say. This was not the image reflected by the window before him. Today he looked tired and drawn, his long gray hair unkempt, the shadow of a beard marking his face, his suit crumpled and sagging. The face he saw was not his face, but rather that of a defeated stranger.

He stood at the window and gazed at the harbor lethargically until he was summoned by one of the secretaries. Marie was on the phone.

"I'm having another bad day," she told him. "Will you be able to come home early?"

"Yes, of course," he said. "I will come now. To be truthful, I'm no good here anyway. It's impossible for me to think about anything but Guy. I'll be there soon."

As he put down the phone, Alain Saillot felt like the most hopeless human being in existence. He loved his wife and he loved his son, almost beyond reason, and he would lay down his life in the blink of an eye for either of them. But now when they needed him most there was nothing he could do.

He must be strong for Marie. He wanted to comfort her and there had been times when he could, but she was growing more distant as the days wore on. He needed her, too, needed for them to be closer again, needed for them to talk and laugh and love as they once had, as they had at a time when life was good, as they had before their world collapsed around them.

He would go home to Marie now. They would talk without saying what they really feared most. They would eat dinner in silence. They would try to sleep. But a darkened room would not hide reality. Sleep would be fitful, marked by brutal nightmares that caused them to wake in states of near-panic. And there was no longer the illusion that a new day would bring new hope.

Alain Saillot locked his desk and was on his way out the door when the secretary called him again. "Agent Schuler at the FBI is on the phone," she said, unable to hide her apprehension.

He rushed back and picked up the phone. "I'm here," he said.

"Mister Saillot, I wanted to let you know that I'm going to Tennessee tomorrow," Anton Schuler said. "I'll be working with an agent from the Knoxville office. We'll find out more from that eyewitness the AP reporter turned up. If the witness is credible, this is the first definite word on Guy's whereabouts since he left Baltimore."

"That would be important, I think."

"Yes, it would. If we can establish that he was there, we're closer to finding out where he went next. But, Mister Saillot, I need to emphasize that this sighting was some time ago," Agent Schuler warned. "It's only a small step in our investigation. It may turn out not to mean much."

"I understand. But at least it is something."

Alain Saillot put down the phone and turned to the secretary, who stood waiting nervously. "They're going to talk with someone who may have seen Guy," he said simply. "But it would have been quite a while ago. I'm afraid it really doesn't mean anything."

Chapter 9

Charlie Monroe was in the office early, as he had been every day for the last ten years. He plugged in the coffee pot, checked his calendar, and leaned back in his chair to watch the September sunrise over the mountains to the northeast. It had taken some time, but Knoxville finally had come to feel like home.

The change had not been easy. Agent Monroe had spent his early FBI years in Charlotte, close to his family roots, and before his reassignment had considered Knoxville almost as remote as if it were in another country. It was, as they used to say, "across the mountains." Nobody went there unless they had good reason.

The negative factor in that indictment, though, referred only to the roads. Even the safest route between Charlotte and Knoxville could be hazardous, particularly if driven at high speed as depicted in movies about moonshine runners in their long-tailed, lowered Ford coupes. Charlie Monroe loved the mountains. He gladly would spend time there whenever he could, but like everyone else he dreaded having to drive through them when he had a tight schedule to keep.

Things in the Knoxville office had been quiet lately. Agent Monroe was restless. He had joined the FBI because he liked action, although one of the great paradoxes in his life story was the fact that a decidedly non-active profession had paved his way into the Bureau. For that, he was indebted to the U.S. Army.

Charlie Monroe had been caught by the nation's first draft law and called into service in the Great War just after he graduated from Furman University. He got a chance to see the world when the army sent him to Europe. Fortunately, while two of his friends died in the ugly trench warfare in France, he was assigned to the supply service and never got close to combat. Instead, the army taught him the ins and outs of accounting. After the war he made a good living as a bookkeeper but was bored out of his skull. When the FBI began to recruit accountants to help combat organized crime he was among the first to answer the call.

Life in the FBI had been good and now, at age sixty, he was looking ahead to retirement. His three children were grown and he and his wife were in excellent health. They wanted to travel and spend more time with their six grandchildren. And watch more basketball. Charlie Monroe loved basketball more than almost anything else in the world—even his silly word games. But while he could play the word games anywhere with anyone, with basketball all he could do was buy tickets and watch somebody else play. He was looking for his 1955–56 Furman schedule when he sensed someone standing behind him.

"Brought you a cup of coffee, Charlie."

He swiveled in his chair to face Allison Pryor.

Allison was the office manager, receptionist, and general knower-of-everything-important who kept him and the other Knoxville agents on the straight and narrow.

"Thank you kindly, Miss Allison," he said. "You look radiant this morning, as usual."

"Flattery will get you everything, Mister Monroe. What time did you get here, anyway?"

"Just a little earlier than I usually do."

"Anything new this morning?"

"Yes, ma'am. I've got a new Father Fletcher story you haven't heard."

"I've heard them all, Charlie."

"Not this one."

"Well, I suppose I'll have to hear it sooner or later," she said with feigned sarcasm. "Go ahead."

Agent Monroe's smile grew wider. "Well then," he began, "I'm sure you haven't heard the funny fable of Father Fletcher's aid to the frugal Freuhlings. You see, Frank Freuhling is an old German farmer up on the French Broad River near a chute of rapids that, on account of the heavy mist hanging over the water, they call the Foggy Falls.

68

So one day Frau Freuhling calls Father Fletcher and asks can he come over, because she and Frank are fighting a family feud. Father Fletcher finds his way through the forest to the Freuhling place, and Frau Freuhling says Frank has a fierce drinking problem and she fears the farm faces financial failure. Further, she says Frank's failing falls partly on her, because of an engraved silver flask handed down for generations and given to Frank by her Finnish father, Franz. She says Frank carries the flask in his coat pocket and as long as he has it he won't stop drinking. Father Fletcher fidgets a few minutes and says, 'I think I have a fix.' 'How in the world?' Frau Freuhling asks. 'It's frighteningly simple, Frau Freuhling,' Father Fletcher says. 'I'll find the finely finished family flask and fling it across the French Broad River to the far side of the foggy falls.' 'Finally!' Frau Freuhling says. 'Father Fletcher, you are a fine friend.'"

Allison Pryor groaned.

"Now, now," Agent Monroe chided good naturedly. "You know you liked it."

"No, I was fixing to say that I failed to find it funny."

"I suppose you think Father Fletcher is a figment of my fertile imagination? He was a real person, you know. He and I went to school together."

"Are you serious?" she asked.

"Oh, yes. And he was a far better student than I. Father Fletcher did not fail his freshman physics final at Furman."

"Charlie! That's awful. Are you ever going to run out of Father Fletcher stories?"

"I sure hope not. We've got to find a little humor where we can. Otherwise life would get awfully dull."

"You have a lame sense of humor, Charlie. Now answer my question: Anything new this morning?"

"No, ma'am, nothing exciting anyhow."

"Just like my life."

"I doubt that you need anything new, Miss Allison. Surely you already have enough excitement in your life."

"Oh, sure. Do the dishes, do the laundry, change the bed linens, try to clean up the spots the dog left on the carpet, take the car to the garage again—any more excitement and I'd probably collapse from the thrill of it all."

"Your car's back in the garage? Didn't you just tell me a few weeks ago that you had that problem taken care of?"

Allison shook her head. "This is a different problem. Now it's something screwy in the steering. Feels like I'm driving on a flat tire or something."

"You know you can borrow my car any time you need to. My wife can always drop me off in the morning and pick me up again at night."

"Well, I'm supposed to get it back late this afternoon. I appreciate your offer, though. You still thinking about a new one? Car, I mean."

"Not any more. We looked around some, but did you know you can hardly get anything for under two thousand dollars these days? There are too many other things we could do on that kind of money. Besides, you get a new car and then you have to keep it all shined up."

Allison smiled. "Oh, come on, Charlie. You've got more money than you know what to do with. Go on out there and buy that Oldsmobile you've been wanting."

She went back to the outer office, leaving Agent Monroe chuckling. Allison had been there longer than he had and all the agents considered her the glue that held the Knoxville office together. Not only was she extremely competent, but also there had been lots of tough days when Allison's unfailing good humor was all that kept a lid on things.

Agent Monroe went back to his search for the Furman schedule. One wall of his office was dominated by framed photographs of Frank Selvy, in his mind the greatest player ever to wear the Furman uniform. Every month or so he reread the *News-Sentinel* story on that amazing performance last February when Selvy scored a hundred points in a game against little Newberry College.

Charlie Monroe still regretted never having a chance to play organized sports himself. He'd been tall and gangling as a youth—suitable for basketball, but basketball didn't count for much in his time. The only popular team sport in his Chester, South Carolina, high school was baseball and he was never any good at baseball.

Except for this, he had lots of pleasant memories from his childhood. Chester offered the best of small town life—genteel people, lots of open space for kids to run and play, and peaceful, tree-lined streets. He played with black boys and girls his age as well as whites, and it never occurred to him that there was anything unusual in his black playmates going to a separate school. That was the custom. He was taken care of by a black nanny that he loved like a grandmother. It was the custom, also, that she could not sit at their table nor participate in social activities with his family. No one talked about such things, but everyone understood.

Agent Monroe eventually found the Furman basketball schedule he was looking for in the bottom of a desk drawer. He'd barely taken a look at it when Allison popped in again and announced a phone call from Baltimore. Agent Anton Schuler was on the line. He picked up the phone and greeted Schuler warmly.

"You hillbillies got anything to do these days besides fishing?" Schuler joked.

"Not much. But then I don't reckon we got near as much crime to worry about as y'all do up there," Charlie Monroe said, affecting a strongly exaggerated Southern accent. "How's that lovely missus?"

After an awkward pause, Anton Schuler said, "Janet and I separated a while back. I guess we're heading for a divorce."

"I'm sorry, Anton. I didn't know. You handling it okay?"

"You wouldn't have had any reason to know. And, you know, I miss the companionship and all, but we'd been heading in different directions for a while now. It just didn't seem to be working anymore."

"Well you know what Shakespeare said: 'Men are April when they woo, December when they wed; maids are May when they are maids, but the sky changes when they are wives.'"

Schuler managed a chuckle, but it sounded like it was forced. "You're the Shakespeare scholar," he said.

"Not much of one, I'm afraid. Anyway, I expect you called me to talk about the Saillot case. I'd be glad to put everything else aside and try to get a handle on it. I hope you've got something new."

"Yes and no, Charlie. We have an eyewitness now who puts him in the neighborhood of Cherokee Lake, but the trail gets pretty cold from there. You want to meet me up there and see what we can shake out?"

"If you say so, sure."

"Get your suitcase packed, then," Schuler said. "I'll get back to you as soon as I can, on my schedule. It'll be good to see you again, Charlie."

Agent Monroe stood and stretched. Although he was a man of average height, his rail-thin body made him look taller. And while his white hair gave him the appearance of an elderly Southern gentleman, his youthful face and energetic movement might have belonged to a much younger individual.

Anton Schuler was one of the best FBI men in the country, and Monroe would be happy to work with him again. The case of the missing man from Baltimore bothered him more than anything else he was involved in just now. Everything he learned about the young Frenchman tended to play on his grandfather sympathies. He wondered if Guy Saillot had grandparents back in France desperately waiting for word from America that their grandson was all right. Missing persons cases like this one made him wish he was back in Charlotte trying to untangle complex tax-evading bookkeeping schemes.

The Saillot case had marked a turning point for Charlie Monroe in a way that surprised him, and in a sense made him ashamed of himself. He had developed a low opinion of the French during his army service in Europe and his dislike for everything French had grown through the years, reaching a peak in the second war when it seemed to him that Americans were fighting where Frenchmen ought to be. He'd even made a sarcastic remark when the first reports on the Saillot case arrived on his desk, bringing a gentle rebuke from Allison. He had come around, over time, as he learned more about Guy Saillot, and he'd recently expressed to Allison his great empathy with the young man's family.

"But you don't like the French, remember?" Allison scolded.

"Not the *French* French, maybe—but this young fellow's French-American," he answered, with his typical Charlie Monroe good humor.

Agent Monroe had entered this case expecting that Mark Kinder, the University of Tennessee student Guy Saillot was supposed to visit, would be the key. It had taken only hours to rule out Kinder as a suspect in any foul play. Monroe felt confident that Guy never made it to Knoxville. But beyond that, who knew?

He went to the outer office to get another cup of coffee and banter with Allison but made it only to the coffee pot before the second call from Baltimore came in. Schuler said he was heading south the first thing in the morning and would plan to meet up with him at the sheriff's office near the Tennessee Bend Motel.

Agent Monroe turned back to Allison. "Check me a car out of the motor pool, would you please?" he requested. "It looks like I'll be heading up to the Cherokee Lake area tomorrow. I hope things may be coming to a head on the Saillot case."

"Saillot? That's the young Frenchman from Baltimore who's missing?"

"Yes. And I don't think the outcome's going to be a happy one. We still don't have much to go on, of course, and he could be alive and well someplace a long ways off. My experience with this kind of case says otherwise, though."

"These cases are hard on you, aren't they." She stated this as a fact, not a question.

"Yes, they are," Charlie Monroe said. "Especially when they involve young victims. Saillot is only twenty years old. He should be looking forward to a long, happy life."

"Which reminds me, it looks like they're bringing those yahoos over in Mississippi to trial for murdering that little boy from Chicago."

"Emmett Till. And I hope they get a conviction, but I don't think I'd count on it. As bad as race relations are in Tennessee, I guess they're a lot worse in Mississippi. But the South is changing. It has to. The rest of the country simply won't stand by much longer and see human beings treated the way we've treated our Negroes. The Supreme Court's ruling on school segregation was just the beginning."

Allison Pryor's expression showed her concern. "How's that going to turn out, Charlie? I mean, there's a lot of people who just aren't ready for their kids to go to school with Negroes. I know it's the right thing, but if I had young children I might feel different."

"I know. It's easy to condemn. But prejudice is an unpastured dragon, Allison. Let it loose, nurture it with a little ignorance and fear, and pretty soon it's in all the dark places and if we're not careful we'll all be devoured in its ugly flame. Change won't come as fast as it ought to, I expect, but it will come. There'll be a good many hurdles to get over and too many missteps along the way, but change will come. We all have to inhabit the same space on God's good green earth. Maybe there'll be a day when those who come after us won't have cases like the Emmett Till murder."

"Lord I hope so," Allison said. "I surely hope so."

Agent Monroe left the office and went home to pack. He had mixed feelings about tomorrow. He looked forward to seeing Anton Schuler again. The two had worked together on a few cases in the past, and Monroe had great respect for his Baltimore counterpart.

Surely there was good potential to move forward on the Saillot case, otherwise Schuler would not be making the trip down to Cherokee Lake and wouldn't have asked him to. But at the same time, the thought that there might be progress in the case filled him with dread. As he'd just told Allison, he didn't expect this one to have a happy ending.

Chapter 10

Feigen's telephone conversation with Bill Skyles had brightened her outlook somewhat, although she wasn't sure why. Perhaps it was the sense of security her editor always left her with, the sense that what she was doing was important, that he was behind her all the way. And then there was the promise—or more accurately, the hint of a promise—that Agent Schuler finally might be about to do something. She took satisfaction in this, too, since it was her digging that had turned up an eyewitness and provided the impetus.

Although the sun already was high when she walked out of Room 10, the morning was still cool compared to the suffocating heat of the afternoon before. The view of Cherokee Lake's sparkling waters was even prettier than she remembered. She paused to take in the view.

Feigen hadn't been close to the lake, and suddenly she wanted to. It was Cherokee Lake that brought others here and, who knew? Perhaps Guy Saillot had been attracted to it as well. Regardless, she felt the pull of east Tennessee's natural beauty more strongly every time she stepped outside and a good share of the credit went to the slender arm of the lake visible from where she stood.

In the motel office, Effie Catlin was nowhere in sight. Barney Vidone was busy checking in four men from Indiana. They had reservations for the night before but they'd been delayed and were only now arriving. They were here to fish, they said, making their annual pilgrimage. Barney was joking with them, something about being Hoosiers and what the hell was a Hoosier anyway? It seemed they had stayed here before and knew their way around.

"How's the fishing, Barney?" one of the men asked.

"I've seen some real good strings of walleye and crappie. Some bass, too."

"Big John's still serving those fantastic ribs?" another man inquired.

"Still the best ribs this side of Kansas."

"What the hell do they know about ribs in Kansas?" a third man asked good naturedly.

"Well, I always heard that Kansas was cattle country," Barney said. "I figured people in cattle country would know about ribs. To tell you the truth, though, I've never been to Kansas and probably wouldn't care to."

The fishermen laughed with him, and Barney Vidone obviously was enjoying the camaraderie with his new guests. It occurred to Feigen that this enigmatic man might be pleasant company in the right setting. She stood aside and listened until Barney suddenly looked up, as if he'd only now noticed her presence.

"Good morning, Miss Feigen," he said. "Are you going to be with us a while longer?"

She told him she would be staying for at least one more night and asked how to get to Cherokee Lake, a place where she could actually get to the water. Barney suggested a boat launch site that was near and explained the easiest way for her to find it. She'd be there in twenty minutes, he said, and she would be able to park and enjoy a pleasant view of the lake. The four Indiana fishermen nodded agreement, as if they knew the site well.

"If we weren't too tired from driving overnight, we'd be right behind you," one of them said. "I'm sure ready to get that boat in the water and wet a line or two."

Barney's directions proved to be precise and accurate. Feigen was soon parked at the lake shore, her new Chevrolet fitted into a row of other cars and pickup trucks in an area adjacent to a boat ramp.

She joined some dozen other people who sat on a low stone wall that edged the parking lot, in front of their parked cars and trucks, looking out over the calm lake surface. At their feet, along the edge of the water, bees and butterflies competed for nectar among the flowers of an irregular patch of Spanish needles and a pair of dragonflies darted about like tiny helicopters operated by drunken pilots. Feigen immersed herself in this restful setting and it wasn't long before she sensed a calming of the tensions that had gripped her for the last several days, but particularly since she left Baltimore.

It was hard to sort out her feelings about the South. This quiet scene of natural beauty was what the South should be, and there was no reason to believe that the people around her now were anything but good and virtuous human beings. She had expected to find prejudices in Tennessee and she had. But of course she'd found Agent Schuler in Baltimore to be just as bad, at least so far as his homophobia was concerned. She had no basis on which to judge whether he was guilty of racial prejudice or, for that matter, whether he might consider her inferior simply because she was a female.

Perhaps Sergeant Campbell at the sheriff's office was an anomaly. A misfit among his own people. Effie Catlin had impressed her as a very nice woman, and so had Mandy. Feigen remembered an aphorism of her father's, "You can't judge a book by its cover and you can't judge a dog by the length of its tail. Take the full measure of a person, Rachel and Morrie, take the full measure."

Judge Max Feigen was a very wise man. She never had questioned his advice.

There was a stir at the boat ramp where two men were trying to launch a small, flat-bottomed fishing craft which they had backed into the water on a trailer hitched to a dilapidated Ford truck. One of them was in water up to his waist at the back of the trailer. It looked as if he was having a problem loosening one of the ties and clearly he was losing his patience. Everyone within hearing range was treated to his ugly litany of profanities.

The boats already on the clear blue water reminded her of Baltimore, although these were fishing boats with outboard motors rather than the pleasure craft sailboats she was accustomed to. Most were at anchor or moving slowly across the glassy surface so quietly they might have been giant lily pads propelled by a gentle breeze. The men aboard cast their fishing lines in rhythmic arcs, and here and there a partner hoisted a net to help land a reeled-in catch. One in the distance to the north was coming at high speed, though, heading in her direction.

Feigen watched as the boat grew near and raced toward the launch site, the young woman in control waiting until the last minute to cut the power of its motor. The boat skidded up onto the gravel beach beside the ramp and the young woman and two young men jumped out, pulled the boat to higher ground, then ran to a red pickup truck and roared out of the parking lot and onto the highway.

"Well, I wonder what's got them in such a hurry," said a heavyset woman close to Feigen, shaking her head as if she disapproved. She apparently expected an answer.

"It looks like they had an emergency of some kind," Feigen said. "Nothing obvious that I could see."

The woman shuffled her sitting position until she could turn her head far enough to speak with Feigen face-to-face. "Might be nothing at all, though," she said. "Kids today are always in a hurry. They get a little older they'll slow down."

"This is the first time I've been here," Feigen said. "Is it usually this busy?"

"Sometimes a lot more than this. Right here's one of the best places on the lake to put out your boat. It's fun to just set and watch some of them ole boys get their boats off the trailer and away from the ramp. You'd think they'd never launched a boat before. Of course we get fishermen from all over. I've seen 'em drunk and sober, old and young. You name it. You set here long enough, you're likely to see just about anything."

Feigen smiled. "I take it you live nearby," she said.

"Just up the road yonder. My husband used to fish Cherokee Lake every day of the year. He passed a year ago in November, but I still like to come out here and watch what goes on—just in good weather, though."

"Oh, I'm sorry for your loss. That's never easy."

"You get over it, but your life's not ever the same again." The woman leaned toward Feigen and extended her hand. "My name's Rachel," she said. "It's from the Bible."

"No kidding? My name's Rachel, too!"

The woman seemed pleased. She looked older than Feigen had thought, but her face was still pretty and her dark eyes lit up as she talked. "I'm happy to make your acquaintance, Rachel," she said. "I suppose there's quite a lot of us—a lot of us named Rachel, I mean. You don't sound like somebody from around here, no offense intended."

"None taken," Feigen replied. "No, I'm from Maryland. Baltimore. And originally New York."

"I've been to Baltimore. I thought it was a pretty place. My late husband and I used to travel some, even if we never took a real long trip. But I was always glad to get home."

"Like they say: Home is where the heart is."

"And that's true. I was born and raised around here, and Jack—that was my late husband's name—Jack and I got married before we were twenty years old. He was a good man. We never wanted to live anywhere else."

"It sounds like you've had a good life," Feigen said warmly. "And this is a beautiful area. I can see why you wouldn't want to leave."

"I suppose some would say the Lord gave us paradise to live in. I'd rather think he loaned it to us and we're responsible for keeping it the way it is so the ones who come after us can enjoy it as much as we do."

With some difficulty, the other Rachel pulled herself up to a standing position. She stooped over to pick up a thick blue beach towel she'd been sitting on and groaned as she straightened up. "Honey, getting old isn't much fun," she said. "You get a new pain somewhere every day." But her tone was cheerful. "Have you had lunch yet? I was about to head on down to Big John's Place and get a bite to eat. I'd be more than pleased if you'd like to join me."

"You know what? I've not even had breakfast. You bet I'll join you. I'm hungry."

"Then let's go. I could eat a horse!"

Feigen followed as the other Rachel, driving an older Buick sedan with faded blue paint, drove straight to Big John's Place. The parking lot was half full and two other vehicles arrived at the same time they did. A middle-aged couple got out of one, a black Lincoln with Virginia license plates, and two men in overalls climbed out of a rusty and dented old Dodge pickup truck. These four and the two Rachels entered together. Mandy was on duty at the hostess stand and greeted them with a smile.

"Are y'all together?" she asked.

That brought a prompt universal denial from the six patrons, after which Mandy seated the Virginia couple and returned. It seemed as if she had not recognized Feigen until now.

"Sorry, I didn't notice who you were in the middle of all the others," Mandy said, obviously somewhat embarrassed by her failure. "Any progress on your investigation?"

"Nothing to write home about. So far, you've been the biggest help of all. But I'm not done yet."

The other Rachel looked somewhat startled. "Are you a police woman?" she asked. "I mean, not that it makes any difference, I just—"

"No, no," Feigen interrupted. "I'm a reporter, here working on a story. Mandy gave me some important information, otherwise I might be gone by now."

Mandy seated them at a table near the front. A waitress Feigen hadn't seen before took their orders and soon had two generous chef salads and tall glasses of sweet iced tea on the table. The other Rachel commented on the menu and made small talk about the pleasant atmosphere at Big John's, the efficiency of the staff, and how she and her late husband always enjoyed eating here. After a few minutes, she abruptly stopped speaking. Feigen searched for words to break the difficult silence.

"I'm sorry if coming here brings back painful memories," she said. "I wish I could have known your husband."

"You would have liked him. Everyone did. And please don't worry about the painful memories. There are lots of happy ones, too, and he always enjoyed it here. Just now I realized that I must sound like a lonely old widow woman so anxious for company she grabs onto strangers so she'll have somebody to share a meal with. I'm not like that at all, really. I'm a friendly person and I take to new people pretty easy, that's all."

Feigen put a hand on the other Rachel's arm. "I didn't think that," she said. "To be honest, I'm the one who was pretty desperate for company. I feel like I'm a long ways from home in a strange place—strange to me, I mean. I've not spent much time in the South."

"Well, there's plenty of folks around here who'd think darkly on you because you're a Yankee," the other Rachel said, laughing. "Please don't judge us all on the likes of them. If God created one of us, he created us all."

"Even the Negroes?"

"Even the Negroes. Rachel, there's not a racist bone in my body. I have black and white friends that I love equally, and there are blacks and whites both that I don't think too well of. The color of their skin doesn't have anything to do with it. My husband always said we're good or bad on the inside, and our insides look pretty much alike."

"Your husband sounds like a very wise man."

"But tell me all about you, now," the other Rachel said. "What kind of story is it you're working on? I didn't know there was anything exciting enough around here to bring a reporter down from Baltimore."

"Maybe there isn't," Feigen said. "I'm trying to trace a missing man—a boy, really—who got to somewhere around here and vanished. I've not had much luck."

"Oh, that's terrible. And he has a family back home?"

"Yes. His parents are worried sick." Feigen took Guy Saillot's picture from her purse and put it face-up on the table. "From what I can tell, he's a kind young man who's never been in any type of trouble. I'm hoping to find out he's all right, but the longer this goes on the more concerned I become."

"That breaks my heart," the other Rachel said. "The world can be a hard place." Tears suddenly welled up in her eyes. "Jack, my late husband, always said that. The world can be a hard place. I heard him say it many a time."

Recognizing that their conversation was causing the other Rachel unnecessary emotional distress, Feigen quickly changed the subject. She asked about the history of Cherokee Lake and was surprised by the extent of the other Rachel's knowledge. She asked about winters in east Tennessee, how people made their livings here, whether there were incentives for the young people to stay in the area, other things that were not trivial, things she really wanted to know. To every question, the other Rachel offered full and insightful answers. By the time they'd finished lunch Feigen had come to feel that she'd learned more in this unplanned social event than she often had during formal interviews with so-called experts.

The waitress brought a tray of appetizing desserts, but neither woman felt she had room for anything more. There was no longer any excuse to delay going their separate ways.

After they'd said their farewells at the door, each promising to stay in touch, Feigen turned back to bid goodbye to Mandy. Before she had a chance to speak, Mandy called to her, "Have you heard all the excitement? The car in the lake and all? Sounds like something big for around here."

Feigen was instantly fixated on what Mandy had to tell her. "What car in the lake?" she demanded.

"Three young people boating on the lake saw a car in the water. They said it was deep down, and they probably never would have seen it except for the high overhead sun. It was up near—"

"When did this happen?"

"Sometime this morning," Mandy said. "Some fishermen staying at the Tennessee Bend were in the lobby when these three came running in all excited and said they needed to call the police. Barney gave them a hard time, but finally let them call the sheriff's office."

"So that's why they were in such a hurry. I saw them at the lake, Mandy. But they left from the boat launch area. With all the boats in and out of there wouldn't you think someone would have seen the car earlier? I mean, assuming it's been there for a while."

"From what I understand, it's in deep water up by the hickory bluffs."

"Hickory bluffs?"

"Yes. That's an area only a few miles north of the boat launch where the lake bank is a high cliff. Deep water right up to the edge. But there's no road that goes up to the bluffs."

Feigen could feel her heart pounding in her chest. Her hand shook as she reached out to put it on Mandy's arm. "Do you know anything about the car? Was it a two-tone green Ford? Could they see it that well?"

Mandy shook her head. "I've told you all I know," she said. "I'll bet there's plenty of talk up at Barney's motel, though."

As she drove back to the Tennessee Bend, Feigen's palms were sweaty and she could feel the goose pimples on her arms. If the car in the lake should turn out to be Guy Saillot's green Ford there was a chance he was in it. Or rather, his body. All the worst possibilities she'd dreaded all along. If it was his car and there was no sign of Guy, there would still be some hope, although it would be diminished.

"Oh, dear God," she whispered, "let it be somebody's old junk Plymouth."

Chapter 11

There was a small knot of men in the lobby of the Tennessee Bend. Barney Vidone was nowhere to be seen. Feigen asked if any of the men, all of them apparently motel guests, knew anything about the car found in Cherokee Lake.

"I seen a sheriff's car out there in the driveway a little bit ago," one of the men said, "but I don't know what it was about."

Another man had more information. "Yeah, they were talking about a car in the water," he said. "I didn't hear where it was, or any more about it. The deputy said maybe somebody could take a look at it this afternoon but it didn't sound to me like he was in any big hurry."

A new wave of fear tightened Feigen's chest. If there was no road leading to the high bluffs as Mandy said, this would mean the car was deliberately driven over the cliff and no doubt meant foul play. And if it was Guy's, she would have to accept the likelihood that something terrible had happened to the young Frenchman. But there was no evidence that it was his car, she reminded herself. *Don't throw in the towel yet, Rachel. Don't assume the worst!* The voice in her head, this time, was that of Bill Skyles.

As she approached the check-in counter, Effie greeted her pleasantly. Feigen got straight to her foremost concern: "Have you heard anything about the car they found in the lake? Anything new, I mean."

Effie looked at her blankly. "I'm sorry, I don't know what car you're talking about," she said. "Somebody found a car in the lake?"

"Yes. I'm surprised you haven't heard. Three kids saw it in deep water up by the something bluffs. I forget exactly what they called it."

"Hickory bluffs, I'd suppose. But I don't know how a car would get in the water there. There's no road. Unless somebody wanted to get rid of it, of course."

"How do I get there? From what I heard, the sheriff was going to look into it this afternoon."

Effie was clearly skeptical. "Our sheriffs down here don't usually get around to anything that fast," she declared. "I'll grant you that this young Sheriff Carter's better than what we're used to, though. Time was it likely would have taken a couple of weeks to get to it. Unless some political big shot showed an interest, then they could move like a scalded dog."

"Oh, yes, I got a taste of your sheriff's office first hand."

"Well, like I said, Sheriff Carter is turning out to be a big improvement. He's still stuck with some of the old deputies, though. You might as well hang around a while and have a cup of coffee with me, Miss Feigen. Nothing's going to happen on any car in the lake this fast."

Feigen thanked her for the invitation, but said she needed to get on to other things. Effie Catlin gave her directions to the hickory bluffs—warning her to beware of copperhead snakes—and she went back to her room and tried to call Bill Skyles. He was out of the office, Ken Maddow told her, and likely wouldn't be back until the middle of the afternoon.

"Tell him they found a car in Cherokee Lake, Ken," Feigen said. "That's all I know about it for now, but I'll get back to him as soon as I find out anything more."

Maddow promised he would deliver the message. She thanked him and hung up.

There was no point in waiting around for her editor to get back to the office, and she had a strong urge to get busy. The hickory bluffs were not far away. She wanted to see something happening and maybe, just maybe, the sheriff would choose to act a little faster than Effie predicted. She quickly changed into jeans and walking shoes and set off for whatever lay ahead.

Finding the hickory bluffs was not as easy as Effie had led her to believe, but after an hour of false turns and backtracking and nearly being run off the road by a logging truck she found what she hoped was the right place. The region was aptly named; tall hickory trees interspersed with oaks and sweet gum formed a dense forest that spread over high, rocky ridges separated by deep valleys.

She found a clearly defined trail to the lake, and quickly learned to pick her way carefully along the rough footpath. At several points it went up or down steep inclines and it was strewn with rocks and occasional fallen branches. Even more hazardous were the tree roots that crossed the path and were easy to trip over. Where the trail crossed a rocky creek, she paused briefly beside a pool of stagnant water and looked up at what probably would have been a forceful waterfall before the dry season set in.

Feigen had forgotten Effie's warning about copperheads until she was startled by a sudden movement in the dead leaves beside the path. Her heart skipped a beat and she jumped sideways. She studied the ground carefully before she took another step, but she never saw anything that might have moved. From this point on, though, her heart pounded a bit faster.

After nearly an hour of difficult walking, she found herself at the edge of a high bank looking down on Cherokee Lake. She guessed the drop from here to the water to be at least thirty feet, maybe more. Estimating distances never had been one of her best talents.

But how could anyone have managed to get an automobile to this location? Somewhere, there must be a passable trail wider than the footpath she'd just taken. It would have to wind its way from the highway, two miles back, by some route that avoided the steepest inclines. Feigen assumed that she had missed the actual point where the car went into the water, but she hoped she was close. She stood and looked out over the water. The bright sun reflected off the surface of the lake in millions of sparkles. It would be nice just to sit back against a tree and enjoy the magnificent view. Surely, in this natural paradise, people should be content with their world. But as Bill Skyles had told her once, "Face it, Rachel. A lot of people are just no damned good." Wherever there were human beings, he said, there always would be trouble.

Much as she might have liked to, there was little reason to stay at this place. She'd found the hickory bluffs and seen Cherokee Lake from this high vantage point, and there was nothing more for her to do here. Feigen somewhat grudgingly turned her back on the lake and started back to her car. She walked for twenty minutes or so, then sat down to rest. The afternoon temperature had become tortuously hot again and she was grateful for the shade. The woods was quiet except for songbirds and chattering squirrels.

She stopped longer than she had intended, listening to the birds and squirrels and trying to forget the misfortune that had brought her here in the first place. But in her mind's eye there remained that image of Marie Saillot, the heartbreak in her voice, the pain in her words. Where was Guy? This challenge had not lessened and Feigen knew it would be her driving force until she found resolution.

Later, back at the Tennessee Bend Motel, she showered and got ready for bed. Although the air conditioning had been running full blast, the room was warm and she decided to abandon her night clothes and sleep naked. She lay tossing and turning on top of the sheets for a time, then got up and went to the bathroom and splashed cold water on her face. She studied herself in the large mirror on the wall, with no particular interest in what she saw, and went back to bed. When she finally did go to sleep, her sleep was not peaceful. She had nightmares about Guy Saillot and deep, dark water.

The Tennessee Bend was buzzing with activity when Feigen woke on Wednesday morning. She'd intended to be up early, but it had been nearly dawn when restful sleep finally came and it was eight-thirty when she woke. Three sheriff's department cars were in the parking lot, along with one from the Tennessee Highway Patrol. A small crowd milled about. She saw two of the Indiana fishermen, who nodded politely, as she walked to the lobby.

Inside, three people whom she recognized as the young woman and two young men who discovered the car in the lake were seated on a couch, facing a uniformed officer and two other men who were dressed in dark blue suits. The uniformed policeman and the two men she assumed to be plainclothes officers all had pens and notepads and were furiously writing down everything the young trio said.

She edged closer. The uniformed officer noticed her and immediately stood up and hurried to confront her.

"This is private police activity, ma'am," he said.

"I'm Rachel Feigen, Associated Press. What's going on?"

"I don't care if you're the editor of the *New York Times*, lady. I told you, this is private police business. Now please move along and don't interfere."

Feigen was frustrated by the rejection, but she knew she had no grounds for pushing herself into the ongoing police investigation. She would have to bide her time. She saluted the officer, as if acknowledging orders, and went to the counter where Effie stood watching.

"It looks like the action has picked up," she said.

Effie's face lit up with excitement. "Oh, boy," she said. "I'll say it has! There've been more cops in and out of here this morning than I've ever seen in one place before. Sorry you missed it."

"I overslept. I guess I wore myself out yesterday going up to the hickory bluffs and checking things out. It's pretty up there, but apparently I wasn't at the right place. There was nothing moving but me and the squirrels. And, of course, maybe a copperhead or two that I didn't see."

Effie Catlin looked surprised. "Then you missed the big event," she said.

"What big event?"

"They raised that car out of the water. I heard they hauled it off somewhere and locked it in a garage."

Feigen caught her breath. "Effie, do you know—was there a body in it?"

"I didn't hear one way or the other," Effie said. "But chances are, word would be out by now if there had been. My guess is it was empty."

"And you don't know where they took it?"

"No idea."

"Think these cops here know?"

"Sure they do, but I don't think they're into giving out information just now. They look to be busy collecting it."

"Yeah, I see your point," Feigen said. "That means a trip back to the sheriff's office. One of my favorite places to visit."

"I think Barney went over there a while ago, but I don't know why."

"Well, I need to go call my editor then I'll be heading over that way. I'll see you later."

When she got back to Room 10, the door was stuck. Feigen was about to throw her shoulder into it when George came from out of nowhere and shoved it open for her. He was gone before she had time to express her thanks. She remembered what Mandy had told her and made a mental note to try and make better contact with

George when she returned to the motel later in the day, even though she still had not come up with a way to communicate with him in a meaningful fashion.

She put in a call to Bill Skyles, who answered on the first ring. "Maddox said I missed your call yesterday," he said. "Anything new?"

"Bill, I went up to look around the area where they found that car in the lake. There's no way anybody could have driven into the water at that place by accident. It's way back in the woods and there's no road to it."

"Listen to me, Rachel. I don't want you to push too hard on this one. Let the cops do their job, okay? You'll have plenty of time to pick up the facts as they come out."

"I know, Bill. But the local law enforcement establishment is not what you'd call real eager to put out information."

"Give it time, Rachel. Do you need anything from me?"

"No, but I wish you were here."

"I'll be there tonight."

"So you really are coming? That's great. You can't get down here soon enough."

"I'm leaving within the hour. Until I get there, you keep your head down, kid, and be safe."

As she hung up the phone, Feigen stared into the large framed mirror that dominated the room. The face looking back at her was that of a woman she hardly knew. She wanted to see contentment but there was none. The face was marked by concern, uncertainty. It looked worn and haggard. She hadn't slept well since she arrived at the Tennessee Bend Motel and she was terribly worried about Guy Saillot. The myth that professional journalists are not supposed to get personally involved in their stories had never given her pause, and even if it had there was no way she could stand aside and not have feelings about this one. All she had to do was remember the pain in Marie Saillot's eyes.

Although she knew little more about Guy than she did when she started to work on this story, she had come to think of him almost as if he was a personal friend. She remembered Marie's description of her son: "He is so good to everyone. He wants to understand the world and make it better."

Feigen had come up with nothing to contradict this view. Who would want to harm him? She needed to know about the car that had been raised from the deep water of Cherokee Lake, but she really didn't want to. She had tried hard not to expect it to be Guy's green Ford. But she did.

Still, all she could do for Guy Saillot—and for Marie—was to find the truth. Feigen felt a new wave of determination. Damn it, she was a reporter. She had a job to do. She needed to go do it.

Minutes later, at Big John's Place, she got the information she hoped for. Mandy was there, to Feigen's surprise, trading work schedules with another hostess. And Mandy had information. She said the car that had been pulled from the lake was impounded on a securely fenced storage lot just past the sheriff's office. The gate would be locked and no one would be permitted to go in, but on the back side of the lot, away from the road, the enclosure was nothing more than open chain link fence. Feigen would be able to see the whole storage area from there.

Too excited to want breakfast, Feigen hurried to her car and drove straight to the sheriff's office, slowed in front of the building and kept going. A hundred yards beyond she saw what she was looking for. Although there was no sign to tell what it was, off the road on the right was an area fronted by a high board fence with a chained and padlocked gate marked by a crudely painted "No Trespassing" notice. She parked on the narrow driveway that led to the gate.

An open strip of recently mowed grass ran along the fence. Feigen walked fast, across the front of the lot parallel to the road, then along the side. The storage lot was not large. She quickly came to the back corner and turned, and had a clear view of all the impounded vehicles. There were only three. Two were pickup trucks. The third was a two-tone green Ford with Maryland license plates.

Feigen had to stifle an urge to scream. She felt faint. She wanted to shout to all humanity that life is unfair, the world an ugly place. "Guy didn't deserve this," she said to herself, aloud, her words edged with bitterness. "Poor, poor Marie. I'm so sorry."

But she still had work to do—now more important than ever. *Get a grip on yourself, Rachel. Be a reporter.* She must get back to the challenge that brought her here in the first place. No matter how bleak things looked, Guy Saillot was still missing. Her determination was fueled by new anger. For better or worse, whoever was responsible for his car being driven over the high bank into Cherokee Lake knew where Guy was.

Feigen half walked and half ran back to her car, the sparkling new Chevrolet which she had taken so much pride in only a few days ago. Its only meaning now was its function, transportation, a means to get her where she needed to go. Pride in material things truly would be vulgar compared with personal tragedy, loss such as Marie Saillot surely had felt for weeks. Feigen had not fully appreciated that loss before. Although it might be slim, there had been hope. But any hope that Guy would turn up alive evaporated with her first glimpse of that two-tone green Ford on the sheriff's impoundment lot.

She drove back to the sheriff's office, prepared to confront Andy Campbell, the vulgar desk sergeant, with her demands. A young man she had not seen before sat at the counter where Sergeant Campbell had been when she was there earlier.

He greeted her politely.

Feigen was momentarily flustered. She had steeled herself to do battle with the nemesis of her previous visit. "I'm with the AP," she said, showing her press card. "I need some information."

"Yes, ma'am?"

"The car that was pulled out of Cherokee Lake—what can you tell me about it?"

"Not much, I'm afraid. There was no sign of anyone inside the vehicle, but that's all I'm authorized to say. The sheriff will have a news conference when there's more information. Sorry."

"What about the registration?" she asked. "It had Maryland plates?"

"Ma'am, the sheriff has not released that information yet. People need to be contacted and all that."

"Any guess about how the car got into the lake? I mean, there's no road—"

The young officer maintained his pleasant demeanor. "I'm sorry, I don't have anything on that, either. We won't be releasing any more information pending the arrival of the FBI from Knoxville. I'd expect they're going to take control of things."

"The FBI? Why?"

The young man smiled. "Well, as I'm sure you know, ma'am, when there may be a crime across state lines, we call in the FBI. If they find reason to be involved, they like to run things their way. But you probably know that, too."

"You've been helpful, and I appreciate it," Feigen said. "Do you have any guess as to when there might be more information available?"

"Like I said, the sheriff will have a news conference. But don't be surprised if all he has to report is what I've already told you."

This time, Feigen left the sheriff's office feeling good about the way she'd been treated. She had known going in that not much information could be released until people had been contacted, as the young deputy said. "People," in this case, meant Alain and Marie Saillot. And she knew, of course, that the FBI already was involved.

And where in the hell was Agent Anton Schuler? Was he going to just sit on his fat butt in Baltimore and wait for the Knoxville office to tell him what was going on? She might not like him, but she wished he was there.

Chapter 12

It was sweltering hot outdoors, but Barney and Harlan McElroy and Bishop Collins had moved to the Tennessee Bend Motel parking lot to deal with a situation they would rather not talk about where someone else might hear. There was a problem they needed to do something about. Right now.

Once they got their heads together they were quick to reach a consensus; Barney and Harlan readily concurred in Bishop Collins's self-assured declaration that they were doing only what had to be done. The uppity jewgirl had left them no choice, Bishop declared, driving up in her shiny new Chevrolet with Maryland tags and checking in at the Tennessee Bend and starting to ask questions about things that were none of her business. Andy Campbell said she'd been to the sheriff's office a couple of times and they had heard about her sticking her nose in other places where it didn't belong for a couple of days now. It was time to act.

Bishop had an audacious plan.

"We'll lock her in a room with a couple of good nigger boys and let nature take its course," he explained. "She'll get her comeuppance when the boys' jungle instincts take over, and in the morning we'll drag the boys out and teach them better than to mess with a white woman. Probably nothing more than a good whipping—unless they give us trouble. And maybe we ought to have her cook us up some bacon and eggs while we're at it, too."

Harlan took a final puff on his cigarette, dropped the butt at his feet, and ground it into bits with his boot heel on the asphalt surface of the parking lot. He spit and wiped his mouth on his shirt sleeve.

"Okay, Harlan, you got a problem with all this?" Bishop Collins demanded.

Harlan rarely questioned Bishop's ideas, but this time he had one concern: "Since the jewgirl's from the city, she's probably a whore and she might enjoy it. Don't you think?"

Bishop Collins assured him that her city background wouldn't matter. They'd find a pair of sturdy young bucks who would be more than she could handle even if she was a whore. She would be pleading for mercy before the boys were done with her. Harlan was satisfied.

To Barney Vidone, Bishop's plan promised more excitement than anything the three ever had done together. He'd been careful for two years not to let slip the fact that he bought the Tennessee Bend partly as a means to his own entertainment, but now, struck by a sudden impulse to make a singular contribution to Bishop's scheme, he decided to divulge his secret.

The primary instrument of Barney's amusement was Room 10. He had devoted hours of his own labor to this room, painting and repainting, installing sparkling new bathroom fixtures, laying new carpet, bringing in nice furniture. Then he cut an opening in the inside wall and covered it with a stylishly framed two-way mirror—a mirror so dominant it begged to be made use of. Behind the mirror was his pit room, a darkened and cramped little closet of a space where he could sit, beer in hand, and leisurely enjoy a full view of everything that went on in Room 10.

"With what Bishop's come up with, it'll be even better," Barney said. "She's already in there. All we have to do is put the boys in with her."

If Bishop Collins was surprised by Barney's revelation, he didn't show it. "You creepy little prick, I always knew you were getting your kicks somewhere in that damned firetrap," Bishop said. "I reckoned you were getting the real thing, though, not just watching the action through a peephole."

Harlan was not so receptive. "Dang it Barney, what if it was my wife in that room some time?"

"Oh, hell, Harlan, your wife's way too skinny to interest even a little creep like Barney," Bishop Collins said. "Anyway, why would she be spending the night in the Tennessee Bend Motel? You don't think she shacks up, do you?"

Harlan's anger was palpable. His neck reddened almost to his chin, then the coloration crept up one side of his face. "That's not funny, Bishop," he protested.

"Harlan, you're too damned sensitive."

"No, I ain't. You wouldn't want somebody making fun of your wife!"

"Making fun? I'm just telling it like it is."

Harlan stepped forward, toward Bishop Collins, and raised his massive right hand in a threatening gesture. Barney quickly jumped in between them. Harlan stood mutely for an instant, dropped his hand and grinned. Bishop Collins reached out and slapped him on the back and both men laughed.

"We got to get along," Barney said. "We're all in this together. We can all three fit in the pit room, too. May be a little crowded, but I think it'll be worth a little bit of rubbing shoulders to see the jewgirl put in her place."

"You got any more secrets?" Bishop asked.

Barney shook his head. "You fellows know everything there is to know," he said.

Harlan's demeanor had turned pleasant again, as if he was happy to have the subject turned back to the jewgirl instead of his wife. He clearly was eager to get on with Bishop's plot, but now he had more questions: "I been wondering how we can lock them in from the outside? Can we do that?"

"Yessir," Barney said proudly. "There's a hasp on every door. I padlock some of the rooms during the off season when I don't need all of them."

"Couldn't they bust out a window?"

"Wouldn't do 'em no good. Windows all got bars on the outside."

"Okay, then. But where we going to find the two nigger boys?"

Bishop Collins looked at Harlan with an expression bordering on scorn. Then he laughed. "Harlan, you just may be the dumbest white man I know," he said. "We could find a nigger boy behind every tree. What in the hell do you mean, where we going to find them?"

Harlan was defensive again. "We can't just drag a couple of them from out behind trees, Bishop. We got to get a drop on them first. We ain't talking about some old men outta the woods. You said sturdy young bucks. And we're talking about two of them, right?"

Bishop's impatience was beginning to show. "Shit, Harlan," he grumbled, "how hard's it going to be to find two sturdy young nigger boys? Hell yeah we want them one at a time, but that sure ain't no problem. We can hole the first one up in another room while we get the next one. Leave him there all day if we have to."

"That wouldn't be a problem at all," Barney said. "Like I said, every room has a hasp on the door. And I've got good strong padlocks, too."

"You got any other problems, Harlan?" Bishop said.

Harlan looked embarrassed and shook his head. "You always think of about everything there is to think of, Bishop," he declared meekly.

Barney had been reluctant to express a worry of his own, but this seemed to be a good time to bring it up. "When the jewgirl checked in, she said she didn't know how long she'd be staying. Unless we get the boys in Room Ten with her tonight she might be gone. I guess we'd be rid of her, though, and maybe wouldn't have to do anything."

Bishop Collins scowled. "Come on now," he said. "I know you wouldn't want to rob us of all that fun, would you? What I'd like to know, though, is how 'n hell did you manage to keep that room secret? Effie not know about it? I'll bet George—"

"But we all know George ain't gonna make no racket about it," Harlan interrupted, and roared with laughter.

"Effie might have suspected something," Barney said, "but from inside Room Ten everything looks normal. She's never seen the pit room. You've got to go through double doors in back of the supply closet in my office to get to it and I keep the second door locked. The key's right here in my pocket. George knows the pit room's there, but he's way too dumb to figure out what it's for."

Bishop Collins was ready to move.

"If we get down to the business area we might be able to get them boys yet today," he said. "It'd be nice to have 'em there when the jewgirl gets back to the motel. Harlan, you got a gun or two in your truck?"

"You ain't never seen me without one, have you?"

"We're not talking shotgun or deer rifle here. You carrying a pistol?"

"Damn right I am."

"Okay, then. Let's get down to the bus station and see what we can find. Some boy just passing through gets off a bus ain't nobody going to miss him. Now look, when we see a boy we want, let Barney go up and start him talking. Barney, be sure and get right in his face, nose-to-nose. Then you and me, Harlan, we'll come up to him from behind. You stick that pistol in his back and tell him if he moves his black ass will be dead before he hits the ground. You ready, Barney?"

"Yeah, but I need to go in and let Effie know I'm leaving. She'll take care of things till I get back."

Bishop Collins already had started walking toward his truck. "Okay, then," he called to Barney over his shoulder, "leave the Studebaker here and ride with me."

"Fine. Long's I don't have to ride in that rattletrap old GMC of Harlan's."

Barney ducked into the motel office while the other men went to their trucks. He told Effie he might be gone for a few hours. Then he hurried out, before she could raise questions, and joined Bishop Collins in his red Ford pickup with its flashy chrome plated custom running boards. Bishop floored the accelerator and screeched out of the parking lot and Harlan followed.

A few minutes later, Bishop Collins eased his truck into the Greyhound bus station parking lot and stopped in the shade of a sickly tulip poplar tree. Harlan drove up alongside. A Knoxville-bound bus sat idling not far from the front entrance to the small terminal, the foul odor of its diesel exhaust unavoidable even in the open air. Its door stood open and a small group of passengers milled about inside the waiting room.

They sat tight until a young black man left the station and walked nonchalantly toward the open bus. At Bishop's signal, Harlan and Barney climbed out and followed Bishop toward the building, meeting the young man half way to the waiting bus.

"Decent day, isn't it?" Barney said, greeting him with a friendly smile. "On your way south?"

"Yes, sir."

"Travelin' or heading home?"

Before the young man could answer, Harlan jammed a pistol into his back and commanded him to be quiet. The smile on Barney's face became a mean scowl, and Bishop Collins took a firm hold on the man's right arm. The young black man did as he was told and made no protest. He stood still and quiet, as if afraid to move.

"Let's get in my truck, here," Bishop ordered. "Just do what we tell you and you won't get hurt. We don't want no trouble."

"Who the hell are you?" the black man said angrily.

Harlan slid his gun up to the back of the man's head. "Right now we're the ones who're going to blow your head off if you don't do what you're told," he said. "Earl Warren ain't around to help you now, boy."

The young black man got in the truck and Barney took Harlan's pistol and climbed in beside him. He kept the gun low and out of sight. Bishop Collins started the engine and gunned the pickup back onto the highway, pointed toward the Tennessee Bend, and Harlan followed close behind.

No one spoke during the short drive to Barney's motel. When they got there, Bishop drove the full length of the parking lot, to the far back side. "Which room you want to put him in?" he asked Barney.

"He can cool his heels a while back there in Room twenty-nine," Barney replied. "There won't be anybody in yelling distance of these rooms back here."

Their captive slid across the seat of the pickup and crawled out behind Barney. "What do you want with me?" he demanded. "You want my money? What? Just take it and let me go."

"Just shut up," Bishop Collins ordered. "You're going to have a real good time before this is all over if you just do what you're told. But you give us any trouble, boy, and your own mama won't recognize you when they find your black-assed carcass rotting away out there in a hole in the ground someplace in the woods."

Barney unlocked the door to Room 29.

Bishop shoved the young man through the door. "Jes make yo'self to home," he whined. "We'uns be back fo' yo' in a little bit." He laughed heartily, as if he considered his crude imitation of the local black accent extremely funny. "Be sure and put that padlock back on there, Barney. This one's a real keeper. And you better give Harlan back his pistol before he gets scared of hisself."

Sergeant Willie Jamison heard the lock snap shut on the outside of the door and knew he was in serious trouble. There was a number on the door marking this as Room 29, but he had not been able to see the name of the establishment. It would be some time before he learned that he was a prisoner in the Tennessee Bend Motel.

He looked about the shabby room. The walls were dark green, with splotches of lighter color where damaged areas had been repaired and repainted. There were the bare essentials common to a cheap motel: a sagging double bed with a washed-out, olive-colored spread, a compact dresser, and a round, Formica-topped table with two chairs. The carpet was worn and dirty and the drapes over a single window were shabby and almost colorless. There was no closet, only a wooden rod fastened between two panels that jutted out from one wall and formed a narrow compartment without a door. Two bent wire hangers swung from the rod. The only lamp sat on a nightstand next to the bed. There was no telephone.

The heat was stifling. If the room had air conditioning, it had not been turned on. He looked for any type of controls for heat and cooling but none was visible.

The door to the bathroom stood half open, and Jamison took a quick look inside. To his surprise, the room was reasonably clean. There were white bath towels stacked on a shelf above the toilet and a pair of yellow hand towels on a rack beside the mirror. He unwrapped the tiny bar of Ivory soap that lay on the sink and washed his hands, then cupped them and brought warm water up to his face. He dried with one of the yellow towels.

The image in the mirror paralleled the self-image he carried in his mind. He looked like an American soldier, hard and tough. He was six feet tall and muscular. His hair was close cropped and he was clean shaven, his civilian clothes as fresh and neatly pressed as his military dress would have been had he been in uniform. But there was something else. He could see the fear in his own eyes.

Willie Jamison was not easily intimidated, but he had heard enough about racial tensions in the South to know that a black man merely passing through could disappear from the face of the earth and nobody would know. It would be three days before someone noticed that he had not checked in at Fort Jackson when he was supposed to and commence to look for him.

I'll be listed as AWOL soon, he thought. *I wonder how hard they hunt for an AWOL soldier?*

They'd start with what they knew: He departed South Korea a

month ago with a thirty-day leave before reporting to his new duty station. If they checked with his mother in East St. Louis, Illinois, she'd say yes, he spent a good part of his leave there with her. But he left home a week ago to visit his uncle in Pennsylvania.

His uncle would tell them he was on a bus on his way to South Carolina—*and that's where my tracks would end.* Nobody would remember seeing him anywhere along the way. They'd say one black man looked pretty much like another, especially since he wasn't wearing his uniform.

His anxiety deepened.

He sat on the edge of the bed and pulled a pack of Camel cigarettes from his shirt pocket. Only five cigarettes left. He lit one and drew the smoke deep into his lungs. He felt the comforting burn, the sense of release that surged through his body when the nicotine hit his blood stream. This temporarily helped calm his frayed nerves and he was grateful for even the slightest relief.

Bone weary, Jamison finished the cigarette and lay back on the bed and studied the ceiling as if it might hold hidden clues. Who were these crazies and what did they want? He'd faced imminent danger in Korea, but faced it on equal terms. He knew who the enemy was and he had the means to defend himself. *After all I've been through, getting lynched in the backwoods of Tennessee would be a hell of a way to end up. And if I died here right now what would my life have amounted to?*

He was too agitated to stay still. He got up and paced the floor for a few minutes, then returned to the bathroom. It was small and cramped and it reminded him of the one in the rundown apartment where he grew up.

His early years in East St. Louis had left an indelible mark on Jamison's view of the world. By the age of twelve he had given up on himself, spinning down a path hell-bent for destruction. And he didn't care. In spite of his mother's pleading, he had made no effort to turn himself around. It was chilling now to realize how close he'd come to being lost.

If he wanted excuses he had plenty. Living in poverty with nothing more to look forward to than being accepted by a street gang, no father, a mother who worked two and sometimes three jobs to keep herself and him afloat. It had not been easy.

But Jamison wasn't one to make allowances, and he took little credit for his own salvation. Two things happened that proved turning points in his young life. First, he was caught trying to steal a knife in a sporting goods store, and second, his Uncle Jerome came to visit. The awkward and shameful attempt at stealing threw him headfirst into the juvenile justice system, where he was put under the thumb of a dedicated probation officer who refused to let him slip through the cracks. And then Uncle Jerome came, on two week's leave from the army, and for the first time in his life he had a good role model who took the time to show him that things could be different.

Jamison sat on the bed again, then lay back and relived those two weeks in his mind. Could it really have been that long ago? Uncle Jerome, his mother's younger brother, was tough as nails but gentle as a kitten. He would put on his uniform and walk with his nephew through the crowded downtown streets of East St. Louis at almost the midnight hour, pushing his way through the drunks and pimps and whores and the young hoodlums looking to stir up trouble. He was not afraid and he would not be intimidated.

Uncle Jerome would be his model. Jamison promised himself that he'd stay calm, do whatever it took to escape this place, and eventually show up for his new assignment at Fort Jackson. His outlook brightened as he looked ahead. He was a good soldier and that meant being where he was supposed to be, when he was supposed to be there.

South Carolina was segregated. He needed to get ready for a world in which he would be treated as an equal as long as he was on the military base but face an insurmountable wall between himself and the white population as soon as he stepped through the gate. Not that racial prejudice was something new, of course. He had seen it everywhere he'd ever been, and in many ways the only real difference between Illinois and South Carolina was that the Southern state embraced official segregation while his home state disallowed it as a matter of law but made little effort to deal with it socially. There had been precious few white faces in the schools he went to.

Jamison thought about his uncle in Pennsylvania, long since retired from the military and beginning to show his age. He was glad he'd taken the time to go by and visit. In his mind's eye he could see the pride in his uncle's eyes when he showed up in uniform. Uncle Jerome had been filled with questions about his service in Korea, his experiences along the demilitarized zone that separated the two parts of the divided country, his new assignment at Fort Jackson.

There were tears in the older man's eyes when they parted at the bus station and Jamison had promised to visit again as soon as he could.

But he couldn't escape reality. All the memories, all the optimistic looking ahead could not change his present situation. He had been taken at gunpoint by a trio of racists and locked into a room somewhere in Tennessee. He was ready to put up a fight if he had the chance. But wherever he was and whoever these men were, Sergeant Willie Jamison feared that the odds were very much against him getting out of this alive. He had no doubt that his fight, if it came, would be a fight for his life.

Chapter 13

With the first new player essential to their amusement securely locked away in Room 29, Bishop said it was time to head back down the road and look for the second. Harlan drove in front this time, and Bishop Collins got right on his bumper.

"Let's see how fast I can make Harlan nervous," he said to Barney. "You ever ride with Harlan? Somebody gets too close behind him it scares him shitless. He always thinks there's somebody out to get him, riding his ass and fixing to run him off the road or something. I asked who in hell would be out to get him, given that he ain't got no money or anything, and he just looked at me funny. I told him if he gets rear-ended he's got the law on his side, but Harlan don't always get your point."

"How come you let him work for you at the sawmill?" Barney Vidone said. "Can he handle the job?"

"Aw, I don't give him anything to do that takes any brainpower, just heavy lifting and packing things around that need to be moved. He's strong as an ox. Mainly, I just let him work once in a while to help him out."

"That's generous of you, Bishop."

"You know me, Barney. I help them that helps me. You know how me and Harlan got together in the first place, don't you?"

Barney said he didn't, even though he'd heard the story a dozen times at least, and maybe more.

"He come along one day when I'd been boar hunting and got my truck stuck in a ditch. I swear he very near lifted it out with his bare hands. Anyway, we got to talking afterwards and I found out he saw things pretty much like I do. You and me was already set up to torch that ACLU billboard down there towards Knoxville and I asked did he want to come help."

"Yeah, I remember that one," Barney said. "That was the first time he took part."

Harlan turned in at the Shell gas station directly across the highway from the Greyhound terminal. Bishop stopped beside him and told Barney to roll down the window on his side of the truck, then motioned for Harlan to do the same.

"This ought to be a good place," Harlan said. "Don't you think so?"

"You done good, Harlan," Bishop Collins answered, shouting across Barney and over the noise of both engines. "We're going to pull up over yonder a ways and watch. You set tight till you see us get out. Then you get to us fast."

Bishop drove to the opposite end of the station's driveway and turned around, then backed up to the base of the tall Shell sign. That left them facing the pump islands. They waited and watched. The first five cars that stopped had white occupants. The sixth car, a blue Oldsmobile sedan, was driven by a lone black man.

Bishop Collins was cautious. "Let him get out where we can see him, in case he's an old man. We need us another sturdy young buck."

After an attendant had filled the Oldsmobile's fuel tank, the driver got out and went inside. He was a young man, tall and strongly built and well dressed.

"That boy will do just fine," Bishop Collins said. "We'll grab him soon's he comes out. I'll take Harlan's gun and hold on him and make him drive his own car back up to the motel. You bring my truck."

He quickly scooted from the pickup and motioned for Harlan. Barney got out and rushed behind. Harlan met them in the middle of the driveway, not far from the blue Oldsmobile at the pump island. Through the station's front windows, they watched their prey pay for his gas. When he came out he went around to the side of the building and entered a restroom that had a conspicuous sign marking it as the one for "COLORED MEN."

"Wait till he's almost back to his car," Bishop Collins directed.

"Then that boy's ours. See, Harlan, like I told you, this was easy as falling over drunk."

The young black man was inside the restroom for only a few minutes, then came out and headed in their direction. Barney again made the first contact. "Decent day, isn't it?" he said, figuring that this approach had worked well the first time and he might as well use it again.

"Yes, it's a very nice day," his target answered, smiling. "Excuse me, please."

He started to walk past Barney, but at that instant Harlan and Bishop closed in and Harlan pushed his pistol hard into the young man's back. Like Barney, they repeated the routine they had used earlier.

"Where are your white sheets?" the victim said angrily.

"We don't wear no white sheets because we don't take no orders from nobody," Harlan said. "Around here, we give the orders."

"So then you're just ignorant local rednecks?"

Harlan jabbed harder with the pistol. "Don't get smart with me, boy!" he growled.

Bishop Collins had a secure grip on their victim's right arm and Barney moved around to the other side. The young black man followed Bishop's orders and quietly got behind the wheel of his car. Harlan held the gun on him until Bishop was set in the passenger's seat and then passed the pistol through the window. They quickly formed a three-vehicle caravan en route to the Tennessee Bend Motel.

By the time Barney and Harlan reached the back of the parking lot, Bishop Collins had their captive standing beside the Oldsmobile with both hands on top of the car. Bishop was holding Harlan's pistol, almost casually, and the two looked to be engaged in conversation.

"Looks like you got yourself a new friend, Bishop," Harlan called as he and Barney approached.

"This boy ain't too bad for a nigger," Bishop replied. "Fact is, I kinda like him. I been telling him we're setting him up for a real good time."

Barney fished the key to the padlock on the Room 29 door from his pocket and said, "Bring him on over here. Maybe him and the boy that's already in there will have something to talk about while they wait for the party."

"White women, most likely," said Harlan.

Willie Jamison heard a noise outside and bolted up from the bed and started toward the door. He had a fleeting plan of attack, to stand beside the door and jump the first man through. This might be his last chance. He heard the snap of the padlock opening. The door swung inward, as if pushed violently, and a young black man was shoved inside. Then the door was pulled shut with a loud slam and Jamison heard the padlock snap shut again.

He and the other man stood and looked at one another for a moment and then the other man said, "Who are you?"

"Sergeant Willie Jamison, U.S. Army. Who are you?"

"My name is Loman. Do you have any idea what this is all about?"

"Crazy rednecks, is all I know."

"How long have they had you locked in here?"

"I don't know, two hours maybe."

As they stood face-to-face, Jamison could see that Loman was a couple of inches taller than he was and probably outweighed him by twenty pounds. And no flab. This guy was big. He felt a surge of relief to have another person in the room. Not that they were any closer to being out of the woods, as far as he could tell, but surely two men had a better chance than he would have had by himself. He needed to feel Loman out, see what he brought to the game.

"Where'd they grab you at?" Jamison asked.

"Coming out of a gas station. You?"

"They got me at the bus station. Three guys. One had a weapon."

"We need to take stock here, Jamison. I think we're in real danger. Will anyone know you're missing?"

Jamison told the newcomer what he already had worked out in his own mind. "It will be a couple of days or more before they miss me," he said. "I'm supposed to report in at Fort Jackson, South Carolina, the day after tomorrow. Probably be another day after that before they start looking for me."

"So if I understand this correctly, you're actually in the army now and on your way to a new post. Right?"

"You got it."

"And you were traveling by bus?" Loman asked, shading his question as if calculating the answer in advance.

"Yes."

"Okay, this could be important. What kind of luggage did you have?"

"Luggage? I'm in the army, man. I had a duffel bag."

Loman smiled. "Yes, of course," he said. "It has your name on it and it's still on the bus. When that bus gets to South Carolina and you're not there to pick up your duffel bag somebody has to notice."

Jamison returned the grin.

Loman extended a hand. "My name is Quintilius Varus Loman," he said. "The whole mouthful. Call me Quint."

"Quintil . . . what? Where in hell did you get a name like that?"

"Quintilius Varus Loman. My father was a history professor at Alabama State University. He wanted me to have an illustrious name."

"Well, you got a name all right. I don't know about illustrious. Glad to meet you, Quint. And by the way, my full name is John William Jamison Junior, but as far as I know I never set eyes on John William Senior. I've been called nothing but Willie since the day I was born."

"That keeps it simple. We're Quint and Willie."

"So what got you into this shit?"

"I'm a civil rights lawyer on my way to Mississippi," Loman told him. "I expect you heard about the kid from Chicago, Emmett Till?"

"Yeah, I guess, if that's his name. I hadn't heard about it, but my uncle was talking about something going on down there."

Loman looked surprised. "It's hard to believe that you hadn't heard about it. It took the death of a kid to get the press interested in a black person being murdered in Mississippi. But the Till case has had pretty extensive coverage."

"Look, damn it," Jamison said, suddenly tensing, "I was in Korea watching over the gooks. We didn't do a whole lot of newspaper reading over there."

"Gooks? Why would you call another human being a 'gook'?"

The question flustered Willie Jamison, who never had faced it before, but also overrode his irritation that the new prisoner appeared to be accusing him of ignorance. He started to speak, then closed his mouth firmly.

"Forget it," Loman said. "We can talk human relations at a later date. Right now, we need to concentrate on getting ourselves out of here."

Jamison was relieved. "Okay, let's start with that bunch of crazy rednecks that shanghaied us and brought us in here," he said. "None of them are too smart, but that big guy is so dumb he probably hasn't figured out that eating beans makes him fart."

Loman tried to suppress a laugh, but couldn't. "You have a colorful way of putting things, sergeant," he said.

"Hey, I'm sorry if I don't talk like a lawyer. We didn't rub asses with too many of you guys on the streets of East St. Louis."

Now it was Loman who tensed. "Look," he said firmly, "don't try that poor, underprivileged black boy crap on me. I came off the mean streets of Birmingham, Alabama."

Jamison saw the steel in the other man's eyes. "Hey, I didn't mean it like that," he said. "We're in this together, man. But how the hell did you make it from Birmingham, Alabama, to being a big time lawyer?"

"I was a good athlete. I got a football scholarship to the University of Wisconsin, and made it from there into the Michigan law school. It wasn't easy, but I got through."

"You still got people in Alabama?"

"Yes. My mother's still living. And an aunt and a few cousins. My brothers and sisters all moved away. How about you?"

"My mother in East St. Louis and an uncle in Pennsylvania. She's a saint and I probably wouldn't be here today except for him."

Loman raised an eyebrow. "Oh? Wouldn't be here as in not enjoying a trip to the sunny South, or wouldn't be here as in you might have departed this glorious life?"

"It's a long story. You know, I lost the girl I loved, tried to drink myself to death, all the usual crap."

Jamison had no desire to tell this stranger about Paris. He hit only the high spots of the story.

He was seventeen the first time he saw her and Paris was fifteen and surely the most beautiful girl in the world. He envied her because she had a father. Her father named her after the French city he saw in a movie theater travelogue just before she was born. Paris hated that her four siblings got common names while she was stuck with one people laughed at, but Willie Jamison loved her name almost as much as he loved her.

"Yeah, we talked about getting married when I finished school and got a good job," he explained. "I walked the streets of East St. Louis or crossed the river to the city every day looking for work. Never found anything, though, and it didn't matter."

It didn't matter, he told Loman, because Paris was mugged and robbed on a busy street in broad daylight. Her skull was fractured by the blunt object the mugger used as a weapon, bone fragments piercing her brain, and she never regained consciousness. She died two days later at St. Mary's hospital, the place where both she and Willie Jamison were born. He got drunk as soon as the funeral was over and tried to drink himself to death, was not truly sober for a month, hardly ate or slept, and almost killed his mother with worry.

"I was done for if Uncle Jerome hadn't showed up again," he said. "No question he saved my life. He convinced my mother that the army offered me the best way out of East St. Louis and the rest, like they say, is history."

"So the army worked for you?"

"Just like home. You don't have to worry about where your next meal's coming from and they keep you in good boots." He wouldn't tell Loman that the best part was the small monthly allotment he was able to send to his mother.

"Were you in combat?"

"I was lucky. The war was over when I got there."

"Better to be lucky than to be good sometimes," Loman said. "That's what they say, anyway."

Jamison was eager to change the subject, especially not to get an image of Paris stuck in his mind. "How about you? Got a heartbreak story for me?"

"No, I guess I've been too busy. The heartbreak probably will come when I wake up someday and find out I've missed the boat spending too much time on going to school and trying to change the world."

"How come you're going to Mississippi?"

"They're about to bring the Till murder case to trial. The Philadelphia Urban League office is sending me down there to monitor it."

Jamison finally had lightened up. He managed a smile, even. "Okay," he said. "I'm a soldier and you're a lawyer. You come up with a plan to get us out of here and I'll take the fight to the enemy. Your brain and my killer instinct. They'll be damned sorry they tried to mess with the likes of this team."

"I like your confidence."

"Confidence, hell. I'm bluffing."

Loman seemed to appreciate the joke. "So okay," he said, "if it worked on me it might work on them. We might be able to convince these dumb asses that if they mess with us they're going to rouse your killer instinct and end up in a world of hurt."

"Oh, yeah, no doubt about it," Willie Jamison said sarcastically. The fear he'd seen earlier in his own eyes still was there.

Chapter 14

Barney Vidone felt a rush of smug satisfaction when the second young black man had been shoved into Room 29 and the door locked behind him. He often had sensed that Bishop Collins did not fully appreciate his contributions to the group, this trio of upright, God-fearing citizens who had given a great deal to the community and, in Barney's opinion, deserved greater recognition than they had yet received. He'd never really expected public acknowledgment, though, and he cared nothing for what Harlan thought, but he looked up to Bishop Collins and craved their leader's respect.

In the back of his mind, Barney always had believed that one day his Tennessee Bend Motel would come to play a significant part in their work. Bishop Collins said derogatory things about it from time to time but now he'd see how important the motel was in carrying out their plan to put the uppity jewgirl in her place. And the icing on the cake was Barney's unique creation, Room 10, which was about to offer his two cohorts some of the same grand entertainment he'd enjoyed for the last couple of years.

It had been hard for Barney to reveal the secret of Room 10. His voyeuristic trait wasn't something he was particularly proud of.

He had high moral standards, and he had no truck with those who would mistreat Christian women or be cruel to animals or children. He had always treated the black people fairly, and the day they accepted their proper place in society and black men gave up their lust for white women he would happily let them live in peace. He would, in fact, be relieved, because he would no longer be burdened

by the obligation to protect the white way of life that God had be-
stowed upon the faithful.

Just now, Barney was a bit concerned that Bishop might be more
interested in having fun than he was in putting the jewgirl in her
place. But he already had made a solid commitment to their
scheme—to say nothing of giving away the secret of his voyeur's
window—and there was no way he could back down. The two young
black men were securely imprisoned in Room 29 and it was only a
matter of time before the jewgirl returned and all three of them were
thrown together in Room 10.

"These boys won't be going anywhere till we come back and let
'em out," Barney declared. "This door's solid oak. It'd take a truck to
bust through it."

"And a lot stouter truck than your little Studebaker at that,"
Bishop Collins taunted, elbowing Harlan in the ribs as a signal that
Harlan was supposed to laugh.

Harlan responded on cue, though it seemed to Barney that the
laughter was somewhat painfully forced. Harlan had never been
much good at faking anything. He did his best, though. "Yeah, Barney, it'd take a stouter truck than that little Studebaker of yours to
bust through that door."

Barney was irritated, but he pretended to take the ribbing good
naturedly. "You fellows are just jealous because my truck is prettier
than either one of yours," he said, and faked a chuckle of his own.

This was the kind of thing he wished Bishop Collins wouldn't do
so often. Barney was proud of his truck and Bishop knew it was a
sore spot. When it came to style, his Studebaker was way ahead of
Harlan's old rattletrap GMC or Bishop's Ford. It was exactly what he
needed as a businessman who wouldn't be hauling hay and hogs and
firewood like Harlan did or greased-up old machines like the one in
the back of Bishop's truck right now. And he kept his truck clean. It
had "Tennessee Bend Motel" painted neatly on each door and Barney felt that it was always important to his business to present a good
image.

"Well, okay now, we got our two nigger boys," Bishop Collins
said. "How much time you think we've got to kill before that jewgirl
comes back? I wouldn't mind running down to Big John's Place and
seeing is his beer cold today. What y'all say?"

Barney knew Bishop Collins well enough to recognize what was happening. Bishop had to get serious again to prove that he was still in charge. Barney was willing to play along. "I'd say nothing's going to happen until after dark, so we've got three or four hours probably," he offered. "Nobody's keeping time on us."

"Well let's get the hell outta this hot sun, then," Bishop said. "You coming, Harlan?"

Bishop Collins and Harlan climbed into Bishop's truck and drove out of the motel parking lot, turning toward Big John's Place. Barney stopped in the office to check with Effie Catlin and make sure everything was all right before he went to join them. Effie was on the telephone. He waited patiently until she was finished.

"Some woman from New Jersey wanting to know if we had high quality rooms," Effie explained. "I told her hell yes, the Tennessee Bend is a high quality establishment. But maybe I didn't sound convincing or something, because she didn't make a reservation."

"Don't matter. We'll fill up before the weekend, with this nice weather. There's going to be lots of fishermen wanting to get on the lake. You need me around here for a couple of hours?"

"I wouldn't think so. I expect it'll be pretty quiet for a while now."

"Then I'm going to run down to Big John's and have a beer with Bishop and Harlan. They've been helping me with some things out back. You know where to call me if anything comes up."

Barney whirled and started to leave, eager to escape before Effie had a chance to lecture him. George was coming in. He backed up, stepped to one side, and held the door open for his boss. Barney gave him a friendly pat on the arm and George smiled.

When he got to Big John's Place, Barney was surprised to find Bishop Collins and Harlan still in the parking lot. Had they waited for him to get there before going inside? Harlan promptly set him straight. "You missed a right good fight, Barney. A couple of dumb peckerwoods had had a little too much beer and was taking their disagreement out on each other right out here in front of everybody."

"Yeah, well. The show's all over," Bishop Collins proclaimed. "I'm thirsty. Let's drag our sorry carcasses inside and see what we can do about it."

They went in and Mandy greeted them with a fake but obligatory smile. "Do you fellows need a table, or are you headed for the bar?" she asked.

"Straight to the bar," Bishop said loudly. "But you can go ahead and show us the way just like we were going to the dining room. That way I can watch your little round behind while you walk in front."

"You better not drink too much beer tonight, Bishop," Mandy answered. "Sounds to me like you're already a little bit rowdy."

"Rowdy or randy, take your pick," Bishop Collins said.

"Rowdy or randy!" Harlan snickered. "That's a good one, Bishop. Rowdy or randy!"

It was early for drinkers. The bar was deserted except for one old man sitting at the far end smoking and nursing a glass with only a few drops of beer left in it. Ben Catlin and a man none of them knew sat at a table near the door. Barney greeted Ben, then Bishop led his team to his favorite spot and Barney scooted onto a stool on one side of him while Harlan took one on the other side. The bartender, a young man they didn't know, took his time about acknowledging their presence.

"Get your ass in gear and get us some beer," Bishop demanded. "Big John ain't paying you to stand around and ignore his best customers!"

The bartender hurried over, his face quickly beginning to flush with either embarrassment or anger. "I'm sorry, sir," he said. "What can I get for you gentlemen?"

"Some of that warm horse piss you got on draft," Bishop Collins said.

"It's good beer, sir. Big John is——"

"Oh, hell, I know it's good beer. Elsewise I wouldn't be asking for it, would I?"

"I'm sorry, sir. I just meant——"

"Dammit," Bishop said hoarsely, "don't take it so serious. We're here to enjoy ourselves. Ain't that right, Barney?"

Harlan responded before Barney could say anything. "You got that right, Bishop. We're here to enjoy ourselves."

The young bartender, his face reddening even more, turned and drew three glasses of beer from the tap. He set the first one in front of Bishop Collins then retrieved the other two and placed one in front of Barney and one in front of Harlan. He stepped back and waited to see if Bishop had further orders. When Bishop began to drink his beer, the young man hurried to the end of the bar as if he needed to check on the old man.

"Tell me something, Harlan," Bishop Collins said, "you ever put it to a Jew?"

Harlan was busy lighting a cigarette. Bishop's question apparently took him by surprise, but he still managed a quick answer: "Hell, no. I ain't never been close enough to one."

"How would you know, in the dark?"

Barney watched Harlan's face in the mirror behind the bar. Harlan was taking Bishop Collins seriously. Barney took advantage of the opening to add his own jab. "Harlan's been too busy puttin' it to old man Windsor's cows to go looking for jewgirls, Bishop."

"That ain't funny, Barney," Harlan flared. "I've got a wife. My wife didn't run off and leave me like yours did. Me and Bishop are both still married."

Barney cringed, but made no response. Bishop Collins, obviously aware that Harlan had touched on a sensitive topic, jumped in to block any more fuel from being added to the fire he'd inadvertently ignited. "Harlan, lest I forget to mention it later, you did a good job when we went out to get them two boys," he said. "You too, Barney. The three of us make a pretty damn good team when we want to. Seems to me like we ought to get a little more active."

Harlan took the bait. "What have you got in mind?"

"Heck, I don't know," Bishop Collins responded. "It just seems to me like we work so good together we can do about anything we set out to. Wouldn't you say, Barney?" Without waiting for an answer, he went on. "With all the damage the Supreme Court's doing up there in Washington, it seems to me like free-thinking citizens like us may have to get more active. Nobody's going to do it for us."

Harlan caught Barney's gaze in the mirror and looked his reflection in the eye. "You didn't answer him, Barney," Harlan said. "You think we work good together?"

"Sure. Real good. Like the three musketeers."

Bishop Collins spread his arms like a mother hen taking in her chicks and slapped both of them on the back. "That's the spirit, boys," he said. "Like I was just saying, we can do about anything we set out to. Harlan, give me a cigarette." And in a loud voice, "Barman, get us some more beer over here. And don't take all day!"

The young man behind the bar hurried over and took three fresh glasses from the shelf and filled them at the tap, then carefully set a glass in front of each of them. He picked up their old glasses and dumped them into a tank of dishwater. Then he turned back to Bishop Collins. Bishop stared at him but said nothing. The bartender blushed again, and again looked for something else to do. This time he turned back to the tank of dishwater and pretended to be totally absorbed in the task of washing glasses.

Barney hardly noticed any of this. He was still smarting from Harlan's upbraiding. Having his wife walk out on him was the most humiliating thing that ever had happened to him and it was something he'd rather no one mentioned, something he tried to pretend never took place. It had been almost fifteen years now since Eva left him, packing a handful of things and moving out without a word. He simply came home one day and found her gone.

Eva had never found happiness in their marriage. Barney went through a great deal of self-examination trying to understand why, but never reached any firm conclusion. He suspected that she didn't fully understand her role. Preacher Ward always made clear that the wife was to be submissive, that the husband was the master of the house. Barney had been firm in his decisions the way Preacher Ward said, but tried not to be overbearing—to give his wife direction without resorting to commands. He had hit her only twice that he could remember and those were times when she'd blatantly disobeyed him.

Eva had never been one to complain, but on the other hand she'd never showed much appreciation for the way Barney supported her. He was pretty sure he had offered her a better way of life than she had before she became his wife. He always let her buy new shoes when her old ones wore out and a new dress every spring.

He was grateful for one thing, and that was the fact that their brief marriage hadn't produced children. And he really did not miss Eva all that much. It was the humiliation that was hard for him to take. Before he moved into the Tennessee Bend and had to give them up, he had a beautiful pair of golden retrievers and he probably would have felt much the same if one of them had run away. But there never had been any danger of that. He fed his dogs well.

Chapter 15

Quint Loman had a real bitch of a headache. This was not unusual when he traveled, because he always pushed too hard to get where he was going, drove too many hours without taking a break. He had been under enough stress already, on his way to Mississippi for a trial that would not be easy for him to sit through and at the end of which justice was not a certain outcome. In the two years he had worked for the Urban League, he had not been involved in anything that would bring the anguish of this case—two Mississippi white men accused of murdering a teenaged black boy from Chicago.

His colleagues in Philadelphia assumed that Loman was the perfect one for this assignment, being from the deep South himself, and he'd been reluctant to say otherwise. He had not been willing to tell them that reports of the murder of Emmett Till had sharpened memories of an event he had futilely tried to forget for two decades, an event that had brought his first hard brush against the most hateful of human nature when he was only eight years old.

Like any black child in Alabama, Quint Loman had seen and felt racism from as early as he could remember. But not the terrible, gut-wrenching meanness on display that tranquil Sunday afternoon when his fifteen-year-old cousin was beaten to death by a gang of white youths, his battered body thrown into the back of a pickup truck and hauled like the carcass of a slaughtered animal through town and back again and then hanged from the lowest branch of an ancient live oak tree in his grandmother's front yard. His cousin's offense? He was too arrogant. He had refused to step aside and make way for the white boys coming toward him on the sidewalk. No charges ever were filed. Authorities said they could not identify the murderers.

It never would be possible for Loman to forget that day, never possible for him to bury it deep enough in the dark recesses of his subconscious mind that it would not rise at unexpected moments and strike him anew with the same searing pain he'd felt at the time. His best hope always centered on moving forward, working for better days ahead, concentrating on the fact that even in Birmingham, Alabama, things were better now than they were then. But this best hope often was overtaken by reality—reality like the murder in Mississippi of a black teenager from Chicago.

Quint Loman felt fortunate that he'd been able to escape the South. His ability to catch and hang onto a football drilled into his midsection by a strong-armed quarterback had proved a simple blessing. Not that he hadn't encountered racism in the North—far from it, he had seen plenty. But it was less vicious. And it wasn't institutionalized the way it was in Alabama.

Given the gravity of his present situation, though, all this might as well be ancient history. Here he was, locked in a room with another black man, both of them taken at gunpoint by a trio of racists whose motives were as mysterious as the landscape on Mars. If he wasn't afraid, Loman certainly was worried.

"I'd feel better if I knew what these guys are up to," he said to Willie Jamison, who'd just gone into the bathroom to get a drink of water. "I keep thinking about them individually. Trying to break down the group, comprehend who they are. I just don't have a clue what they want with us."

"Tell you one thing, man," Jamison said over his shoulder, "whatever it is, it's not good."

"Did you look this place over thoroughly? I mean, to make sure there's no way out."

"You got it. That door is solid oak and it'd take a cutting torch to get through the bars on the window. I even studied the ceiling, thinking maybe there was an opening of some kind. We're stuck in here, man."

"So what's the bad news, sergeant?" Quint Loman said, trying to sound less apprehensive than he really was.

Jamison came out of the bathroom and stood directly in front of Loman, looking him square in the eyes. "The bad news, lawyer man, is that sooner or later them guys will be back. And I doubt they're going to be bringing us fried chicken and watermelon. We ought to be working on a plan—you know, not just set around and wait for our guardian angels to pluck us out of here."

"You're right, Willie. Any ideas?"

"Okay, to start with, we're not going to break out of this place. Like I said, it's a fortress. We're going to have to make our fight when they come back."

Loman rubbed his chin. "We have nothing to fight with, and they've got guns," he said. "Have you seen anything we could use for weapons?"

"There's a steel rod holding up the shower curtain, if we can bust it loose from the wall. Looks heavy enough to do some real damage with a good swing. Let's take a look at this bed—see what kind of frame it's on."

Jamison stepped across the small room to the bed, tossed the covers aside and lifted the badly stained mattress and shoved it against the wall. A box spring foundation sat beneath the mattress and he pushed it aside as well. This revealed a poorly constructed platform, made from sheets of plywood nailed together to form an upside down box that held the springs perhaps eighteen inches off the floor. There were no drawers or openings, meaning that there could be no cleaning under the bed. It also meant there was nothing there which would be easy to turn into a weapon.

"Won't help us," Jamison said. "The only thing I see is maybe smashing a chair and making clubs out of the legs."

"Smash it quietly, okay? My head is about to split with this headache."

"Shit, man. You got a lot more to worry about than a headache. Your head may get split anyway if we don't do something to get ourselves out of this fix."

Loman smiled weakly. "I know that, Willie," he said. "But I still wish I had an aspirin for my headache right now. Go ahead and smash a chair, though, and let's see what kind of weapons we can create."

Jamison picked up one of the chairs, lifted it high over his head, and brought it crashing to the floor. The chair splintered into several pieces, none large enough to make a suitable club. Without comment, he picked up the second and swung it against the floor as well but this time not as hard. Three of the four chair legs broke loose. The sergeant picked up one and examined it for splinters. Then he tossed it to Loman.

"Here," he said. "Take a practice swing or two with this. Maybe you can split somebody else's head."

Loman studied the thin stick of wood. It was light in weight—not nearly heavy enough to make an effective weapon. Still, he felt good to have something in his hand that might give him even the most modest means for fighting back. He grasped it like a baseball bat and swung it hard. The makeshift club whistled as it slashed through the air.

"Yeah," he said, "just give me a head to split! Do you have a plan for getting the drop on those imbeciles?"

"I'm thinking about that. It won't be easy."

Jamison checked out the other two chair legs, chose one, and took a couple of practice swings of his own. He laughed sarcastically. "We're just trying to fool ourselves, lawyer man," he said. "Them guys are packing guns. A couple of pieces of a busted up chair won't get us out of this mess. You hear what I'm saying?"

"I hear you. And I know you're right."

"But we're still not going down without a fight, right?"

"We'll give it our best shot, Willie."

Willie Jamison fell quiet, and Loman tried to think through the situation logically. Jamison was correct; their captors would be armed and there would be little or no chance to overcome them with clubs. Even with the element of surprise—if they could accomplish it—they'd still be outnumbered. So what alternatives did they have? If attempting to fight their way out was not a practical option, what should they do? It would help to know what those righteous defenders of Southern honor planned to do next. Would there be a better chance of escape later? Were their lives at risk? Who were these men anyway?

His headache pain was not going away. The suffocating heat made it worse. He wanted to cover his eyes to block the light and he yearned for an ice bag to hold against his throbbing temples. Anything that would bring even the slightest relief.

Jamison was back in the bathroom, trying to pull down the steel rod that held up the shower curtain. Loman heard the sound of something being ripped from a wall and assumed the sergeant had succeeded. Then swearing. Jamison emerged, blood streaming down his forehead, and held the steel rod aloft as a sign of triumph. "I got it," he proclaimed. "This is a lot better club than a flimsy chair leg."

"What happened to your head?"

"Nothing much. I fell backward when this thing come loose and then hit myself in the head with it. Just split the scalp a little, it looks like."

"You'd better get back in there and wash it up. You don't need an infection from attacking yourself."

"Ha, ha. You should have been a comic, not a lawyer."

"Yeah, whatever. Anyway, I thought you'd given up on the idea of trying to arm ourselves with clubs and taking them by surprise."

Jamison was bending over the sink with the water running. Either he did not hear the last comment or chose to ignore it. Loman smiled. He was beginning to like John William Jamison Jr. He admired the sergeant's spirit. If there was going to be hand-to-hand combat with the three rednecks who had kidnapped them and obviously had further designs on their lives and freedom, there was nobody he would rather have beside him than Willie Jamison. By the same token, though, his new friend deserved a better fate than to be dragged into the woods and murdered for no reason other than being black.

When Jamison finished in the bathroom and turned back his way, Loman told him, "You're a trained soldier, Willie. You know a lot more about this kind of thing than I do. So far as I'm concerned, you call the shots from now on. Just tell me what to do."

"Yeah, I'm trained for combat—even hand-to-hand," Jamison said. "But you can't put up much of a fight if they shoot you first. You think it's even remotely possible they might come after us without their guns?"

"No, I don't."

"Me neither. The odds are against us, lawyer man."

"Willie, the odds were against you and me the day we were born. I didn't get where I am by giving up, and you didn't either. Like you just said a while ago, we're not going down without a fight."

Willie Jamison stepped forward. Loman reached out to him. The two men clasped hands and looked each other square in the eye. "If we don't make it out of here," Loman said, "I want you to know that I admire and respect you. You're a good man."

"That makes two good men," Jamison responded. "It wouldn't be fair for two good men to be brought down by some idiot backwoodsmen out in the middle of nowhere. I never worried about dying young, man, but I always thought if I did it would be in war. I don't intend to be lynched, not now and not ever."

An hour later, Sergeant Willie Jamison sat stiffly on the floor, his back against the plywood frame that had held the box spring and mattress before he dismantled the bed, his jaw set hard and his anger growing by the minute. The fatalism that had marked much of his time in Korea was at play here, too, and he was thinking that in the end there might be little or nothing he or Quint Loman could do to affect their own fate. Whatever would come, would come. But he was not inclined to take it lying down and allowing himself to be overpowered without exacting as much blood as possible.

What infuriated Jamison more than anything else was the fact that he could make absolutely no sense of the situation he was in. He had taken the hardships and dangers of Korea in stride for almost two years, but he always understood why he was there. Now, locked in a room in a cheap motel somewhere in the backwoods of Tennessee, he had no clue why he was being held prisoner. Who were these men, and what did they plan to do?

Quint Loman sat on the opposite side of the makeshift platform, facing the wall. The chair leg that was to pass as a club lay on the floor at his feet.

"Lawyer man," Jamison said flatly, "I keep changing my mind. I'm ready to put up a fight as soon as somebody steps in that door. Then I think that since there's three of them and they're armed we wouldn't stand much of a chance. And now I don't know what I think. But what the hell? We're going to fight, right?"

"To the last breath," Loman answered. "But how much of a fight can you put up with the barrel of a pistol staring you in the face? Or more than one barrel, probably. These guys are cowards, Jamison. I don't see them walking in here without their guns."

Jamison studied the metal shower curtain rod he'd ripped from the bathroom wall. "We just need to pick our time so's we got the best advantage," he said. "Then whatever happens, happens."

"That dumb one is the one that scares me," Loman said. "He's likely to flare up at the least little thing and decide to blow somebody's head off."

"Yeah, and on top of that I'd guess he's itching for an excuse to shoot us anyway. I see him as a guy who'd see two dead niggers as two good niggers."

Loman was pensive. "Yes, I think you're right," he said. "Except I also see him as an insecure man who's afraid not to follow orders, and they obviously want us alive for something. They have a plan for us, otherwise they wouldn't have gone to all this trouble. It's possible that making a stand here is our last chance, Willie, but I think it would be suicide under the circumstances we're looking at here."

Jamison drew himself up from the floor. He flexed his arms and legs. "I've already give myself in to that," he said. "We're in a tough spot here and I know our odds are not all that good. But I swear it'd be worth it if I could take that guy that's calling all the shots with me." He swung the rod viciously. "Gimme one good chance!"

"A heroic act like that just might earn you your place in paradise, Willie. That one, especially, strikes me as a danger to the civilized world."

Loman stood and stretched, as if following Willie Jamison's example. Jamison went into the bathroom and ran cold water on his hands, then pressed his fingers firmly against the gash on his head. He had managed to stop the bleeding earlier, but it was starting to ooze blood again. Keeping one hand on the wound, he turned back to Loman and said, "So you're a lawyer for the Urban League? That means you must be a smart guy. Maybe you can tell me something."

"What? You need legal advice?"

"No, not legal advice. I just want to know who is Earl Warren?"

Loman grinned. "You're being facetious, right?"

"What the hell does that mean?"

"I mean, you're joking, right?"

Jamison made no effort to hide his irritation. "Damn it, man," he said, "one of them rednecks was talking about Earl Warren like I ought to know who he was. I never heard of him. You going to tell me or not?"

"Don't get mad," Loman said. "I was only surprised that any black person in the United States wouldn't recognize the name Earl Warren."

"Well like I just said, I never heard of him."

"Then I suppose you never heard of *Brown v. Board of Education.*

It was an important case ruled on by the Supreme Court, and Earl Warren is the Chief Justice. How could you miss all that?"

"Look, man. Don't treat me like some dumbass guy just fell off the watermelon truck on my head. I've been in Korea, and there wasn't a whole lot of news got to us over there. Cut me a little slack, okay?"

Loman stepped closer and put a hand on Jamison's shoulder. "I'm sorry," he said. "You've been carrying a load over there that most of us would find way too heavy, I expect, and I'm grateful for what you did. They say war is hell and from what I've heard Korea ranks somewhere below that."

"Forget it. We're in the same deep shit here. We need to be pulling together."

"Absolutely. And it's this Supreme Court thing that's got these racists all fired up. They've spent their lives congratulating themselves that separate-but-equal scheme was fair and just and the court knocked the pins right out from under them. They blame Earl Warren."

"Okay, so what exactly does all this mean? Without the lawyer talk."

"It means they can't legally send black kids to different schools solely because they're black and say they're getting just as good an education. The Warren court said there's no reason black and white kids shouldn't go to school together."

"And it took the Supreme Court to decide *that?*"

Loman laughed. "I expect you and I could have told them, right? The problem is, you and I don't have a whole lot of weight to throw around in places like Alabama and here in the wilds of east Tennessee."

Jamison smiled, but quickly sobered. He sucked in a long, deep breath and exhaled slowly. His eyes flashed with anger. "I wish we'd get a chance to throw some weight around right here," he said. "A fair fight, I mean. Take their weapons away from them and let us go hand-to-hand. There's not much I can think of right now that'd make me feel better than busting some white noses. How in God's world can idiots like the ones that locked us in here think their kids are too good to go to school with black boys and girls?"

"I know the question," Loman said. "But not the answer."

Jamison retrieved the shower curtain rod that he had stood on end in the bathroom. He was afraid he was going to lose control of himself. He swung the metal rod hard, crashing it down on the table, then swung it again and again, raining thunderous blows until he had vented much of his fury. Loman stood by and looked on sympathetically.

"I'm sorry, lawyer man," Jamison said after he had calmed down a bit, "I want to do something so damned bad. Anything! But we're totally helpless."

Loman took a few seconds to respond. "I wish they'd come on," he said finally. "Whatever they plan to do with us, let's get the show on the road."

Jamison put a finger to his lips. "Somebody's out there," he whispered.

They froze in position, waiting, listening, barely breathing, watching the door. Jamison fingered the metal rod and motioned to Loman that he should pick up the chair leg. Loman grabbed the makeshift club and slipped silently to a post tight against the wall, next to the door. Jamison followed, taking up his watch on the opposite side of the room's only entrance.

They heard nothing for the next several seconds. Then muffled footsteps along the outside of the wall, moving toward the barred window. A shadow slanted across the pane in the afternoon sunlight and in an instant they saw a face, barely above the middle level of the window. The person was short. It looked to be a black man, although they did not have a clear view through the thin curtain behind the drapes.

Willie Jamison pounded on the wall and shouted, "Hey! Help us get out of here!"

There was no response from outside. As quickly as it had appeared, the face was gone. Whoever it was, was moving away.

"Call the cops!" Jamison yelled, banging on the wall again.

"I don't think you need bother with that," Loman said. "My guess is that that poor guy is way too smart to get involved."

"But at least somebody knows we're in here. Somebody besides the three slave traders who locked us up."

Quint Loman smiled, and almost laughed out loud. "Like I said before, Willie, you have a clever way with words," he said. "That would be funnier if it wasn't so close to the truth. I feel almost as vulnerable right now as all those kidnapped Africans must have in the belly of slave ships on their way to America."

    "Oh, yeah," Jamison said. "America, land of the free."

Chapter 16

The possibilities offered by Barney's secret Room 10 were just beginning to sink in on Harlan MacElroy. While he and Barney and Bishop Collins had carried out more than their share of the violence and intimidation against local black people, the Hebrews, as Harlan called them, had not been of much concern in their part of Tennessee. Harlan hadn't been outwardly fervent over Bishop Collins's plan before, but after he had given it more thought the notion of watching the gang rape of a jewgirl or any other female left him almost trembling with excitement.

Still, Harlan had a problem. When it came to giving the two boys a whipping for messing with a white woman, he wasn't at all sure he wanted to go through with that. Getting what you could off a girl, no matter how you did it, was natural for a man. He never had supposed it was much different for black men than white, as long as it was among their own kind.

And as far as them raping a white woman, he hardly considered a jewgirl white. He wanted to ask Bishop Collins about that but he was afraid it was a dumb question.

Harlan never had been much for interfering in matters between men and women. He understood Bishop Collins's enthusiasm for having a little fun with the two boys they had locked up in Room 29 of Barney's motel, because Bishop liked to prove he was as stout as any man in the county and could whip most anybody around in a good fight. But if a black man took advantage of a black woman or a Jew, Harlan had a real hard time figuring out how that was white people's business.

He would go along with it in this case, though, because he did not want to get on the wrong side of Bishop Collins. Bishop had a way of making you feel important when you did things his way.

Harlan had never hated anyone. His view of life was pretty much hands off—everybody ought to mind their own business and leave everybody else alone. If they did, and if everybody stayed in their places, life would be a lot more simple.

This was his only quarrel with his colored friends and neighbors; sometimes they didn't want to stay in their place. He had never gone to school, but if he had he was confident he wouldn't have wanted to go to the same school as the nigger kids. Papa Puckett, the old man who raised him, called the little ones "alligator bait" so they evidently didn't count for much, and Harlan was afraid of the older black boys.

But now, according to what Bishop Collins was saying, some big judge somewhere up North was making black and white kids go to school together. Why couldn't he just leave things alone and mind his own business?

"That court you was talking about," Harlan said, turning to Bishop on the barstool beside him, "is that the one that said white kids and niggers had to go to school together?"

"You got it," Bishop Collins said. "Supreme Court of the U.S.A."

"I'd sure hate for Emmie to have to go to that kind of school. Mary Rose, too, when she gets big enough. You think that court up North could make our kids down here in Tennessee go to school with niggers, Bishop?"

"Harlan, it's the high court for the whole country, up in Washington, D.C. They expect their rulings to be carried out all over, including here. But that don't necessarily mean we're gonna do it. If you don't want Emmie going to school with niggers, who's gonna make you?"

"I reckon it'd take a whole lot more than some judge up there in Washington to make me—"

He was interrupted in mid-sentence by Barney. "What's the matter, Harlan? Are you afraid Emmie might take up with one of them big black boys? Maybe get you a spate of little half-nigger grandchildren?"

"That's not funny, Barney," Harlan shot back. "You wouldn't

like it neither, if you had kids."

Barney said nothing more, but Bishop Collins picked up right where he had left off. "That Earl Warren needs to be got out of there," he said. "If the black folk having their own schools has been good enough for 'em all these years, what in hell gives him the right all at once to change it? I expect they don't have a lot of niggers out there in California where he comes from."

"So what you're saying is, Earl Warren is a judge on that court?" Harlan asked. "Is that why they call him a nigger-lover?"

"Yeah, Harlan. That's why they call him a nigger-lover."

Harlan grinned, pleased to be enlightened. "I didn't know that. I wondered who he was."

"Well, shit, Harlan. Now that you've added two and two and come up with something besides five, I reckon you understand why we got to get rid of him."

"You got that right, Bishop," Harlan said loudly, looking about the room to see if others might be in hearing distance. The two men who had been sitting at a table were gone, though, and except for the old man at the far end of the bar no one else was present. But he could see Bishop Collins's face in the mirror. He could tell that Bishop appreciated his support.

Harlan had been working hard today to firm up his standing with Bishop. Maybe he could strengthen it a little more. "Even if I was willing, there ain't no way Mama Grace would let them kids go to school with colored boys."

Bishop Collins's reaction was not what he had hoped for.

"Harlan, how come you call your wife 'Mama Grace'?" Bishop asked. "She ain't your mama, no matter how often you suck a tit."

Barney roared with laughter and Harlan could feel the heat creeping into his face. He didn't have a quick response, nothing clever to say the way Bishop Collins would. And sometimes, Barney. It was a great frustration to Harlan that he always thought of a smart comeback hours later, when it was too late. No one had ever accused him of being quick-witted. But he was determined not to let Bishop's challenge go unanswered.

"I s'pose it's because that's what the girls call her," he said. "She started it, too. When they was little she'd say to them, 'come and tell Mama Grace what's the matter.' They probably took that to be her name, so they called her that."

Barney leaned forward so that he could see around Bishop and look Harlan in the face. "What do they call you, 'Papa Dimwit'?" he snickered.

To Harlan's immense relief, Bishop Collins jumped in. "Now, boys," Bishop said, "remember, we're a team. We don't want good natured joshin' to get out of hand. Harlan here's an important part of the team, Barney, and y'all ought not to talk down to him like that. I know you was just kidding, and Harlan does too, but if somebody else overheard they might think you was serious. We can have our fun, but let's stick together and make sure we're all headed in the same direction here."

"Shit, Bishop, everybody gets a little ribbing now and then," Barney said. "You didn't think I meant anything by it, did you, Harlan?"

"Naw," Harlan told him, "you was just carrying on, like always." But his response belied his true instinct. Barney talked down to him because he thought Harlan was dumb.

Right now that didn't matter much, though. Harlan was about to burst with pride. Bishop Collins—*Bishop Collins*, this man he admired and looked up to, this man he wanted to be like—had stood up for him. And called him an important member of the team. For one of the few times in his life he quickly thought of the right thing to say. "We should drink to that, Bishop." And then, in a loud and demanding voice, just like he knew Bishop Collins would, "Barman, another round of beer over here. And don't take all day!"

"That jewgirl won't be giving us any more trouble after tonight," Bishop said, swiveling on the stool so that he could speak face-to-face with Barney rather than talking to an image in the mirror behind the bar. "I'm kind of itching to go over to the sheriff's office and tell Andy she's on her way out of town."

"I'll bet she's on the road tomorrow, all right," Barney said. "She's not likely to get much sleep tonight."

"I guess there's a lot of them up there in Baltimore where she come from, but we sure don't need any more coming in and trying to tell us how to run things in Tennessee. The governor ought to give us a medal for chasing her out before she causes some kind of big stink. Too bad we can't do it like Adolph Hitler did."

Barney had just taken a slug of beer and paused to wipe his

mouth with a shirt sleeve before he answered. "You'd know more about that than me," he said.

Bishop assumed that Barney was referring to the fact that Bishop served in Germany during the war. He still regretted his role in the fighting, even though he'd had no choice but to follow orders. But how could he feel good about killing Arians whose supposed crime was the elimination of Jews? The German soldiers had fought gallantly and had every right to be proud. At one time Bishop had dreamed of a ruler like Hitler taking control in America, but that hope had long since vanished.

He envied Barney, who had been sent to the Pacific to fight the yellow Japs. Barney never wanted to talk about it, but Bishop Collins was sorry he'd never had Barney's opportunity to help rid the world of non-whites.

Bishop was grateful, though, for some of the things he had learned in the army. He'd been handling rifles and shotguns all his life, but his military experience taught him that shooting at human targets was a lot more fun than shooting squirrels and deer. And he'd learned about high explosives you didn't shoot from a gun. With all the work lying ahead, this last one might be especially good to know.

"I'd a been glad to be on the opposite side from that little Hebrew squad leader we had," he said to Barney. "Did I ever tell you about him?"

Barney indicated not, although Bishop was pretty sure he had. Anytime somebody got to telling war stories he was most likely to tell them about Corporal Haim Gorleki, the cocky little Jew from Brooklyn, New York.

The two biggest negatives he experienced in the army were having a Jew as his most immediate superior and having to kowtow to officers who were younger than he was and hadn't nearly as much good sense. Fortunately, the little Jew didn't last long and once he recognized that the officers got commissioned only because they came from privileged backgrounds and went to fancy schools and knew people in high places Bishop tended to find them more comical than threatening. You weren't afraid of a man you could laugh at.

Right after his infantry company got to North Africa as part of the American invasion in Operation Torch, Corporal Haim Gorleki became Bishop's squad leader. Gorleki took his low-level authority much too seriously and seemed to find pleasure in making life miserable for the men in his squad.

Bishop Collins remembered clearly the day a dozen years past when his company first made contact with the enemy. They caught up with a small band of French stragglers who probably had no desire to fight, but a couple of the American riflemen, nerves on edge, opened fire and a wild shootout quickly developed. Corporal Gorleki ordered his men to take prone positions for cover. Bishop kept his eye on Gorleki, who lay in a shallow depression only yards away. He saw his squad leader raise his head and shade his eyes trying to see the French positions, and he saw the impact of the bullet that ripped through the corporal's shoulder and tore off huge chunks of flesh and bone.

Gorleki collapsed face down in the dirt, bleeding like a stuck hog. Bishop Collins made no move. Haim Gorleki, the young Jew who had parents, grandparents, and three siblings waiting at home in Brooklyn, went into shock and bled to death without ever receiving medical attention.

Gorleki was replaced as squad leader by Corporal Jesse Cross, a lanky, red-haired boy from South Carolina. He and Bishop Collins got along very well.

Bishop was about to tell all this to Barney when Harlan, who apparently had missed their whole exchange, starting with Bishop's praise of Hitler, nudged his way back into the conversation. Harlan still had his mind on the government forcing his Emmie and Mary Rose to go to school with colored kids, as if that discussion had not been interrupted.

"What do you reckon nigger boys need to go to school for anyway?" Harlan asked. "It don't take much learning to lift and tote."

Bishop Collins had no problem with changing the subject back to school integration. Right now, the biggest danger he saw to maintaining the white Christian way of life was that contemptible ruling handed down by Chief Justice Earl Warren's Supreme Court. If he had his deer rifle and Judge Warren in his sights . . . But even if he did it would be too little, too late. The damage was done.

"Tell you what, Harlan," Bishop said, "let's not ruin our fun by dwelling on things like un-American court rulings. I guarantee you there'll be time to act on that sooner or later, but right now we got something real nice set up back there at the Tennessee Bend Motel and I propose we have another round of beer and look forward to tonight's entertainment."

"You got that right, Bishop," Harlan answered, but not so loud this time. "Come on, barman, get over here and bring us another round."

Chapter 17

Hunger pangs reminded Rachel Feigen that she'd had nothing to eat all day and it was well past noon. Okay, she thought, it's Big John's again, and maybe Mandy's still there. She hurried to Big John's Place, then sat for a minute in the car while Fats Domino's "Ain't That a Shame?" finished playing on the radio.

The hostess station was not staffed when she entered. A "Please Seat Yourself" sign was posted instead, and Feigen went straight to the empty dining room. A young blonde waitress rushed over to meet her and showed her to a table. Feigen asked for coffee and ordered a chef's salad with shrimp. The service was swift and efficient and she was half way through lunch when she saw Mandy approaching.

"Did you find what you were looking for?" Mandy asked softly.

"Yes, I'm sorry to say I did."

"Sorry? Why?"

"Because it was the car I was hoping it not to be."

Mandy pulled out a chair and sat down across the table from Feigen. "The missing Frenchman's?" she said. "I'm real sorry to hear that."

"I'm not surprised, of course. But like they say, no news is good news. Until I knew for sure, I had hope. Now I have to face the cold facts."

"So where does this leave you?"

Feigen hesitated. "I don't know. I'll just have to wait for the FBI to get here and do their stuff on the car and see where it goes from there. And my editor is on his way."

"From Baltimore?"

"Yes."

Mandy reached across the table and put a hand on Feigen's arm. "Are you going to be all right? I mean, you're not in any danger here, are you? You're more than welcome to come home with me tonight. I can't promise that my place is as fancy as the Tennessee Bend, but the air conditioner works and the couch makes a pretty good bed."

"I'll be fine," Feigen responded. "But you're an angel to care. I'll never forget it."

"You be careful, though. Look, I worked the early shift today and I'll be heading home as soon as I get my things. But, here, I want you to take my phone number, just in case. Okay?"

Feigen said sure, she'd be glad to have it, and Mandy printed her number on a napkin and handed it across the table. Leaving the dining room, she turned and smiled, as if wanting to show that she felt better about things. Feigen returned the smile and waved her hand. Mandy already had turned her back and was through the door and never saw the gesture of farewell.

Bill Skyles hadn't had time to make the drive from Baltimore yet, but Feigen wanted to be there when he arrived. She rushed through the rest of her lunch and went straight to the Tennessee Bend Motel. Effie was busy on the phone. She didn't see Barney Vidone. She sat in the lobby for a few minutes watching hopefully through the window for her editor's car, a red Buick that he kept shined to a mirror finish.

But this is silly, she thought. *He hasn't had time to get here and he'll call when he does. Unless it's real late, and then he'll leave a message for in the morning.* Rather than waste time watching for her boss when it was very unlikely he would get there, she might as well go to her room and see if she could do something productive. And if not, she could lie down and maybe catch a nap.

On her way to Room 10, she watched for George. He didn't seem to be anywhere on the grounds. The door to her room opened easily this time. She went into the bathroom and washed her hands and face and dried hastily with one of the yellow towels. Sitting on the edge of the bed, she twirled the tuning knob on the radio until she found a station that played something besides hillbilly music.

Al Hibbler's "Unchained Melody" suited her mood, and anyway she loved his powerful voice. She listened through the record and waited to see what the DJ chose to play next. This turned out to be The Platters singing "Only You," another song she liked.

With time to kill, Feigen listened to a few more records on the radio and straightened up the clothes she'd unpacked. The room had a closet nearly as big as the one in her bedroom at home and ample drawer space.

She was relaxed and comfortable and she almost could have forgotten what brought her to the Tennessee Bend Motel in the first place. Bill Skyles's arrival would snap her back to all that soon enough, and she needn't worry about watching out for him because he'd call when he got there. She wanted to lie on the bed and listen to the music and not think about Guy Saillot and Marie's tears and the green Ford that had been pulled from Cherokee Lake.

There was no use trying. Guy was still missing, Marie was still shedding tears, and the green Ford pulled from the deep waters of the lake painted a sinister picture of what may have happened. Guy would never have abandoned his car and left himself stranded. It might have been stolen, but he would have reported that. The alternatives were what Feigen was trying not to think about.

Reporting on the courts in New York City, she had heard her share of gruesome crime stories. There had been cases where people did things she found almost unimaginable. She had sat in the courtroom and watched men who were accused of heinous crimes sit stone-faced and listen while the evidence against them was spelled out in shocking detail. It was as if they were outsiders looking on while the trial focused on the acts of others.

Given her own sheltered life, she might have been ill prepared for such violence, but Feigen had learned a great deal about the meanness of human beings through her study of history.

She always had been fascinated by the stories of the ancient Greeks. They were supposed to be highly civilized, and Homer wrote that the Greek soldiers took their bathtubs with them to fight the Trojan war. After a day of combat it surely must have felt good to bathe and have their bodies massaged with olive oil. Civilized? The next day they went back to hacking and spearing the Trojans in bloody hand-to-hand combat. As Homer put it, a Greek sword pierced a Trojan's breast and another Trojan "bit the dust." There was lots of dust biting at the hands of those civilized Greeks.

She'd learned early in her studies that some of the most terrible things human beings had done to other human beings were done in the name of the law. In the seventeenth century, the highly civilized Brits took down the bodies of convicted criminals who had been hanged and carried out the imposed punishment of drawing and quartering. Drawing and quartering was a sentence often meted out to citizens deemed guilty of political crimes.

"You couldn't cross a king and expect to get away with it," her favorite history professor declared.

As a city girl who never had seen livestock slaughtered and butchered, Feigen didn't understand the concept of drawing and quartering. But an enthusiastic graduate assistant had explained it quite clearly.

"Drawing and quartering consists of cutting the body open and disemboweling it, then lopping off the head and cutting the body into four pieces, or quarters," he told the class. "And after this delicate procedure had been carried out the civilized Brits rather liked to put the head and body parts on public display as a lesson to others who might be inclined toward disloyalty."

He went on to explain that the Brits "perfected" the art of drawing and quartering, only partially hanging the convict first—that is, leaving him alive to experience the procedure. Oh, and cutting off his genitals and burning them before his eyes. Yes, highly civilized.

So perhaps civilization had progressed some, after all—at least in terms of punishment meted out by the courts. So far as the criminals were concerned, they didn't seem to be getting any better. She recalled the case of a repulsive old scarecrow who called himself "the Pope," a murderer and rapist who traipsed about Manhattan chanting sermons in Latin. One of his victims was a middle-aged nun. He waited for her after her school let out, dragged her into his car and drove her out through the Hamptons all the way to Montauk Point, tortured her until she begged for mercy, then raped her repeatedly. Then he slashed her throat.

Prosecutors said he wanted a keepsake or two, so he cut out her vagina and slashed off a breast and carried them around in his coat pocket for a couple of days. "She was so beautiful," he told an investigating detective, "and she gave me so much pleasure that I just couldn't let her go."

Without realizing what she was doing, Feigen stood in front of the large framed mirror on the wall and studied her own body, trying to imagine how the victim would have been carved up the way the police described. The murderer would have had to use his knife like a butcher, literally. How could he do it? He obviously was insane, but his attorney made no effort to launch an insanity defense.

She always discussed the cases she reported on with her father, usually after her stories made it into print. She tried not to be too obvious about her personal opinions. But there were times when she couldn't hold back, times when she expressed outrage over the viciousness of the crimes and wondered aloud whether harsh enough punishment even was possible. Judge Max Feigen always responded the same way; justice, he said, must be tempered by mercy.

Feigen had been trying to push the Saillot case from her mind, but she had managed to do just the opposite. She had reminded herself how truly brutal people could be. Guy had vanished and there was virtually no limit to the possible reasons why. He could have been the victim of a crime as horrible as any she ever had reported on in New York. She suddenly felt ill, and saw in the mirror that she was as pale as a ghost.

After a couple of deep breaths, she went into the bathroom and drank a glass of water and soaked a washcloth in cold water and pressed it to her forehead. She went back and sat on the edge of the bed and then lay down. Another Al Hibbler song was playing on the radio. Minutes later she was sound asleep.

Guy Saillot haunted her dreams.

When she woke she had no sense of the time, nor how long she'd slept. Was it possible that Bill Skyles had arrived at the Tennessee Bend and tried to call her? She had slept so hard she might not have heard the phone. She sat on the edge of the bed and started to call the motel office and ask. When she picked up the phone, it was dead.

"Damn!" she exclaimed, "Damn this rotten place, damn Cherokee Lake, damn Tennessee, damn, damn, damn!"

Pent-up emotions that had been building over hours and days suddenly erupted in an outpouring of fury. She threw herself across the bed and pounded a pillow with both fists. Her body shook with the force of her rage, frustration, fear, agony over what probably lay ahead. The action was cathartic. She beat the pillow savagely until her energy was spent and the emotions that had driven her gave way to fierce resignation.

She sat up and tried the phone again. Still no dial tone. She punched the switch beneath the handset several times but nothing happened. She got up and returned to the bathroom, repeated the face washing, and set out for the motel office. Her door was locked. From the outside.

Effie Catlin left work early. This was rare under any circumstances, but even more so to do it at Barney's behest. Her boss usually needed her to stay around the Tennessee Bend as late as she could and help him with the books. Barney was good with people, but he never would be good with the business end of things. Effie often wondered if the motel would survive for long without her.

But she wasn't one to question authority—especially when authority told her to take time off. She spent too much of her life at the motel and not nearly enough of it at home. This was a chance to have a couple of hours more with her husband, and she rushed to get away before Barney changed his mind.

George was in the lobby, collecting the day's rubbish from all the trash cans, and smiled that sweet smile that made him one of her favorite people. She signaled goodbye with a slight wave of her hand and returned his smile. He looked at the clock, then turned back to her with a puzzled look that was almost comical.

"Yes, I'm going home early," Effie told him. "Barney told me to go ahead and take off."

She knew that George couldn't hear her words, but he could read the expressions on people's faces and Effie had learned that if she merely talked to him as if he could hear he often got the message. Or, at the very least, the spirit of the message. George smiled again and returned her hand wave and went back to work. There was no doubt in her mind that he was highly intelligent and probably was much more capable of functioning in society than people gave him credit for. It was an open secret that he could tell time, for example, though Effie could never understand how he had learned.

Once her old International pickup truck was out of the driveway and headed toward home, she quickly forgot about Barney Vidone and George and the Tennessee Bend Motel. She lived less than ten miles away, but there were times when the drive seemed long. She thought it was because of her eagerness to get home—the drive to work in the morning always felt like a short one—but Ben insisted it was because of all the faster drivers who passed her as she lumbered along in the old truck. He couldn't account for the difference between going to work and coming home, but Effie never pushed the discussion.

She stopped at the Piggly Wiggly and picked up a loaf of bread and a pound of freshly ground hamburger meat. Ben liked hamburger almost as well as he liked steak. Which was good, because they couldn't afford steak very often. Ben wasn't able to work anymore, and Effie hadn't had a raise for over two years. Two or three times she'd tried to get up her courage to ask Barney for more money, but each time she had lost her nerve before she had the chance. She liked Barney and she liked her job, but her financial straits were getting somewhat dire.

The closer to home she got, the better Effie always felt. She never failed to get a sense of contentment when she turned off the highway into the narrow lane that led up to the old house where she and Ben had lived ever since they got married. It was a small house, but plenty roomy for the two of them. Ben had kept it in good repair and the clapboard siding rarely went for too many years without new white paint.

Effie was the one who took care of the yard. She was most proud of the azaleas that surrounded the house and brightened the winter-dulled setting with a glorious profusion of pink, red, and yellow flowers in the spring. All of the spring and summer flowers were gone now, of course, and the yard looked parched and brown. There was a visible path worn by a pair of red foxes that had taken up residence in a burrow just a little ways up the hillside from the back of the house and made countless trips across the yard when they hunted. But the same hot, dry spell that had been hard on the lawn had left the sweet gum trees with the brightest colors Effie could remember. They stood out vividly in the woods that stretched away from the house on three sides.

Whatever the season, this place always looked beautiful to Effie. She could not bear the thought of being away from it for any length of time. Ben loved it, too. He had said many times that he would not trade their modest Tennessee home for the Taj Mahal and Buckingham Palace combined.

Ben was sitting on the porch when she drove up to the house, gently swaying back and forth in the bench-like swing suspended from the ceiling by lengths of chain. He planted his feet on the floor to stop the movement and sat stoically while she walked toward him and climbed the eight board steps to his level. He smiled, but waited for her to speak first.

"I got off early," she said.

"So I see."

"Have you had a good day?"

"Nothing special."

"I stopped at the Piggly Wiggly and got us some fresh hamburger meat. Would you like for me to fry up a couple of patties for supper?"

"Yeah, that sounds good," Ben said, and she believed she heard some enthusiasm in his tone. "I'll help."

Effie went inside and he got up from the porch swing and followed. The house was unbearably hot. She put down her grocery bag, pushed open the kitchen door, latched the screen door, and turned back to face her husband. "How come you've got everything closed up like this?" she asked. "It's like an oven in here."

"I've been gone," Ben told her. "I just got back a little bit ago, myself."

"I didn't know you were going someplace today. Did you get a ride?"

"I went with Randolph over to Big John's Place and had a beer. You don't mind, do you?"

"Of course I don't mind," Effie said. "I just didn't know you were going, that's all. You took me by surprise."

"I was surprised, myself. It wasn't something we'd set up in advance or nothing like that. Randolph just drove up and asked did I want to go and I said yes. I kind of enjoyed it, too. The getting out as much as the beer, I think."

"I'm glad you went, honey. You need to get out more."

Effie put the hamburger meat on a platter and formed patties with her hands, careful not to make them too thick because Ben liked them well done all the way through. She salted and peppered each patty, first one side and then the other, and pulled a blackened cast-iron skillet from a lower cabinet. She soon had four generous hamburgers sizzling in the pan. The cooking meat smelled delicious.

Ben got two glasses from one of the high cabinets and filled them with ice cubes from the freezer, then took a pitcher of sweet tea from the lower part of the refrigerator and placed it and the glasses on the table. "Think we need silverware?" he asked. Effie said she believed not, and he put out bottles of mustard and catsup and added plates and napkins to his place settings.

Effie was surprised at how good the fresh-cooked meat tasted. She should have bought buns, too, but Ben said the sliced bread was fine, it was the meat that mattered. They ate like hungry sailors who'd been at sea too long without food and quickly finished the hamburgers and most of the pitcher of tea. Although he didn't say it, she could tell that Ben enjoyed the meal.

"I don't know why Barney thought I should go home early," Effie said. "He usually wants me to stay around as long as I'm willing but he acted like he sure wanted me to leave today."

"Was he drunk?"

'Why, no, I don't think so. I've never seen him drunk, come to think of it. How'd he be able to run the motel by hisself if he was drunk?"

"Well, I was just wondering," Ben said, "because him and those two he hangs out with put away a lot of beer at Big John's Place this afternoon."

Effie was skeptical. "Oh, I don't think Barney drinks very much. I knew he was there, though. I don't think Bishop Collins is a good influence on him. And that other one, Harlan whatever, doesn't strike me as all that bright. But Barney likes them and I guess that's all that matters. It's none of my business who he drinks beer with."

"It sounded like they had big doings going on tonight, anyway," Ben said. "That dumb one was all excited about something. You hear anything about it?"

"Tonight? Barney came back to the motel. I don't see how they could be up to anything tonight. But I'm just nosey enough to smell around tomorrow. Like I said, I don't trust Bishop Collins. I've always been afraid he'll get Barney in trouble one of these days."

Chapter 18

Quint Loman heard a sound outside the door. It took him an in-stant to realize that it was someone opening the lock, and then it was too late. The door to Room 29 flew open and three men, led by Harlan MacElroy with a double-barreled shotgun, burst in before Loman could move. Willie Jamison, lying beside him on the dirty mattress they'd thrown back on the bed frame, tried to grab the metal rod lying on the floor but couldn't reach it. Even if they had settled on a firm plan to spring an ambush when their captors showed up, the prisoners had been taken by surprise.

Harlan's eyes were alive with anticipation. "Get your black asses up and get moving," he yelled, motioning toward the door with his shotgun.

Barney Vidone looked about the room. "What the hell you boys done here?" he sang out. "You sure as the devil are going to pay for all this damage!"

"You can worry about the damage later," Bishop Collins said. "Right now we've got bigger fish to fry. The sooner we get these boys up to Room Ten, the sooner the fun begins."

"You got that right, Bishop," Harlan said loudly. "Let's get these boys moving. You, get up!" He prodded Jamison with the barrel end of the shotgun. "Get on your feet, boy!"

Loman saw the hesitance and confusion on Willie Jamison's face and thought the sergeant might try something. It would be suicide if he did. Loman had no doubt that the shotgun was loaded, and no doubt that the man who carried it would shoot at the slightest provocation. Jamison would be cut in half by the blast. Jamison looked up and Loman shook his head. "Do what he says, Willie," he said quietly. "We're about to find out what these delightful hosts have in store for us."

Harlan roared with laughter. "Delightful hosts?" he mocked. "You boys are going to find out pretty soon who's a delightful host. And it ain't none of us. Right, Bishop?"

"You're always right," Bishop Collins said sarcastically. "Now come on, gentlemen, let's move out of this nice room Barney set up for you and see if we can find better accommodations. I believe he said Room Ten is ready." He stood back and gestured toward the door. "Let's all go on over and check it out."

Harlan motioned with the shotgun. Jamison stumbled over a piece of broken chair but quickly regained his balance. He squared himself in front of Loman, who nodded in the general direction of the door. "After you," Jamison said. Loman stepped to the door and out into the humid night air, with Jamison close behind. Harlan's shotgun was inches from Jamison's back. Barney pointed the way and the five men moved quickly along the dimly lighted pathway, rounded the end of another section of the motel, and stopped at the door of Room 10.

Barney produced a ring of keys. He fumbled at the lock for a minute, then stepped back, out of sight to anyone inside the room. Harlan pushed the door open and shoved the two prisoners through it. Rachel Feigen confronted them with an angry challenge: "Who the hell are you and what the hell is going on here?" Bishop Collins quickly replaced the heavy padlock that again imprisoned the two black men and, now, the uppity jewgirl from Maryland.

"Let's get on to the room where we can see, Barney," Harlan urged. "Ought not to take them boys long to start on her, do you think?"

"Oh shit, Harlan, don't be in such a damned hurry," Barney said. "We've got all night."

Inside room 10, Feigen pulled back, moving to a defensive position that placed the bed between her and the two men who had just been thrown into the room. "Who are you?" she yelled again. "What do you want? Why are you in my room?"

"Ma'am, we don't want anything of you," Sergeant Willie

Jamison assured her. "We were kidnapped, and we've been held prisoner for most of the day in another room. What's your story?"

She kept her distance, but was somewhat less frantic. "Somebody just locked me in a little while ago," she said.

"But you weren't brought here against your will in the first place?" Loman asked.

"Certainly not. I'm checked in like any other paying customer. I found out the phone was dead and started to go to the office and the door was locked from the outside. I've been pounding on the wall and yelling, but nobody seems to have heard me."

"It doesn't take a genius to know that we're all in danger here, Miss. Look, my name is Quint Loman and this is Willie Jamison—John William Jamison Junior, if you want me to be formal. Whoever you are, it looks like we're all in this together now."

Feigen extended her hand. "Rachel Feigen," she said.

"And you have no idea what this is all about?" Loman asked.

"Of course not. And you don't, either?"

"Ma'am, we were taken at gunpoint," Jamison said. "Not at the same time, but they locked us in the same room. Neither one of us has ever been here before. We were just passing through."

"It's hard to see that we have anything in common," Loman said. "You may be worth holding for ransom, but Willie and I are not. Unless they're simply looking for bodies to feed to their wolves or something, I'm at a complete loss to understand what their motives are."

"It's possible they don't like me because I've been asking too many questions," Feigen said. "I'm a reporter for the Associated Press in Baltimore. That's what I came down here for, to ask questions. Now what about you two? Why were you here in the first place? You don't strike me as fishermen from Indiana come down here to wet your lines in Cherokee Lake."

"As Willie said, we were just passing through. I'm an Urban League attorney from Philadelphia on my way to Mississippi for a trial. Maybe you've heard about the Emmett Till murder case?"

"Of course. And you, Willie?"

"I'm a U.S. Army sergeant, just back from Korea and on my way to Fort Jackson, South Carolina. They shanghaied me at the bus station. I'm from East St. Louis, Illinois."

"Well, now we're the three musketeers," Feigen said. "So what do we have in common? Maybe I'm missing something obvious, but damned if I see it. A woman reporter, a lawyer for the Urban League, and an army sergeant. Either of you see anything?"

"No," both men said in unison.

"Okay, I'm going to venture a guess that neither of you ever heard of a young man named Guy Saillot. He's from Baltimore and he's been missing for a couple of weeks now. The last he was heard from, he was staying here. Here at the Tennessee Bend Motel. That's what brought me down here, and with any luck the FBI will be right behind me."

"FBI?" Jamison said. "I wish they'd hurry up and get here. But from what you said, somebody knows you're here. That's different from the lawyer man and me. Nobody keeping track on us."

Feigen started to speak, but was brought up short by a curious noise. There was a slight thump, as if something or someone had bumped the wall from the other side, followed by a brushing sound. She and the two men froze and listened intently but heard nothing else.

Willie Jamison broke the silence. "Probably a cat outside or something. Or whoever it was that looked in the window at us in that other room and didn't pay any attention when we yelled at him. It wouldn't surprise me if everybody in ten miles of this place is involved. I wonder if they even have any police around here."

Feigen laughed sarcastically. "Oh, yeah, sheriff's office right down the road. But they don't seem to have any interest in looking for the bad guys. They don't have time to bother with missing boys or answering questions from a Jewish reporter from Mary Land."

"So you're Jewish?" Loman said. He seemed surprised.

"What? You didn't notice my big Jewish nose?"

"No, I didn't. But you may have hit on something we've been overlooking. Think about it. There are people around here who don't like black men like Willie and me, and some who apparently don't care too much for Jews. See what I'm getting at?"

"Yes, maybe I do," Feigen said. "But I wasn't taken at gunpoint the way you were, and most people here have treated me respectfully. On the other hand, the fellow at the sheriff's office—"

"Treated you like a Jew," Loman interrupted.

"Yes, exactly."

Willie Jamison had taken a seat at the table, in a straight-back wooden chair similar to those he had broken up for weapons in the other room. "Looks to me like they treat Jews better than black men, though. You got a nice room. Notice anything real different, lawyer man?"

"Oh, yes," Loman responded. "This one is air conditioned. I might survive the night in here." He turned to Feigen. "The room we were in must have been a hundred degrees. I'm surprised they weren't worried about Willie and me leaving our nigger smell."

Feigen managed a slight smile. "So you think maybe I got a cool room so that I'd not leave a Jew smell?"

"You two are getting way ahead of me," Jamison said. "That's probably because I'm too hungry to think straight. You don't have anything to eat in here, do you? Loman and me haven't had any food all day."

"Don't make a big deal of it, Willie," Quint Loman chided. "Just pick up the phone and call room service." They all tried to laugh, but just now laughter was hard to come by.

The total vulnerability of their position was beginning to wear heavily on Willie Jamison. He saw little hope of escape and Quint Loman's theory that all this had something to do with the fact that the two men were black and Feigen was a Jew had added to his trepidation. No one knew they were being held captive and if they were in the hands of extreme racists they had to expect the worst.

"We might have a better chance of understanding what we're up against if one of us was a Southerner," Feigen said.

"Loman is," Jamison answered.

"You?" She turned and addressed Loman sharply. "I thought you said you are from Philadelphia. I don't hear a Southern accent."

Loman smiled. "I lost it somewhere along the way," he said. "But, yes, I am a native of Alabama. I spent my formative years in that black boy's paradise."

Feigen turned to Jamison. "And what about you, John William Junior? I suppose you're going to tell me you're really from Mississippi or Georgia and not Illinois?"

"No way," Willie Jamison replied. "First of all, call me Willie. So far as I can tell, John William Jamison Senior was a figment of somebody's imagination. He sure as hell never showed up in my life. And I hardly set a foot outside East St. Louis before I got in the army, which is why I'm grateful to Uncle Sam. I wasn't the great football player Quintiloonus here was. Football gave him—"

"Quintiloonus?" Feigen tried not to laugh.

"Quintilius Varus Loman, at your service," Loman said. "Something I owe to my history professor father."

Feigen sobered. "And you know who Quintilius Varus was, I assume?"

"I know."

"And it doesn't bother you to carry that name?"

"Look, Feigen, I got the name when I was born. Like I just said, my father was a history professor. He wanted me to carry a distinguished name. Or maybe a distinctive name. I didn't have much say in the matter."

"And you never once asked him about it? Never complained?"

Loman was about to answer her when Willie Jamison spoke up loudly. "What the hell are you two talking about?" he said. "Maybe I didn't go to college, but I know a whole lot about people. Both of you cool down. We got enough trouble, without fighting among ourselves. Anyway, what's got you all fired up? You better talk to the sergeant and let's get it out of the way. Right now!"

"You're right," Quint Loman said. "We don't need to quarrel among ourselves."

"Then tell me what's going on."

Feigen clearly was still agitated. "What's going on," she said, "is that either your friend Mister Loman is completely ignorant when it comes to history, or else he has no sensitivity whatsoever when it comes to the persecution of Jews. I suppose he wouldn't mind if his father had named him after Adolph Hitler, either."

"Oh, that's a bunch of crap!" Loman said angrily. "I know who Quintilius Varus was. But my God, that was nearly two thousand years ago."

This time, Jamison stepped between them. "Not another word! Don't either one of you say another word. If you're going to act like third graders, I'm going to act like your teacher. I want both of you to shut up before you both get mad and say things you don't mean. Don't we already have enough to worry about?"

"You're right," Feigen said. "I blow up too fast sometimes. But when you are a Jew, you're taught about the persecution of the Jewish people. Quintilius Varus earned his place in history by slaughtering two or three thousand Jews celebrating Passover in the temple in Jerusalem because they didn't want to be under Roman rule."

"Okay, so he was a badass," Jamison said. "That probably ain't Quint's fault."

Loman smiled at Willie Jamison, but his expression was stern again when he turned back to Rachel Feigen. "You're skewing history to suit your own purposes. Quintilius Varus is in the history books because he got whipped by the Germans and lost three Roman legions in the process. A failure like that doesn't go unnoticed."

Feigen was equally stern. "Everybody makes excuses! If your father were here right now, I'd welcome the chance to ask him whether he was more impressed by Quintilius Varus's losing a battle against the Germans or winning a so-called battle with the Jews. What do you think he'd say?"

"My father never needed me to speak for him. Do you speak for yours?"

"Nobody speaks for Judge Max Feigen."

Loman reacted as if she had said a nasty word. "So that's why your name was familiar! Judge Max Feigen. We studied one of his cases in law school."

"I'm not surprised. My father's held in high esteem in the legal community."

Loman snorted. "Yeah, maybe so. But the case we studied was an example of judicial prejudice. Your father railroaded a poor guy he thought was a Nazi sympathizer. I can give you the—"

"That's ridiculous! My father never railroaded anyone. And since when was being a Nazi sympathizer a criminal offense anyway?"

Jamison held up his hands, trying to intervene. Neither Feigen nor Loman paid any attention to his efforts.

"I didn't say the man was charged with being a Nazi sympathizer," Loman said hotly. "He was charged with simple assault or vagrancy or something. But Judge Feigen disallowed compelling evidence of his innocence, and that was clearly because he thought the man was a Nazi sympathizer. The poor guy didn't have any money and his lawyer never sought to get the decision appealed. He spent a year in prison for something he likely was not guilty of. That's judicial prejudice."

Feigen started to answer, but this time Jamison would not be denied. "Shut up, now, both of you!" he yelled. "Whatever the hell

151

Quintiloonus did, it sounds to me like it was a long time ago. And who cares if a Nazi sympathizer had to spend some time behind bars. We need to be talking about how to get out of here, not the slaughter of Jews or Germans or Romans or who the hell ever a couple of thousand years ago. Now are the two of you ready to act like grownups again, or not?"

"You're right," Loman declared. "We could end up like those Jews in the temple or the Roman legions in Germania. I think slaughtered was the word she used."

Feigen was coming around. "Yes, and right now that doesn't appeal to me. But I'm glad you acknowledged the slaughter of the Jews, Quint. Or should I say Quintiloonus?"

"Like Willie says, if we don't come up with a way to get out of here you can call me dead meat."

"That wouldn't be kosher."

Her quip was a hit with Loman, who burst out laughing, but puzzled Willie Jamison. But who cared? He had grown impatient with their petty quarrel and he'd had more than enough of their grandiose conversation. They might be better educated that he was, but he suspected that neither one of them could fight their way out of a paper bag.

Loman already had passed the decision making over to him if it came to a physical confrontation and now they had a woman to look after. Any more talk about Roman legions or the slaughter of Jews or any other ancient history that nobody cared about and he'd be more than ready to leave them to their own devices. Right now, their survival rested on his strong back.

Jamison had decided once again that the best chance the three of them had to get out of this alive was to ambush their captors, let the chips fall where they might. He wanted a fighting chance. If he and Loman had made a real plan earlier and stayed alert to carry it out, they might not be here now. Sooner or later the three cowards who locked them in here would be back. This time, he didn't intend to be taken out and moved to the woods or someplace else where their bodies might never turn up. If he was going to die, it would be right here in this room.

In the meantime, he'd just as soon the woman got out of the way. "Ma'am," he said, "why don't you lay down and get some sleep. We'll wake you up if anything happens."

Chapter 19

Barney Vidone led the way. Bishop Collins and Harlan MacElroy followed obediently through the Tennessee Bend Motel office into Barney's private chamber. Without waiting to be asked, Harlan took a seat in the overstuffed chair Barney sat in to watch television. Bishop went straight to the refrigerator and pulled out a cold beer. He took an opener from the top of the refrigerator and crunched a hole in the top of the can and took a long draft, then stood by expectantly, as if waiting for Barney to speak.

"Okay," Barney said, "here's the setup. The pit room's behind the supply closet. I put in a double door so's nobody'd accidentally stumble into it. There's not a lot of space back there but there's a bench wide enough that we can all set down. Everybody will have a good view of what's going on in Room Ten."

Harlan raised his hand, like a child in school. "What about the beer?" he asked.

"We'll take enough beer with us to last a while, I guess. There's a cooler under the bench. But if we run out it's not much of a job to come back here and get more."

Bishop Collins took another drink, wiped his mouth with his hand, and belched loudly. "Damn, Barney, where do you get this stuff?" he said. "I never had beer this bad in my life. If you drink this regular seems to me like it might turn you off on beer altogether." He held the can out to Harlan and said, "Try this and see if it's not as bad as I said."

Harlan eagerly accepted the can and took a fast gulp. "You're sure right, Bishop," he reported. "This ain't very good beer."

Barney reddened. "This is better than most of what you get at Big John's," he insisted. "I don't buy cheap beer, especially not when I'm getting it for myself. Maybe some people just don't know good beer when they have it."

Bishop Collins was trying to keep a straight face, but couldn't hold it. "I was just shittin' you, Barney," he admitted. "That's real good beer. Don't pay no mind to Harlan. He wouldn't know good beer from 'possum pee. I just figured he'd go along with me like he always does."

Harlan looked confused, as if he wanted to answer Bishop Collins but didn't know what to say. He settled for another taste of the beer he had just insulted and drank until the can was empty. He set the can back on the table, wiped his mouth with a hand the way Bishop had, and said, "I knew you was just puttin' him on, Bishop. Like you said, that's good beer. A lot better than what we got at Big John's this afternoon."

Bishop Collins looked at Barney and winked. "Harlan knows his beer," he said.

"Yeah, Harlan's a man of many talents."

Bishop Collins took on a wistful expression. "You know, Barney, fixing to go back there and watch what goes on with them boys and that jewgirl has got me thinking about that little Bougelais gal. She don't ever come around anymore, does she?"

"She doesn't work for that outfit anymore," Barney said. "Some of the other women turned her in and she got fired."

"Yeah, well, jealousy makes some people do nasty things. Reckon we ought to get on back there? I wouldn't want to miss anything."

"You got that right," Harlan said, standing up from the chair. "We wouldn't want to miss anything. Right, Barney?"

"Well, let's go then," Barney said. "Come right on this way. Be quiet, though, so they don't hear us in there."

He again walked in front, leading them through the supply closet—more accurately a small storage room—and silently opened a door on the back wall. This led to a narrow passageway and, only a few feet farther on, another door. He put his finger to his lips to signal quiet, then gingerly pulled open the second door. The space beyond was almost totally dark. Its single source of light was the radiance from Room 10 filtered through the two-way mirror.

Barney stood aside and motioned for Harlan to go first. Harlan was hesitant, but Bishop Collins nodded and he slipped into the pit room and took a seat at the far end of the bench. Bishop went in next. Barney followed, and pulled the door shut behind him. He eased himself down on the bench next to Bishop.

The window, seen from the other side as a large mirror, gave them a clear view of a good portion of Room 10. They saw the three occupants huddled near the middle of the room. The jewgirl from Baltimore was speaking earnestly and the two black men looked to be listening intently. One of them, the taller one, shuffled his feet restlessly as if he wanted her to stop talking but she ignored him. The other man yawned. She spoke for a moment longer, then the taller man began to talk and the other man took a seat in one of the straight-back chairs.

Harlan leaned forward and turned his face toward Barney. "How long you think it'll be before the action starts?" he whispered.

Bishop Collins shushed him. "Just wait," he whispered back. "Those boys are likely to get after her any time now." Turning to Barney, he said lowly, "We forgot the beer."

Barney put the palm of a hand to his forehead in a sign of self-deprecation. He gave Bishop a thumbs-up signal, raised himself slowly from the bench and eased out the door. He walked quietly through the supply closet and into his private office, started to open the refrigerator door, but turned and went to the motel lobby instead. He looked about for a couple of minutes, checked the front door to make sure it was locked, and returned to the back. This time he opened the refrigerator and took out six cans of beer.

Barney was beginning to wonder whether he might have made a mistake in telling Bishop Collins and Harlan about Room 10. Once the cat was out of the bag, there would be no getting it back in. If the two colored boys and the uppity jewgirl put on a good show tonight, Harlan would want to be back in the pit room seven nights a week. And deep down he feared that someday Bishop would use his voyeur's window as fodder for blackmail. Bishop had a vindictive streak and Barney was careful not to cross him, but someday he might slip up.

Of course, if it ever came to that, Barney had an ace up his sleeve. He always had felt bad about facilitating Bishop's afternoon recreation periods with a pretty little Cajun cleaning woman named

Anne Bougelais. Bishop Collins had been mightily taken with her, and offered both her and Barney money they couldn't refuse. Barney's role merely had been to make sure there was a room available and see that the pair wasn't disturbed.

He had rationalized that he wasn't doing a bad thing because the girl needed the money. But deep down he knew that what Bishop was doing was immoral and he was sorry he ever got involved.

All this didn't matter much, anyway. It was too late to change what he had done and all he could do now was hope that giving away his secret didn't come back to haunt him at some point in the future. Maybe the action had started, and Barney didn't want to miss anything. Harlan and Bishop were expecting their beer and he ought not to keep them waiting.

A floorboard squeaked and Barney froze. Instinctively. Then laughed to himself. With all the soundproofing insulation he put in the walls of Room 10, those inside wouldn't hear any sound from outside and anyone outside wouldn't hear anything from them. But damn, there was no way to soundproof the two-way mirror. He never had worried about that before because he expected to be the only one in the pit room and he would be quiet as a church mouse in wintertime.

Bishop Collins and Harlan were almost invisible in the dark room. Barney carefully deposited his half dozen cans of beer on the bench and slid them toward Bishop, who clasped them against his thigh and held them there while Barney sat down. Harlan seemed unaware that Barney had returned.

"Anything happened yet?" Barney whispered close to Bishop's ear.

"Hell no, they just keep on talking in there."

Harlan heard the whispering and looked up. "I almost went to sleep," he said hoarsely, louder than Barney would have liked. Barney watched closely through the glass for any sign that the three hostages on the other side might have heard. If they had, they didn't show it.

"You got the beer?" Harlan inquired, again too loud.

Bishop Collins shushed him. Barney reached across in front of Bishop and handed him a can of beer and an opener. Harlan made no effort to shield the can and muffle the noise when he punctured the top. The sound bounced around the cramped pit room eerily, echoing off the walls. Barney held his breath. But once again, there was no sign the noise registered on the other side of the glass.

"Keep the noise down, Harlan," Bishop Collins murmured. He turned to Barney and whispered, "Can they hear us in there?"

"They can if we make too much noise."

Barney leaned down and opened the cooler under the bench and began to deposit the new supply of beer. Bishop turned back to Harlan and put a finger to his lips. Harlan nodded and raised his drink to his mouth and began to gulp it loudly.

Barney was starting to worry. The three people on the other side of the glass had not behaved the way he expected. He had accepted Bishop Collins's theory that the two niggers would jump the uppity jewgirl's bones as soon as they were alone in the room with her and so far nothing had happened. The three just kept talking, like ordinary people. He had been trying to figure out where Bishop's plan went wrong.

"I got it," he whispered.

"Got what?" Bishop Collins whispered back.

"I know where we made our mistake. We put them boys in the room too early. We ought to have waited till she went to bed. They'd have been on her like dogs on a bitch in heat."

"You may be right. Too late to do anything about that now, though."

Harlan leaned forward and looked Barney in the face. "You think they're going to get after her pretty soon? I need to get home before too much longer. Mama Grace gets worried if I'm out too late."

Bishop Collins snickered. "She probably thinks you're jumping some little gal's bones, yourself," he teased. "You gonna go home and tell her what you been doing?"

"I expect she wouldn't like it if I did."

Harlan straightened up and scooted back until he was sitting tight against the wall. The pit room was commencing to stink of beer and sweat. On the other side of the glass, Room 10 had grown darker. One of the lamps no longer was burning. Barney wondered whether one of the caged hostages had turned it off, or maybe its bulb had burned out. He always tried to cut down on expenses whenever he could and buying cheap light bulbs was one way to save money.

The pit room was getting very little light through the window now, so that it was hard for him to see the faces of Harlan and Bishop Collins. He could hear Harlan sigh impatiently and Bishop shuffle his feet on the rough board floor. His guests might not be willing to wait much longer for the entertainment to begin.

Barney had hoped for a good show, like any number of the scenes he had enjoyed from this vantage point. There had been weeks when he put women in Room 10 four or five nights in a row. Some led to disappointments, of course, like the attractive young Florida girl who got into the room and undressed and took off her wig and makeup and turned out to be a man. Barney had found her—or him—so repulsive he almost shut down the pit room. But two days later a pair of young newlyweds from New Jersey checked into the Tennessee Bend and he put them in Room 10 and spent one of the most thrilling nights of his life watching all the action.

Barney wasn't hard to please. Any woman, young or old, who unwittingly gave him a flash of bare flesh made his little hiding place worthwhile. If a couple had sex, that was just icing on the cake. Most of the time that happened in the dark, though, leaving much to his imagination. He would try to recall every detail of how the woman looked in the light, pretend that he was in the man's place, hope he would perform well and make her night one to remember.

It wasn't always women. He got a mild rush of exhilaration from looking on while appealing young men stood naked before the two-way mirror and admired themselves. He still had fond recollections of a muscular Marine who spent half an hour striking poses and flexing his muscles as if he were performing on stage. As to perverts like the one from Florida, Barney rationalized that given the vulgar tenor of the times he was lucky there weren't even more. There had been others, worse, and he had seen unnatural acts he found completely abhorrent. So far, he had been pretty successful in blocking these from memory as he relived the good times spent in the pit room viewing the performances of his guests in Room 10.

Chapter 20

Agent Charlie Monroe made it to the sheriff's office just down the road from the Tennessee Bend Motel late in the afternoon, after a pleasant and leisurely drive from Knoxville. He had stopped at a Dairy Queen and picked up a strawberry sundae for lunch and he had not pushed the speed limit. Driving through the beautiful Appalachians at the height of their autumn glory was not something to rush.

Having grown up in the South Carolina piedmont, he always took mountains for granted. There were any number of monadnocks, the ambitious little pop-ups that might or might not be part of a larger chain, between Chester and the Blue Ridge and Smokies. Little Mountain, Caesar's Head, Glassy Mountain—as a boy he had learned the names of all of them. Others in his family most often opted for the beach as their preferred days-off site, but Charlie, given a choice, always took the mountains.

Although he never recalled a time when there wasn't beauty to be found in the Appalachians, Charlie Monroe liked the colorful fall season best. Twice on his way from Knoxville he bowed to the temptation to pull off the road on a scenic byway just to get a closer look. Both times he had been glad he did.

Anyway, he knew it would take Agent Anton Schuler a great deal longer to get down from Baltimore.

Agent Monroe ducked into the office just in time to catch Sheriff Asa Carter before he headed to Big John's Place for dinner. The sheriff greeted him enthusiastically and Charlie Monroe responded in kind. "We still miss you down in the agency, Ace," he said. "You were one of the best young techs we ever had. Have you had any regrets about going into politics?"

The sheriff smiled. "I could do without the politics, but I like my job," he replied. "If I can get reelected I'll be happy to stay right where I am. I was about to get some supper. Like to come along?"

Charlie Monroe accepted the invitation. He had looked forward to a visit with Asa Carter and a chance to talk about old times in the Knoxville office. Carter had come to work there right out of the University of Tennessee, and planned on a career in the FBI. He started as a crime technician and hoped to become a field agent. Then the longtime sheriff in his home county decided to retire and Asa went back to his roots and got himself elected without opposition.

In a matter of moments they were seated in the dining room at Big John's. Monroe had forgotten how young Asa Carter was—at least in comparison with himself. The sheriff was tall and heavyset, with a red face that always looked sunburned, and had his hair clipped so short it was hard to tell whether it was brown or black. His dark eyes were lively, as if hiding a secret he wanted to tell. But if Asa Carter looked like a kid, still wet behind the ears, the FBI man knew this was misleading. The young sheriff already had developed a tough, law-and-order reputation.

"This place has the best pepper steak in Tennessee," the sheriff said. "Pretty generous serving, too."

"You sold me. I don't believe I've had a good pepper steak in a couple of blue moons."

They gave their orders to Kathy and drank coffee while they waited for their food. "I suppose being the sheriff carries a lot of weight around here," Agent Monroe said. "Being a local boy to begin with probably didn't hurt, either."

"Yes and no. Being sheriff is an important responsibility, given the scarcity of other law enforcement in an area like this. Being a local boy helped me get elected, no doubt about that. But in the long run it's not going to make me any more popular. Maybe just the opposite."

"Really? Why is that?"

"People know my roots. They know I'm a lot like them—growing up with the same ideas they did, all that. We're going to be in for some hard times, Charlie, and I'm going to have to enforce the law whether I like it or not."

"You're talking about race relations?"

"You got it. Supreme Court ruling and all that. I can't say that I don't feel pretty much like everybody else when it comes to my kids going to school with black kids. I'd rather not see it happen. And that's just the beginning. But I have to put my own feelings aside and enforce the law. That's not going to set well with people who expect me to take their side. Do you see what I mean?"

"I see what you mean, Ace. Lawmen face that dilemma more often than we realize, I guess. It takes guts."

Kathy brought their steaks, served with boiled potatoes and fried okra. As Asa Carter had promised, the steaks were large. She placed garden salads and a basket of hard-crusted dinner rolls on their table, poured more coffee, filled their water glasses, and left them to their conversation.

"I expect you didn't come up here to talk about how I do my job," the sheriff said. "I assume it's this missing person case. Are you running the investigation, or is that the responsibility of the guy from Baltimore?"

"It's his right now. It could become mine, though, depending on what happens next."

"Meaning if you find a body somewhere around here, right?"

"Yes, that certainly would change things."

"Baltimore's on the way?"

"Agent Anton Schuler. You may know him."

Sheriff Carter pursed his lips and showed that he was trying to remember. "I don't believe we've ever crossed paths," he said. "I usually remember an FBI guy when I work with him."

"Schuler's one of the good ones. I expect him to show up about any time now. Meanwhile, you might as well bring me up to speed on what you have. I understand that some reporter claims to have found a witness who says the man was here?"

"So I heard. She was in the office. I haven't talked to her, but I know who she is. What we do have, though, is Saillot's car that we fished out of Cherokee Lake. The guys from the state crime lab went over it pretty well and nothing much turned up. The keys were in it and it looks like the ignition was on when it hit the water, but I'd say it was a dump. Somebody didn't want it found setting around here and got rid of it the fastest way they could think of."

"Nothing to indicate that Saillot might have been in it when it landed in the lake?" Charlie Monroe asked.

Sheriff Carter shook his head. "No. We can't be sure, of course. There's no doubt that somebody drove it over the bank, but my guess is they jumped out at the last minute. A couple of my deputies have been up there scouring the area where it would have gone over but they didn't come up with anything except tire tracks."

"Anything in the car?"

"There was a small suitcase with a few clothes in it in the trunk," the sheriff said. "Everything was so water-soaked it'll take a while to make much out of it, though."

"I'll get some notes down on all this as soon as we get back to your office. Or maybe you're done for the day?"

"Not a chance. I'm at the beck and call of you and Schuler for as long as you guys are here. I'll have my deputies help with any legwork you need. Whatever you want, just ask. We're here to serve."

They finished eating and were leaving the dining room when Sheriff Carter spotted Mandy behind the hostess stand. No one had been there when they came in. "Hey, Mandy," he called pleasantly. "How's the world treating you these days?"

Mandy's eyes brightened and she returned his greeting. "I've got a question for you," she said.

"I hope I have an answer. Mandy, meet Agent Charlie Monroe out of the FBI's Knoxville office. He and I used to work together. What's your question?"

Agent Monroe and Mandy both nodded, but neither actually spoke. Mandy went straight to her question: "That car they found in the lake—have y'all found out for certain whose it is yet?"

"We think so, but I can't release the information yet. The appropriate people have to be notified first. You understand."

"Sure, Ace. I understand. And I suspect those people are in Baltimore, right?"

"Like I said, I can't release that information. But why do you say Baltimore?"

"Because the missing man that reporter's been looking for is from Baltimore. She was hoping it wasn't his car. You needn't tell me anything more, sheriff. I can read your face pretty well."

Sheriff Asa Carter looked at Charlie Monroe with an expression of helplessness. Monroe stepped forward and spoke directly to Mandy. "Miss, do you happen to know where that reporter is? We want

162

to check with her and see what she can tell us."

"She's staying up at the Tennessee Bend. Sheriff Carter knows where it's at."

"Thank you kindly," Agent Monroe said, making a motion with his left hand like he was tipping his hat. Except he wasn't wearing a hat. "We'll give her a call as soon as we get back to the sheriff's office. You have a pleasant evening."

As they stepped outside, the sun was drifting low over the foothills to the northwest. The heat of the day had dissipated.

"Beautiful evening, Ace," Charlie Monroe said. "And feels like it may be cooling off some. This sure has been a hot one for up here in the mountains."

"I think somebody forgot to tell the weatherman we're supposed to stay cooler up here. This summer felt more like the Mississippi Delta."

Agent Monroe looked off toward the sunset. "It's a gorgeous world," he said. "Kind of makes you wonder what it could be like without all the ugliness, doesn't it? I'd rather be up here to go fishing with you on Cherokee Lake than looking for that poor missing French boy. Has anybody told his mama and daddy yet about the car in the water?"

Sheriff Asa Carter's smile evaporated. "The information went to the Baltimore FBI office," he said. "I expect they know by now. As sheriff I have to deal with it, but as a father I can't even begin to understand what it would be like to get news like that."

"I've been in police work a long time, Ace. I suppose I've delivered my share of bad news. I have to tell you, it's one thing that doesn't get any easier with practice."

On the brief drive back to the sheriff's office, they made small talk about family and old acquaintances in Knoxville. Asa Carter reported that his firstborn, a son named Asa Carter Jr., had just turned three. He asked about Allison Pryor. Charlie Monroe brought him up to date, and then they were there. A plain black sedan that both recognized as an unmarked agency vehicle was parked in front of the building, in a space that had been empty when they left for Big John's Place.

Riding with a cop wasn't Bill Skyles' favorite way to travel, but when Agent Anton Schuler suggested that Skyles join him for the trip to

Tennessee in the FBI car, he couldn't think of any reason not to. He wondered if Schuler was sticking his neck out; surely there was an FBI policy on letting civilians ride in agency automobiles, much less taking a journalist along when working on a case. But against the rules or not, it was generous of Schuler to ask.

It was easy for Skyles to rationalize that traveling with law enforcement was a good way to stay on top of a story. He would have a chance to pick Schuler's brain as they rode, and he was sure to arrive in Tennessee at the same time the FBI did. This didn't take into account the agent heading up from Knoxville, of course, but Agent Schuler was certain to be his principal source of information because of the way the case developed and the relationship he and Schuler already had established. The Saillot case belonged to the Baltimore office—so far, anyway.

Anton Schuler was several notches above the average police officer Skyles was familiar with. There was no way he could disrespect Schuler. The more he saw of the FBI man, the more he liked him.

Agent Schuler, on learning that Skyles had been a reporter in Des Moines, brought up the so-called "mad hound" serial killer. "That one went on a while, as I recall," Schuler said. "How come it took so long to catch him?"

"Yes, it did. More than a year," Bill Skyles answered. "I think it took a long time to catch him because there was no pattern to it. He just picked his victims at random, and eventually began to go out into the small towns and rural areas looking for somebody to kill. It was like whoever he happened into when he was in the mood. He had a lot of people scared."

"And this is the one who almost got away? After he was caught, I mean."

Bill Skyles chuckled. "Yes, he did. It's funny now, but it sure wasn't funny then. There had been so much pre-trial publicity the guy got a change of venue to one of the more rural counties. He was being held in a small-town jail and, believe it or not, somebody left the door unlocked."

"That's right!" Schuler exclaimed. "I had forgotten how that happened."

"Well, that's how it happened. Your guys picked him up a couple of weeks later in San Francisco about to board a ship bound for China. He'd hitchhiked all the way across the country and signed on

164

as a deck hand on a freighter. Literally a slow boat to China, I guess."

"Damn, that's bizarre." Agent Schuler seemed to be enjoying the discussion of police work they both remembered. "Sometimes we win the close ones and sometimes we don't," he said.

The drive from Baltimore took longer than they'd estimated, giving them plenty of time to talk. Skyles learned things about Agent Schuler's background that surprised him. When the topic of Rachel Feigen came up, Schuler implied that he held her in high regard and the editor pretended that she reciprocated. But honest consideration of her feelings led him to bring up Guy Saillot's homosexuality

"That way of life is something I never thought much about," Skyles said. "As far as I know, I've never actually known a homosexual. Have you?"

"I had a brush with it once, when I was a kid. It left me pretty disgusted."

"What happened?"

"You probably don't really want to hear this," Anton Schuler said.

"Yes I do—if you don't mind telling me. How old were you?"

"I don't know. Six, I think. I don't mean to imply that something happened to me, it was just something I saw."

"That's enough sometimes."

"It was enough for me, at that age anyhow. And you know, I've never told anyone about this before. There was a park in Stockton that I went to all the time, up until the German-haters drove me away. That's another story, though. Anyway, one day I had to pee and went to the bathroom and saw two men in there engaged in a sex act."

"Not something a six-year-old is ready for, that's for sure," Skyles said.

"I didn't understand what was going on, of course, and I guess I just stood there watching, trying to see what they were doing. I said 'bathroom,' but it was kind of an outdoor shed type building. I was probably twenty feet away. They saw me watching and one of them said 'grab him' and I ran like hell. I don't think they even followed me, but it scared the piss out of me—no pun intended. I ran till I was completely out of breath and got on home as fast as I could."

"I feel honored by your confidence," Bill Skyles said seriously. "Did you ever go back to that park?"

"You know, it's funny but I never associated those men with the park so much. I only thought about them being in the bathroom. I never went to that outhouse again, but I did go back to the park—until they started putting up anti-German signs. That kind of put the queers into perspective, I guess."

Skyles laughed. "That's life. Just when you think something's bad, something worse comes along."

"Yes, it does. And I'm afraid this Saillot case is a bad one, Bill. These missing persons cases don't often turn out well. My gut feeling is that this young Frenchman ran into trouble down here that got him in over his head."

They talked about Guy Saillot. It was apparent to Bill Skyles that Agent Schuler was not prejudiced against Guy Saillot, the individual, but against his way of life. Skyles himself had never had a problem with this, but then he'd not had an experience like the one Schuler had described to him a while back. He had no basis on which to judge the impact it might have on a six-year-old boy but he was willing to cut Schuler some slack.

Just after they crossed the line into Tennessee, they saw the first of several "Impeach Earl Warren" billboards. The signs were a dismal reminder of the deep-seated racial prejudice they could expect to find in the area they were driving into.

Bill Skyles was the first to see a sign for the Tennessee Bend Motel. He wanted to stop there, eager to find Rachel Feigen. Agent Schuler said he was obligated to check in at the sheriff's office first. But don't worry, he said, they would get back up there in short order. Skyles felt better when they found that the sheriff was located only a couple of miles farther on.

Schuler and Skyles were waiting when Sheriff Asa Carter returned, with Charlie Monroe in tow. Skyles was introduced all around and Agent Schuler was introduced to the sheriff and other men in the department.

"My name's Asa, but Charlie here began calling me 'Ace' when I first started down in the Knoxville office," the sheriff said. "Now everybody calls me Ace."

"That just means you owe me a favor," Monroe joked.

Skyles asked to use a phone to call his reporter and one of the deputies directed him to a desk that wasn't in use. He dialed the number of the Tennessee Bend Motel but there was no answer.

"You'd think somebody would be on duty up there this time of day," the deputy said.

"I think we'll be going up there soon. I'm just a reporter, but I'll have you fellows and the FBI in front of me on this one."

Chapter 21

Sergeant Willie Jamison always had been grateful that he never had to use his hand-to-hand combat training. Now, though, he would welcome the chance. He hadn't the slightest doubt that he could take care of any one of the three men who locked him in Room 10 with Quint Loman and the woman, given a fair fight. Fair, in this case, meaning unarmed.

Jamison was grateful to the army for giving him the physical toughness to handle a situation like this if he was able to make a stand. His military training had been intense. Basic combat infantry training at Fort Leonard Wood, Missouri, proved an eye-opening experience for a young man fresh off the streets of East St. Louis, and he made the most of it. He loved the regimentation and the demanding physical drills—both kept him busy and exhausted, easing the pain of losing Paris—and he was happy when the army assigned him to advanced infantry for his next round of instruction.

The young Willie Jamison had never been more alive than he was on those icy winter mornings, marching along one of the post's gritty asphalt streets at sunrise in step with his platoon and singing out the cadence in echo to a drill sergeant's shrill holler:

> I don't know but I've been told
> *(I don't know but I've been told)*
> Eskimo nookie's mighty cold!
> *(Eskimo nookie's mighty cold!)*

Being outdoors in the frigid early morning air made him more intently aware of his surroundings than he'd ever been before. He would never forget the acrid taste and smell of coal smoke from the countless barracks furnaces, the heavy frostings that coated everything with a layer of silver, the cloudless skies that eventually led to a little sunshine and much-welcomed warmth.

He believed he was the only man in his company who looked forward to bayonet drill, the vicious plunging of the rifle-fixed blade into canvas dummies, thrusting and withdrawing to the repeatedly stronger challenge from the instructor, "What's the spirit of the bayonet?" And the inflexible, rote response, more forceful with every reiteration, *"Kill! Kill! Kill!"*

And when it came to hand-to-hand combat training, Jamison had as an incentive the memory of an incident that involved his Uncle Jerome. One night when he and his uncle were walking the streets of East St. Louis they were accosted by a half-dozen teenaged gang members. Young Willie was scared to death, but his uncle stood calmly in the middle of the sidewalk, folded his arms across his chest, and said in a quiet voice, "Gentlemen, I'm a trained killer. I've done hand-to-hand combat with the best fighters in the world. There may be enough of you to take me down, but the first three in reach will be hamburger meat in less time than it takes to spit. So come on. Who wants to be first?"

The young hoodlums backed off and tried to act like it was all a joke. After they were gone, Willie asked his uncle what kind of training did it take to get that good in hand-to-hand combat. Uncle Jerome grinned, then burst out laughing. To Willie's amazement, he admitted that he had no such training and what his nephew had just witnessed was a classic bluff.

The incident left Jamison wishing he really did have that kind of training, and now he had an opportunity to get it. He was extremely competent in hand-to-hand combat when he finished the course.

By the time he got to Korea, he was physically fit and psychologically ready for whatever came next. There was direction now to the mental toughness he'd learned on the streets of East St. Louis. The Korean weather was miserable, there was no longer a civilian population along the demilitarized zone so that the troops felt isolated, and virtually every day brought a new threat of conflict. But he took the hardship in stride and reveled in the constant combat readiness. It kept him sharp.

Service on the DMZ also had kept him from indulging in the debaucheries he heard about among American soldiers stationed elsewhere in the country. Except for a couple of short-leave excursions down to Seoul, he hadn't seen the whorehouses, gambling establishments, and watering holes common in their stories. This suited Jamison very well. In his mind the Koreans were all gooks he would rather shoot than socialize with.

Maybe Loman had a point about dehumanizing other races by calling them names. But philosophy was way over Willie Jamison's head. He'd survived this long by living in the real world, and that meant giving as good as he got. When he joined the army the drill sergeants told him he was training to kill gooks, and that's what he went to Korea for. He just had not had the good fortune to get into combat and see one in his rifle sights.

Jamison respected Quint Loman—had come to like him a lot, too—but he could tell that Loman would rather talk than fight. Personally, he felt the exact opposite. He'd rather fight.

And he still had serious reservations about this woman. Quint Loman was strong enough to put up a good battle if he had to, but what would she do?

"Ma'am, I wish you'd lay down and get some rest," he told Rachel Feigen again. He wanted to add, but didn't, "Stand back and let us men decide what to do."

Feigen didn't bite. "Lie down, hell," she said. "Do you really expect me to sleep in a situation like this? We need to talk, sergeant. Don't you realize what a fix we're in?"

Jamison's anger apparently showed, because Loman jumped in. "I think we all understand what we're up against," he said. "Those men are dangerous. I think Willie knows they don't have good intentions."

"Let's pretend we're all prisoners of war then," Feigen said sarcastically. "What shall we do, sergeant? Merely wait for them to come back and take us out one by one and put bullets in our brains? Or do you think you can get us out of here?"

Jamison was furious, but he managed to hold his temper in check. He pointedly ignored Feigen and addressed himself to Loman. "They caught us by surprise last time. First thing we need to do is make sure somebody stays awake. I'll stand the first watch if you want to sack out for an hour or so."

"I'm with her on that one," Loman said. "Not likely I'd be able to sleep."

Feigen obviously was determined to be included in the conversation. She looked Willie Jamison straight in the eye and said, "I'd like to hear more of Quint's reasoning on why they locked us up to begin with."

"I'm thinking it's pure racism," Loman said. "The same thing that got Emmett Till murdered in Mississippi. These men don't like black people and maybe they don't like Jews."

"Meaning what, in the final analysis?" Feigen asked. "They plan to murder us and dump our bodies in a river someplace like they did Emmett Till?"

"That may not be where they started out, but that's where they are likely to end up. As long as we're alive they face kidnapping charges at the very least. And you mentioned the FBI, right?"

Jamison turned toward the door. "Why in hell would they put a lock on the outside if this is a regular motel? I think we may be in deeper shit than we know. We need to try and bust out of here now instead of waiting for them to come and get us."

His question seemed to hit home with the other two. This room had a lock on the outside of the door and so did the one he and Loman had been held in earlier. If the Tennessee Bend Motel had locks on the outside of its doors, it was a prison pure and simple. Who would make a motel into a prison and why?

"We had better decide what we want to do," Loman said simply. "Things can get out of control pretty fast."

Rachel Feigen's anger was fast becoming fear. She had been angry for much of the time she'd been in Tennessee, facing a mountain of evidence that the people here who mattered most had no concern over the fate of Guy Saillot. Her personal rude reception had been secondary. But if Quint Loman was right, if she was being lumped in with two black men for no reason other than being a Jew, she was in serious danger. Black men were lynched in the South.

Jamison would be a logical target, not because he'd be easy to take down but because he was belligerent. If he got pushed by a white man he sure as hell would push back. Loman was another story. He went to great lengths to avoid any pretense of being a tough guy and she couldn't see him saying or doing something offensive to the local white society. He might insult other Jews the way he had insulted her, but that hardly would have gotten him into this situation—might have earned him a merit badge, in fact. She couldn't make any sense of all this.

The precarious position she was in at least had taken her mind off Guy Saillot. Right now she was concerned for herself. Damned if she was ready to be dragged off into the woods and raped and murdered and maybe have her body dumped in Cherokee Lake. If Willie Jamison wanted to put up a fight, she would be happy to lead him into combat.

"Jamison's right," she said. "I'm not willing to just sit around and wait till they come for us."

"That has a familiar ring," Loman said.

"Martin Niemöller. 'First they came for the Jews, and I did not speak out because I was not a Jew.' Have you read the new book by Milton Mayer?"

"Yes. *They Thought They Were Free.* I wish everyone would—"

Jamison interrupted. "Damn it, people, we don't have time to set here and talk about books. I don't care how good it is, it's not about to help us get out of here. If we want to get out of here alive we better do something. And I mean now."

"Yeah, sorry," Feigen said. "He's right, Quint."

"I know," Loman replied. "We need to keep our heads."

Feigen turned to Willie Jamison. "If anybody is going to come up with an idea, I have a feeling it will be you. What do you think, sergeant?"

"First of all I think we ought to knock out that window. I saw that this room has bars, like the one Quint and I were in earlier. Breaking the glass won't give us a way out, but it might attract some attention. We could yell out of it, anyway. We've got to make some noise, let somebody know we're here. Surely there are people in some of the other rooms."

"That might be a good idea," Loman said. "On the other hand, it might simply bring our wardens running, with their big guns. What do you think, Rachel?"

"I guess I'm with Willie. We have to do something. I don't see how trying to get somebody's attention could be any more risky than just sitting here waiting. God knows those creeps already know we're here."

Jamison nodded. "Our best hope is to get out of here before they show up with their guns," he said. "Meantime, I wish your FBI man would get his ass down here. Where's he coming from? Baltimore?"

"Yes."

Feigen was surprised at Willie Jamison's sudden calm. It looked as if he'd regained his confidence. His palpable anger had subsided, he spoke firmly but not nearly so loud, and she could virtually see the wheels turning in his head. This man was brighter than she'd given him credit for.

Snap judgments had led her into trouble before. Despite her father's teachings that one must always "take the full measure of the man," sometimes she had been guilty of equating character with formal education. She had been brought up to believe that education was the be-all and end-all of a good life and she had too easily translated this conviction into an assumption that educated people would be good people. Her father had warned that this ignored the human factor, which she knew was true.

Jamison might not match her and Loman in schooling, but this man knew human nature. And more important, maybe, he knew how to deal with danger and violence. Quint Loman no doubt had seen his share of these also, but Feigen herself had led a sheltered life. Facing her own limitations now made it easier for her to place her fate into the very strong and able hands of Willie Jamison.

"Willie, I apologize for being snide before," she said. "As far as I'm concerned, you are our best hope. Neither Quint nor I have anything like your training. Whatever you suggest, I'm ready to try."

"I'll buy that," Loman said.

Willie Jamison smiled broadly. He extended a hand to Feigen and then to Loman. "These shitheads can't be any more dangerous than the gooks I stared at eye-to-eye across the line every day," he said. "Of course, the gooks never came charging over that line, so maybe that's not a real confidence builder."

His Alabama upbringing and his vivid awareness of the racial strife that pervaded the nation notwithstanding, Quint Loman had been badly shaken by events of the last several hours. He wasn't surprised that a naïve black teenager from Chicago, not familiar with the ways of the South, would get in trouble in Mississippi. But he had not expected such overt signals of angry discontent as the billboards he had seen along the highway—some decorated with Confederate flags—that demanded the impeachment of Earl Warren, and absolutely nothing could have prepared him for being taken at gunpoint at a filling station by what might yet turn out to be a lynch mob planning his destruction.

Loman fully understood the danger he was in. Growing up in Alabama he had learned that a single racist was bad enough, but get two or three working together and there was hardly any limit on how far they might go.

Aside from being afraid, Loman's most persistent emotion had become an overwhelming sadness. He was a Southerner and there were many things he still loved about the South—the genteel manners, the refined way of life, the generosity and caring of the Southern people. Most of them, anyway. It always had been difficult for him to understand how, when it came to interactions among blacks and whites, men and women who were the most gracious individuals in the world one minute could be vicious miscreants the next.

Not that the meanness had been equally distributed. Far from it. The black people had been subjugated by the iron hand of the whites for too long; few had the audacity to challenge the status quo and seek even the mildest hint of justice. Certainly they would never demand an eye for an eye, or, more accurately, a lash for a lash, a lynching for a lynching, a life for a life.

Loman's hopes for racial reconciliation had been high in recent years. His own experience had proved that a black man could succeed in white society. Likewise, his belief that humanity's better nature eventually would prevail had led him to expect a more positive reaction to the Supreme Court's school desegregation decision in *Brown v. Board of Education*. The near-blanket negative reaction to the ruling across the South had left him somewhat disillusioned.

The essence of the problem, as Loman saw it, was that a white society unwilling to accept the integration of black and white children in the public schools was a society bent on preserving the subservient role of black people across the board. To him, this represented only limited advancement since the days of slavery. He had tried to rationalize the Mississippi situation by concentrating on the fact that the law enforcement axe had dropped fast after the Emmett Till murder. Two men were about to be tried for that heinous act, which was the trial Loman had hoped to attend. But the true ugliness was the killing of the boy in the first place, no matter the trial outcome.

Enough was enough. No more trying to put a prettier face on ugliness.

"Willie," Loman said, "it's time we black people fight back. I'm ready for that fight to begin right here. If it doesn't turn out well, so be it. Like Rachel said, I'm not willing to just sit here and wait till they come for us."

"That's the kind of talk I like to hear, lawyer man. We'll smash that window and yell, but don't be surprised if nobody hears us. We need to be ready when they hit that door. Do you see anything in here we might be able to make weapons out of?"

Feigen said, "If we broke that big mirror over there we might get a few glass shards. I'm ready to slash a throat if I have to."

"That's not a bad idea," Jamison told her. "Wrap the glass in a towel, though, so you don't cut yourself before you cut them."

"Oh, yeah. I'm sure the Tennessee Bend management would hate to get any Jew blood on his floor."

"If 'management' means one of the three piles of crap that locked us in here, when we get done with him his floor's going to be the least of his problems," Jamison said. "Anyway, any blood gets spilled it's going to be theirs."

To Quint Loman, Jamison looked to be spirited and energetic again, determined and ready to fight—the Willie Jamison he'd seen earlier, back in the other room.

Chapter 22

In the pit room behind the mirror, Bishop Collins was on his fourth beer. Harlan was beginning to nod off, his chin drooping almost to his chest. Barney Vidone was seriously concerned that he may have promised too much. Nothing was happening in Room 10. The jewgirl and the two boys just kept on talking, like old ladies gossiping after church.

"Ask Harlan does he want another beer," Barney whispered to Bishop Collins.

Bishop nudged Harlan with his elbow.

"What?" Harlan exclaimed, speaking much too loudly. Then, in a whisper, "What the hell do you want, Bishop?"

"Barney wants to know do you want another beer?"

"How many you reckon I already had? Four or five?"

"How would I know? Ain't nobody appointed me your keeper. You want another one or not?"

"Sure, I could use another one. Did anything happen in there yet?"

"No, they're just talking. Barney, what do you think? We going to get any action out of them boys? Maybe we ought to have give them a few beers before we throwed 'em in there with her."

Barney was reaching down to retrieve a can of beer from the cooler under the bench. The cooler was empty. "Damn," he exclaimed. "We've gone through a lot of beer tonight. I'm going to have to go get some more. Unless everybody's had enough. You sure you want another one, Harlan?"

Harlan had nodded off again.

"I doubt that he needs any more," Bishop Collins said. "Anyway, didn't he say he had to get home to Mama Grace?" He snickered and nudged Barney in the ribs with his elbow. "What kind of man has to get home to mama before midnight?"

Harlan jerked himself up from his slumped position. "I heard that!" he roared, making no effort to hold down the sound. "I heard that, Bishop."

"Quiet!" Barney whispered.

But it was too late. On the other side of the voyeur's window, the trio in Room 10 suddenly stopped talking and looked toward the mirror. One of the black men spun around and started in their direction.

"Let's get out a here!" Harlan cried, jumping to his feet. Bishop Collins was already up. Harlan tried to push him out of the way. Bishop fell sideways, crashing through the mirror and landing on the floor inside Room 10. Harlan took off after Barney, who was rushing away from the pit room.

Rachel Feigen and the two men in the room stood in bewildered silence for an instant, startled and confused. Jamison was the first to move, snatching a chair and knocking the loose glass from the bottom of the mirror frame. As soon as it was cleared, he climbed through the wall and disappeared.

Feigen and Quint Loman ran to Bishop Collins, who was bleeding profusely from a deep gash on the side of his neck. Loman dropped down on his knees beside the surprise intruder and rolled him over, face up. Feigen leaned in close.

"It's one of them, all right," Loman said. "This is not the way I expected them to show up, though."

"He's bleeding bad," Feigen said. "I'd like to let the sonofabitch bleed to death, but I don't think I can."

"You'd get no quarrel from me."

"Grab me a towel or something. And turn that lamp back on. The way his neck's gushing he'll go into shock pretty quick. If you need a rationalization, I want him alive and well to stand before a judge under oath and try to explain what they did to us."

Loman threw her a towel from the bathroom and rushed back to her side. "What they did and what they were going to do," he said angrily. "What happened to Willie?"

"Willie's right here." It was the voice of Jamison himself, coming from the other side of the opening previously covered by the mirror. "Now get through there, you jackass." Harlan MacElroy crawled through the hole in the wall, with Jamison right behind. "I found this one hiding back there in the dark," he said.

Harlan looked like a lost puppy, scared and not sure what was happening. "Barney locked the door after hisself," he said, addressing no one in particular. "I couldn't get out." He seemed to notice Bishop Collins on the floor for the first time. "Bishop, you okay?"

"No, he's not okay," Feigen said firmly. "I won't be able to stop this bleeding for very long. Your friend will be dead if we don't get him to an emergency room pretty quick—if there is such a thing as an emergency room around here. Where's the nearest hospital?"

Harlan was trying to collect his wits. "I don't know, over there somewhere," he mumbled, pointing toward the west. "I ain't never been there."

"Can you get us out of this room?" Loman asked.

"Barney locked the door after hisself. Why do you think he'd do that?"

"You're wasting your time on this one, Loman," Willie Jamison said. "He was already dumb as a stick and now he's drunk on top of that. He don't know his ass from his ankles right now."

Feigen looked up from her patient, keeping the pressure on the towel she had on his neck. "I'm not a doctor," she said, "but I know enough medicine to know that this man doesn't have a lot of time. Guys, we can't save him with just a little first aid."

"What did you find back there, Willie?" Quint Loman asked, motioning toward the opening in the wall.

"Just like the brain here says, the door out of there is locked. It's solid, too, like everything else we've been trying to break through. If we can't get that front door open, that man will just have to lay there and bleed. There's not any other way out."

"I'll bet George has a key," Harlan MacElroy said, almost timidly. "He probably has keys to all the rooms."

Willie grabbed him by the collar. "What did you say? Who's George?"

"I know who George is," Feigen said. "He's the handyman. But he's a deaf-mute, so how would we get him to come and unlock the door even if he does have a key?"

179

"Dang," Harlan said, "I never thought about that."

Bishop Collins coughed, and tried to lift his head. He was pale and looked bewildered, trying to find something familiar in his surroundings. His blood had soaked through the towel Feigen held to his neck and stained the floor around his upper body. He tried to speak, but no sound came from his mouth. He tried a second time but again failed to make a discernible noise. His head dropped back onto the floor and his eyes closed.

Harlan's eyes widened. "He ain't dead, is he?" he whispered, shuffling closer to Bishop Collins.

"No, he's not dead. But he will be soon if we don't get him to a doctor," Feigen said.

Willie Jamison signaled for quiet. There was a sound of muffled footsteps, then a rustling at the door and the clear sound of a key in the padlock. The door suddenly swung open and there were more footsteps, now hurrying away, toward the darkened end of the building. Jamison ran to the door and looked outside.

"I didn't see who it was," he called.

"Don't worry about that now," Feigen said firmly. "We've got to get this man somewhere where he can get help or it will be too late. Hurry! Help me get him into my car. I know the way to the sheriff's office."

Quint Loman already was leaning down and trying to get a firm hold on Bishop Collins. Harlan joined him and the two men pulled Bishop up to a standing position. One stood on each side and propped him up, his arms over their shoulders, his head sagging forward and the bloody towel dangling down the front of his body.

"Run to the office and see if you can find a phone," Feigen said, apparently aiming her words at Jamison. "We might get him help faster if we could get an ambulance."

Loman and Harlan MacElroy already had lifted Bishop Collins by the arms and were dragging him out the door. Jamison rushed out behind them and ran toward the motel office.

"Where's your car?" Loman asked.

"Right there in front of you. The Chevrolet."

"He's going to bleed all over the seat."

"A human life is at stake here, Loman. My car's not that important."

Harlan stopped dead in his tracks, nearly letting Bishop Collins fall. "Ma'am," Harlan said, "my truck's right behind the building. There ain't no need for you to get your nice car all messed up with Bishop's blood. He's my friend. Put him in my truck. I know the way to the sheriff's office, too. I can get him there just as fast."

"You're too drunk to drive."

"No, I ain't. I've drove a lot of times after more beer than this. Besides, Bishop is my buddy."

"I'd do it," Loman said. "A minute or two longer is not going to make much difference. Chances are this guy's not going to make it anyway."

"Get your truck, then," Feigen said. "But hurry."

Harlan left Quint Loman holding Bishop by himself and ran, turning the corner of the building toward the back.

"I hope he comes back," Loman said. "Do you think he's smart enough to realize he can take off now and there's nothing we could do to stop him?"

"We'll know in a minute," Feigen replied.

An instant later they heard the roar of Harlan's old GMC pickup. At first it sounded as if he was driving away, but then the truck came screeching around the far end of the building and raced toward them. It ground to a stop and Harlan jumped out. He ran around to the passenger side and jerked open the door. Loman lugged Bishop Collins to the truck, feet dragging, and Harlan helped get him into the seat. Loman crawled in beside him and Harlan ran back to the driver's side and slid in and the old truck rumbled away.

Feigen barely had time to catch her breath before Willie Jamison returned. He began to shake his head. "Everything's locked up as tight as a jug," he said. "You really think that dumb-assed redneck will do the right thing?"

"Actually, no. But if he doesn't get straight to an emergency room he's about to lose one of his best buddies. And Loman's with him."

"Damn. That could be dangerous. He's probably got three or four shotguns in that old truck. Whose idea was that, anyway?"

"Mine, I guess. I don't take pride in keeping a clear head in an emergency. Loman agreed to it, though, and that bozo may not understand the trouble he's in now but he sure as hell must know better than to get in any deeper."

"I hope you're right. What do we do now?"

"If I can find my keys after all this, let's hit the road for the sheriff's office. We've got a lot to tell somebody."

Jamison followed her back into Room 10, where she quickly found her purse and keys. She led the way out, motioning toward her car. He pulled the door shut behind them.

"My case is cut and dried," Jamison said, as Feigen drove across the motel parking lot. "They kidnapped me at gunpoint. Loman too. Did they do anything to you besides lock you up in your room?"

"No, but probably only because they didn't get to it. Locking me in is still illegal, though. Especially when it's added to a double kidnapping. And that one, like you said, is cut and dried."

Feigen was about to exit the parking lot and drive away from the Tennessee Bend when another car turned off the highway and came toward them. Then there was another, and a third and fourth. She backed out of the way just as a sheriff's department car rolled up beside her Chevrolet. Sheriff Asa Carter got out through the driver's side door and Agent Charlie Monroe got out on the other side. Feigen and Willie Jamison quickly went to meet them.

The second car, a plain, unmarked black Ford sedan, brought Agent Anton Schuler and the most welcome face Feigen could have hoped for: Bill Skyles. The other two cars brought four sheriff's deputies.

Bill Skyles ran to her. "We've been worried about you, Rachel," he said. "Doesn't anybody ever answer the phone at this damned place? The sheriff's guys have been trying to call for two hours. Are you okay?"

"Hey, boss, it's good to see you. Yes, I'm okay. We've had a little excitement around here, though."

Agent Schuler greeted her perfunctorily and introduced the sheriff and Agent Monroe. "The FBI is grateful for your help, Miss Feigen," Schuler said. "We'll get to the eyewitness you found first thing tomorrow. And you know about the car in Cherokee Lake, I take it?"

"Sorry to say, I do. Is there any question that it is Guy Saillot's?"

"No, no question," Schuler said grimly. "The registration confirmed it."

Two deputies who had been checking the area reported that there were no lights on inside the motel office and it was locked up tight, just as Willie Jamison had said. They'd also knocked on the door of the manager's apartment and got no response.

"Looking at the cars in front of the doors, I'd guess a dozen or so rooms are filled," Sheriff Carter said. "I suppose we owe it to those folks not to make any more noise than we have to. Miss Feigen, if we can go to your room where we have some light, we can try to bring everyone up to date."

Feigen agreed and she and Willie Jamison led the way to Room 10. The sheriff, Skyles, and the two FBI agents followed, leaving the deputies to watch things outside. The door to the room stood open and the lights were on. The floor was littered with shards of broken glass and a large stain on the carpet marked the spot where Bishop Collins had lain while Feigen tried to staunch the flow of blood from the gash in his neck. There was a gaping hole in the wall, behind which Barney Vidone's pit room was a dark and empty space that might have been an entrance to a dungeon.

Agent Anton Schuler systematically looked about the room. "Damn! What happened here?" he demanded. "This place looks like a war zone."

"It kind of was," Jamison said. "We've got a lot to tell you guys."

One of the deputies hurried in and caught the attention of Asa Carter. The dispatcher was on the car radio, he said, and needed to talk with the sheriff directly. It sounded like something the sheriff ought to know right now. Asa Carter excused himself and left with the deputy.

Bill Skyles stood next to Feigen and studied his surroundings. He pulled a small reporter's notebook from a jacket pocket and began to scribble. He started to ask a question but stopped short. He clearly was stunned by the blood stains on her clothes, which he was seeing for the first time in the light. "My God, Rachel, tell me that's not your blood!" he said.

Feigen put a hand on his arm. "I've not shed any blood yet," she said calmly. And looking down at the stains herself, "This is my reward for trying to help somebody who probably didn't deserve my help all that much."

Schuler turned to Jamison. "We'll take detailed statements later, back at the sheriff's office," he said. "But give us the skinny on it. Whether it involves the FBI or not, the sheriff probably will want to get some crime lab people in here. To start with, who was in this room?"

"It was my room," Feigen told him. "Then they brought in

Jamison here and a man named Quint Loman and locked the door on us. Oh, yeah, the phone line had been cut or something."

"Okay," Schuler said. "Jamison, I'd guess you weren't a guest in the motel. How did you get into this mess?"

"Me, not a guest? No kidding? They kidnapped me at gunpoint down at the bus station and locked Loman and me in another room before they brought us here."

"Who kidnapped you?"

"Three guys that ought not to be too hard to find. One of them may be dead already, and one of the others hauled him off to the sheriff's office looking for help. I'm not sure about the third guy."

"Do you have any idea why they kidnapped you? What did they want?"

"They never said."

"And so how did you escape?" Schuler asked.

"After the guy fell through that mirror and whoever else was back there ran away, somebody unlocked the door."

"And you don't know who?"

Feigen stepped toward Agent Schuler. "I know who it was," she said. "It had to be George, the handyman. And I think the third man back there, the one who ran away, was Barney whatever-his-name-is who manages this place. The man who hauled off the injured one said the name 'Barney,' and said Barney locked the door behind himself when they both tried to run."

Agent Anton Schuler shook his head, as if exasperated by what he'd heard. "I am totally lost," he said. "It's going to take a while for us to sort this out."

Sheriff Asa Carter walked in just in time to hear Schuler's comment. "I think I can help a little with that," the sheriff said. "I just got a report from the dispatcher that may interest you. Right after we left, two guys showed up in a pickup truck with a man they said was about to bleed to death. That turned out to be Bishop Collins, and one of the men who brought him in was Harlan MacElroy. Collins is a pretty big man around here, but he gets some funny ideas. Harlan hangs around with him every chance he gets. And if they're into something, Barney Vidone is most likely involved. He's the one who owns this place. The three of them together are somewhere between the three musketeers and the three stooges."

"The injured man," Feigen inquired, "is he still alive?"

"Looks like he'll make it."

Agent Charlie Monroe had been quiet. Now he spoke. "From what we've heard here, he's likely facing a federal kidnapping charge if he pulls through. And so is the man who brought him. Your guys on top of that?"

"Yes, sir. They're holding onto Harlan until they hear what to do."

"I think we'd better start looking for the third one, too," Charlie Monroe said. "I'll be getting a report back to Knoxville first thing in the morning."

Chapter 23

When Effie Catlin drove into the Tennessee Bend parking lot just as the sun rose over the Bays Mountains, she was greeted by a sight that caused cold chills to run up her spine. Two county sheriff's cars and two unmarked black sedans that also were unmistakably law enforcement vehicles were lined up near the front door of the motel. Her first thought was there had been a robbery or maybe worse, and she was afraid to think what may have happened to Barney.

She parked her old truck in its usual spot, nervously checked her face in the rearview mirror, hoisted her heavy purse from the seat beside her and, walking as fast as she could manage, went inside. Rachel Feigen was sitting in the lobby. Effie was about to go talk with her when Sheriff Asa Carter approached, coffee cup in hand, and greeted her politely.

"I believe you're Miss Catlin," he said.

"Yes, but please call me Effie. What's happened here? Where's Barney?"

"It will take a while for us to find out exactly what happened, I think. And I was hoping you could tell us where Barney Vidone is. You don't know?"

Effie's nervousness sounded in her voice. "If he's not here he's probably still asleep. He takes care of the office at night, you know. Sometimes he works real late."

"If he lives in the manager's apartment in the back, he doesn't seem to be there. We've banged on the door several times. Does he ever stay someplace else?"

"No. And I don't understand—he wasn't here when you got here? The office should have been locked. How did you get in?"

"George, the caretaker, let us in," Sheriff Carter said. "We need to find Barney Vidone, Miss Catlin. Do you have any idea where he might go when he's not here? Any friends or relatives he might be visiting?"

Effie Catlin felt her legs weaken. Afraid she was about to faint, she quickly dropped into one of the upholstered lobby chairs. "Barney doesn't have any family anywhere close," she said. "He's got lots of friends. I don't know that I'd single out any ones in particular, though. I'm surprised he wasn't here. It's just not like Barney to leave things unattended to. He's never done that before, and I've worked for him ever since he took over this business."

"How long is that, exactly?"

"Exactly? I don't know exactly, but it's been a little bit over two years."

"Do you know Bishop Collins and Harlan MacElroy?"

"Oh, Lord!" Effie clapped her hands to the sides of her face. "Did they get Barney in some kind of trouble? I always knew they would. I warned him, too, I said he spent too much time with them and one day they'd get him in trouble."

Sheriff Asa Carter took a long drink of his coffee. "Did you see either of them last night? Collins or MacElroy?"

Effie shook her head, indicating not.

"When did you see them last?"

"They were here earlier in the day yesterday. But then they left."

"And how about Barney? Was he here last night?"

"Of course," Effie said. "Either him or me has to be here to run this place. He came and asked did I want to leave work early. I don't get to do that very often, so I was glad to take him up on it. But he was here to take care of things."

"And neither Bishop Collins nor Harlan MacElroy was with him?"

"No, sir. He was all alone."

"Could they have been outside? In the parking lot, maybe?"

"No, sir. I left that way. I always park my truck in the same place. If they'd been in the parking lot I would have seen them."

"Could they have been out back, behind the building?"

Effie Catlin slumped in her chair, suddenly become very tired. "Barney came in from the back," she said. "They could have been back there, too, and I wouldn't have seen them. Sheriff, is Barney in trouble?"

"We don't know yet, Miss Catlin," the sheriff said. "We just need to talk to him. I'm grateful for your cooperation, and I'll probably have more questions later. There are a couple of FBI agents here who may want to talk to you, too." He reached out and put a hand on her arm. "Don't worry. We'll get this all sorted out in good time. I know you have work to do now, and we'll try to stay out of your way."

As Sheriff Carter walked away, Rachel Feigen came toward Effie. She looked extremely tired, and approached slowly. Her clothes were badly stained with something dark, like brown paint. Effie smiled and Feigen managed a slightly more pleasant expression as they exchanged greetings. Feigen sat down in the chair the sheriff had just left.

"Do you know what this is all about, Miss Feigen?" Effie inquired.

"Yes, I'm afraid I do. Your boss may be in big trouble."

Effie Catlin burst into tears. "I knew it was going to happen," she said. "I knew it. He spent too much time with those two, and I knew they'd get him in trouble sooner or later. Do you know what they done?"

"I know some of it, but I'm not the one to tell you," Feigen said. "I don't think anything is for certain yet. Are you going to be all right?"

Effie dabbed at her eyes with a tissue and snuffed back her runny nose. "It'll be hard if Barney gets in trouble," she said. "I couldn't run this place by myself. I expect he'd have to shut it down."

"Meaning you'd be out of work, right?"

"Me and George both. I'd make it some way, but what would poor old George do? He'd be out of a place to live, too."

Feigen looked up, as Bill Skyles approached from the direction of the motel business office. "They want to talk to you, Rachel," he said. "Both of your roomies are back there. I think you'll be interested to hear what they know."

Feigen excused herself, giving Effie an encouraging pat on the shoulder, and went to the back. Skyles sat down to talk with Effie. He introduced himself and showed her his press card, asked if she would like coffee. She thanked him and said she'd get some later. He took a reporter's notebook from a jacket pocket and asked her to spell her name and when she did he carefully wrote it down.

"I don't know why you'd want to talk to me, Mister Skyles," she said.

"I'd just like to get some background on this place and on your boss," Skyles said. "We have to report all this, and we want to get the facts correct. You have no obligation to talk to me, of course, but I promise you my only interest is getting it all right."

"And you're Miss Feigen's boss?"

"Yes, but the AP pretty much considers us all equals. It's just that somebody has to be in charge, I guess—you know, take responsibility for making sure everything gets done. Miss Feigen certainly doesn't need me to tell her what to do or how to do it."

"She seems like a very nice lady."

"She is. And one hell of a—excuse me, one heck of a good reporter."

Effie Catlin laughed. "I'm not a prude, Mister Skyles. I hear a lot of pretty crude language around here. We get hunters and fishermen from all over. And some of the regular travelers, you'd be surprised at how nasty they can be if something goes wrong."

"Not me. I'd never be surprised at the nastiness some of my fellow human beings are capable of. How does your manager handle their complaints?"

Effie was beginning to relax. Bill Skyles had a disarming friendliness, to say nothing of the kindest blue eyes she'd ever seen. She chuckled as she told him, "Barney won't talk to them if he can help it. That is part of my job. He always says I can listen to them and say I'm sorry for their trouble and their mad is likely to go away."

"What can you tell me about the handyman, George? It seems like your boss trusts him with keys to everything."

"He does. George came the day Barney took over the Tennessee Bend. Him and Barney go way back."

Effie went on to tell Bill Skyles what she knew of Barney Vidone's background. Barney always contended that the Vidones weren't meant to be mountain people, she said. Barney's grandfather Vidone had immigrated from Italy to West Virginia to work in the coal mines, and Barney's father went to work in the mines at age seventeen. Barney had told her many times how his grandfather and four other miners were buried alive when a mine explosion caused a massive tunnel collapse. Barney's father, newly married, vowed never to go back into the mines and moved to east Tennessee, built a house with his own hands, and started a family.

"Barney says his daddy didn't know how to do anything but work in the mines," Effie said. "He just had to take any kind of job he could get, whenever he could get anything at all. I guess there was lots of times he was out of work."

She said that the way Barney told it, their new white neighbors were mostly Scotts-Irish and at least second generation Americans and never took much to the new Italian family. If he could have, Barney would have changed his name from Vidone to something Irish. "But he says George and the other little black kids didn't seem to care about things like that. Him and George played together a lot. Barney's about the only one that can communicate with George. I don't know how he does it, but George seems to know what Barney wants."

"George looks like a hard worker," Skyles said. "He keeps the grounds spic and span from what I've seen."

"Have you seen his rose garden, Mister Skyles? That's George's pride and joy."

"It was dark when we drove in, and I haven't been outside much this morning. Just a couple of more questions about your boss. Would you say Barney's a racist?"

Effie felt her face beginning to flush. This discussion was taking a direction she didn't like. "I would not," she said forcefully. "He always says the nigras have as much right to their place as we do to ours."

Bill Skyles looked up from his notebook. "What would that place be?"

"Everybody knows that, Mister Skyles. The South has its customs, just like everyplace else. The nigras don't want a lot—just a chance to work and make a living. Nobody begrudges them that."

"Would you say that Barney Vidone is a segregationist, then?"

"I'm not sure what that means." Effie was disappointed in Bill Skyles. He might not be as nice as he seemed. She needed to be careful what she said.

"I mean does he think that black and white people should have separate schools, separate churches, separate restrooms, separate places to eat and sleep, separate places to sit on the bus. All those kinds of things."

"We all think that, Mister Skyles. You would too, if you lived in the South. I get along with the nigras as well as anybody, but I wouldn't want one sleeping in my bed or eating with my fork. If God intended for us to mix like that, He wouldn't have made us different colors to begin with. And now, if you don't mind, I've got a lot of work to catch up on. Barney's likely to be back at any time and I'd hate not to have things in order."

Bill Skyles stood. "Of course," he said. "I don't want to keep you from your work. Thank you for giving me as much time as you have."

Effie rushed behind the counter and began to go over the motel registrations from the night before. To her surprise, Barney had not put them in any kind of order. She needed to organize the forms of people who were expected to check out this morning, make sure they'd paid for their lodging, and be ready to collect their room keys. It looked as if most of the occupied rooms were filled by long-stay visitors—fishing parties, she assumed—so there wouldn't be too many people leaving.

It was hard for her to concentrate on her work. No one had given her so much as a hint about the kind of trouble they thought Barney was in, and she was extremely irritated that those enforcement men had taken over his office. She didn't like having their cars in the parking lot where everybody could see them, either. They might scare away potential customers.

Most of all, Effie hated the implications of what she'd heard so far this morning. It wasn't Sheriff Carter's questioning so much as it was the newsman's. She did not pretend to keep herself well informed, but she had heard enough talk about the Supreme Court and Judge Earl Warren to know that one way or another the government in Washington was again sticking its nose into things that ought to be left to local people. Did Judge Warren's kids go to school with nigras?

Effie Catlin was not prejudiced against black people, and she did not hate anyone. She was a good Christian woman who wouldn't hurt a fly. She knew that most people in east Tennessee were good people, like her, and simply wanted to be left alone.

And she needed for Barney to come back to work. She could

run the Tennessee Bend by herself if she had to, but things went much smoother with Barney in charge.

It took all morning for the authorities to finish gleaning information from the three who had been held captive. Agent Charlie Monroe led the questioning, with Agent Anton Schuler and the sheriff taking part. They talked with Willie Jamison first and then Quint Loman, and finally called in Rachel Feigen. She hadn't been kidnapped the way the two men had, and had less to contribute. Even so, her formal questioning went on for a full hour.

Feigen was intrigued by the efficiency of the three investigators. As a reporter, she was accustomed to asking precise questions. ("Be specific," one of her favorite professors at Columbia had preached. "Ask a general question and you'll get a general answer.") But these men had a way of approaching a question from different directions that she found fascinating. Evading a question was nearly impossible.

Not that she wanted to be evasive, of course. She was tired and hungry and very angry about what she'd just gone through. She was as eager for the blood of those three men suspected of holding her prisoner as the law enforcement men possibly could be.

When they'd finished the formal questioning, Agent Schuler assured Feigen that his original mission had not been lost in last night's goings on. "I'm still here to investigate the disappearance of Guy Saillot," he said. "We got sidetracked by what Agent Monroe expects to put together as a clear case of kidnapping, and since it happened right under our noses so to speak it wasn't something we could ignore."

"That's the last thing I'd be looking for," she told him. "Ignoring what went on here last night, I mean. You bet I want somebody behind bars for what happened to us."

Sheriff Asa Carter shook his head grimly. "You have every right to feel that way," he said. "I have to tell you, you were every bit as much of a victim in this as Jamison and Loman were. It was an ugly little game they planned for Room Ten, and you were to be a star player."

"I haven't the faintest notion what it was all about," Feigen said. "Am I going to find out?"

Charlie Monroe assured her she would. "We're going to explain it," he said. "But if you don't mind, I'd like to bring Jamison and Loman back in and fill in all three of you at the same time. Unless you'd rather do it separately. It may be a bit awkward."

Feigen put on her grownup face and said she was ready. The sheriff left the room and returned with her two new friends. This was the first time she'd seen Quint Loman since he left in the truck taking the injured man to the sheriff's office. She wanted to run and hug him, but settled for flashing him a big smile. Loman returned it. He shook Willie Jamison's hand vigorously and seemed to be in high spirits.

"Just a thought," Feigen said to Agent Monroe, "but if the formal investigation part of this is done, is there any reason my boss couldn't be here? I was way too involved to be objective about it. He's a good reporter."

Charlie Monroe looked about the room and shrugged. The two other investigators said it would be all right with them, and the Knoxville FBI man said he could see no reason Bill Skyles shouldn't be allowed to sit in on the briefing. The sheriff again left the room, and this time returned with Feigen's boss.

"If y'all don't mind," Agent Monroe began, "I'm going to tell you what we know at this point. It didn't take a whole lot of police work to put together what happened here last night. We have sworn statements from Miss Feigen, here, as well as from Mister Jamison and Mister Loman. It's entirely possible that the three of you will be called to Knoxville at some point to testify in court, but given the powerful evidence we have if I was their lawyer I'd be recommending to the three suspects—when we get ahold of them, of course—I'd be telling them they ought to take the best plea bargain they could get.

"First of all, Bishop Collins, that's the fellow that fell through the looking glass and almost got his head cut off, Bishop Collins is going to be all right. Sheriff Carter's men got him to the hospital real fast and they got the bleeding stopped. He's under arrest and charged with kidnapping."

Feigen couldn't resist. She applauded. Willie Jamison and Quint Loman joined in. Agent Charlie Monroe waited until they all had stopped clapping.

"And I've got even better news," he went on. "Harlan MacElroy, he's the chap that took Mister Collins to the sheriff's office in his pickup truck with Mister Loman here, he's told us everything he knows. He's also under arrest and charged with kidnapping. If he keeps on cooperating the way he has been, a good lawyer most likely will be able to cut a better deal for him than for the other two."

Feigen started to clap again, then self-consciously lowered her hands. Quint Loman looked at her and winked.

Agent Monroe went on: "The sheriff's office and the Knoxville FBI office have put out a bulletin on Barney Vidone. We expect he's driving a Studebaker pickup truck with 'Tennessee Bend Motel' painted on both sides of it. That shouldn't be too hard to find. He will also be charged with kidnapping, among other things."

There was a quiet tapping on the door, and Sheriff Asa Carter stepped over and opened it. Effie Catlin stood on the other side. She whispered something to the sheriff and he left the room for a third time, closing the door behind him.

"I was kind of hoping the sheriff would be the one to explain what was going on last night," Charlie Monroe said. "A couple of his deputies took the statement from Mister MacElroy, and Mister MacElroy told them a pretty ugly story. Sorry, I didn't mean to speak in contradictions like that. Anyway, with the sheriff gone, I may as well go on with it myself."

In spite of the embarrassing nature of what he had to tell them, Agent Charlie Monroe pulled no punches. He described Barney Vidone's voyeur's window on Room 10, outlined explicitly what was expected to happen inside the room, and made clear that the real target was Feigen.

"She was the one who stirred things up by asking questions," he said, "and she was the one they wanted to teach a lesson." Quint Loman and Willie Jamison were to be mere tools in their vicious and revolting scheme.

Feigen was astonished at what she heard. She felt as if she'd been put on display, her privacy violated in the most gross manner. Not by the FBI agent from Knoxville, but by the three vile men who schemed to rob her of all dignity. And for what reason? For their own pleasure, to be sure, but principally because she was a Jew. She felt sick, and for an instant thought she might vomit.

Quint Loman was the first to speak. "So let me get this straight. Their entire plan was built on a supposition that, because Willie and I are black, we'd take the first opportunity we had to jump on a white woman's bones?"

"Yes, sir, that states it pretty well," Agent Charlie Monroe answered.

Now Willie Jamison spoke. "What kind of jackasses think like that?"

"Ignorant jackasses, Willie," Quint Loman said. "Welcome to the South, boy! All you black men are animals."

Bill Skyles stood close to Feigen and watched her intently. She realized that he wanted to say something appropriate—if only he knew what it was. Finally, he said simply, "I'm sorry, Rachel." And that was enough.

Rachel Feigen knew that she never would forget this day. She would remember her refusal to believe Agent Monroe's explanation in the beginning, her revulsion when she accepted his words in the end. But she also would take strength from Bill Skyles' unspoken support. Among all the ugly things, that would be a pleasant memory.

Chapter 24

Almost unnoticed while Charlie Monroe was speaking, Sheriff Asa Carter had slipped back into the room. He took a step forward and signaled for quiet. "I have a report that may make everyone feel better," he said. "I just got a call from the office. The Georgia State Patrol reported a little while ago that Barney Vidone is in custody. A state trooper found him sitting in his truck with a flat tire alongside U.S. 41 about half way between Chattanooga and Atlanta. They said he offered no resistance, but begged the trooper not to shoot him. I expect he'll waive extradition, but even if he doesn't it won't be long until he's back in Tennessee."

This time it was Agent Anton Schuler who applauded.

It was clear to Feigen that business here was finished. The law enforcement men had plenty of urgent matters to attend to and Jamison and Loman needed to move on. Sheriff Carter apparently had the same notion. He moved to where Feigen stood with Bill Skyles and said, "We're better people than this, Miss Feigen. I'm sorry."

Willie Jamison stood awkwardly to the side, as if wondering what he should do next. The sheriff turned to him. "Sergeant Jamison," he said, "I understand that you're late reporting to Fort Jackson. Don't worry. We called and let them know what's going on, and we'll see that you get there. Are you a paratrooper, by the way?"

Jamison looked surprised. "Me? Hell no. I wouldn't jump out of a tree."

"Sorry, I just thought because the 101st Airborne was at Fort

Jackson you might be airborne."

"Oh, yeah, I'd forgot. I heard they're moving to Kentucky, Fort Campbell, sometime about now. Don't know if it's happened yet or not."

Sheriff Carter extended a hand. "I wish you all the best, sergeant. I had a friend stationed at Fort Jackson, and he said it's a great place to serve. Lived like a civilian and Columbia is a beautiful city. Big university, lots of pretty girls, all that."

Jamison shook the sheriff's hand. "Sure, lots of pretty white girls at that big university, sheriff. I could be hung just for looking at one of them, much less trying to ride on the same end of the bus. When I step off that base I'm just another nigger, you know that."

"I'm sorry, sergeant," Sheriff Carter said. "Don't give up on us just yet. The South is changing."

He turned to Loman. "Quint Loman. I just realized a while ago why that name sounded familiar. One of the best pairs of hands ever to play the game. Leading pass receiver in the Big 10 Conference two years in a row."

"Ace was an offensive lineman at Tennessee," Agent Charlie Monroe said. "And as you can see, he still has the smashed face to show for it."

"Say no more," Loman answered. "A rock on that line makes quarterbacks and receivers look like all-stars."

The sheriff laughed. "I had to be a rock. I was too damn slow to move. We could have used you at Tennessee, Loman. We gave our quarterback all day to throw a pass but there wasn't anybody who could catch it."

Loman's smile vanished. "Knoxville would have been a lot closer to home for me, too," he said. "But guess what, the University of Tennessee had some colorful reasons why guys who look like me weren't acceptable. I had to go up North where my talents were appreciated."

Sheriff Carter shook his head. "I'm sorry. What can I say? Good luck, Loman. I hope our paths cross again. I understand you're heading to Mississippi for the Till murder trial. Looks like they're trying to get some swift justice."

Loman nodded. "I hope they get it," he said. "All the Urban League ever asked for is equal and exact justice to all men."

"Very well put."

"Give the credit to Thomas Jefferson."

As Quint Loman turned toward her, Feigen gave way to her instincts and hugged him tightly. Then she hugged Willie Jamison. "I'll never forget you two guys," she said. "What say we forget the circumstances we met under and plan a reunion one of these days where we can go out to dinner and enjoy some good conversation without mentioning old times?"

Quint Loman patted her on the shoulder and turned away, toward the door. But not before she saw the tears in his eyes. Willie Jamison was less emotional. "I'm sorry I gave you a hard time," he said. "You're a good woman, Feigen, even if you did save the life of one of the sorriest jackasses ever to walk on two legs. You take care of yourself."

Sheriff Asa Carter had moved outside and stood waiting in the motel lobby. Jamison rushed to join him. Quint Loman walked straight out the front door, turned to his left, and headed toward his car in the back parking lot where he'd left it when his kidnappers locked him in Room 29. Feigen watched when, moments later, he drove slowly down to the highway at the bottom of the slope without looking back at the Tennessee Bend Motel.

Agents Anton Schuler and Charlie Monroe huddled briefly before Monroe headed for his car. Schuler turned back and came over to Feigen and Bill Skyles. "I think this rotten piece of work is about done," he said. "We all need some rest. Charlie and I are staying at a place five miles down the road, a ways past Big John's. It's a nice motel, and I expect they have openings. Pretty good restaurant in it, too. If that's of interest, you can follow us down there, Miss Feigen. Bill, do you want to ride with me?"

Bill Skyles shook his head. "I guess I'll get a lift from Rachel Feigen, ace reporter," he said. "She's got a brand new Chevrolet and I've not even seen the inside of it yet. We'll be right behind you."

After the Tennessee Bend, any accommodations would have looked good to Rachel Feigen. She followed Agent Schuler's FBI sedan to a place called The Dixie Motel—how many of those had she seen?—and could tell from the outside that it was a nice enough place to stay. It couldn't have been more than a couple of years old, had an appealing design, and was beautifully landscaped. Like the Tennessee Bend, it faced east. The noonday sun beat down on the parking lot and heat radiated from the asphalt surface in visible waves.

She parked beside Schuler. Bill Skyles retrieved his luggage from the FBI car and Feigen got hers from the trunk of the Chevrolet. They followed Schuler and Agent Charlie Monroe inside. Feigen had forgotten the blood stains on her clothes until she saw the near panic in the desk clerk's face, but Schuler quickly assured the poor woman that everything was all right.

The clerk said they had plenty of openings, including two on the second floor near those of Schuler and Monroe. Feigen and Skyles checked in and took an elevator up.

"Will you be able to sleep?" Skyles asked.

"Not very well," she told him. "But I'm tired enough to die, so I may do better than I expect to."

Charlie Monroe suggested they all meet at the motel restaurant for dinner at around seven o'clock, but insisted that no one feel obligated. He and Schuler were tired, too, the strain of overnight events showing in their faces.

Feigen was dying for a hot shower. First, though, she needed to call her father.

Judge Max Feigen answered on the first ring. His relief when he heard who was calling came through clearly. "I was worried that you didn't call us last night," he said. "Is everything still all right down there?"

She had not intended to tell him about Room 10 and the voyeur's window and the ordeal she and the two black men had been through, but at the sound of his voice she broke down and began to sob. There was no alternative, then, to relating the whole sordid story. Judge Feigen responded with a mixture of anger and gentle concern, anger at the men who did these things to his daughter, of course, and gentle concern for her. He released his anger first, using language she had never heard from him before.

"I'm sorry, Rachel," he said then, "I suppose a good part of my rant is because of how helpless I feel, sitting here in New York with you way down there. I still want to be there to comfort my little girl when she hurts."

She had regained control of her emotions, and even managed a forced laugh. "I wish you were here, too, Daddy. But just hearing your voice gives me a lift like you wouldn't believe."

"Are you coming home now? You can't get out of Tennessee

fast enough for me."

"It will be another day or so, at least. Agent Schuler and the FBI man from Knoxville promised they'd get right back on the Saillot case. That's what I'm here for, remember. And I don't know if I've talked to you since Bill Skyles got here or not. He came down with Schuler."

"Promise me just one thing, angel," Judge Feigen said firmly. "Promise me you will not stray far from the side of your boss or one of those agents. Agreed?"

"Agreed. I've already had more action than I wanted. And, Daddy, could I ask you about something, one of your old cases?"

"Of course you can. What case is it?"

"I think maybe . . . Oh, never mind. We can talk about it another time."

When the call ended, Feigen undressed quickly and threw her bloody clothes on the floor in a corner of the bathroom. She got into the shower, turned the water as hot as she could stand it and let it pound her body until her skin was red and burned and the steam obscured her vision, then lowered the temperature and stood without moving for another few minutes before she bothered with soap. The powerful spray helped ease the physical aches and nibbled at the edges of the emotional distress that had been building over the hours, but she did not feel clean. She went to bed hoping for little more than a couple of hours of troubled sleep. She woke to a nearly dark room and looked at the clock. She had slept soundly for almost six hours.

The others would be gathering in the restaurant within minutes and she did not want to be late. She dressed with little attention to what she put on—wrapping in a sheet would have felt good compared to earlier in the day—and went downstairs. Agents Schuler and Monroe were there, seated near the back of the restaurant.

Agent Monroe saw her coming and promptly stood. When she got close he pulled out a chair for her and stood behind it until she was seated. He bid her good evening and said, "You look well rested, which I trust means you've had some sleep."

Bill Skyles arrived and joined the trio, and he also commented on Feigen's rested appearance. "After this morning I was afraid you'd have trouble sleeping," he said. "By the way, have you called your father?"

"Yes, I did," Feigen replied. "I broke down and told him a lot more than I intended to. But you know what? I felt better after I did." She smiled at Skyles and the two FBI men. There probably were a lot of bad things happening in east Tennessee tonight, but she felt safe and comfortable in the company of these good men.

At breakfast the next day, although it went unspoken, the two FBI men and the two journalists tried their best to enjoy the occasion and not talk shop. It didn't last long. Sheriff Asa Carter joined them unexpectedly and he had news. A body had been discovered up on the hickory bluffs. "A couple of kids looking for hickor' nuts found it," the sheriff said. "It's pretty far back in the woods, but pretty close to being in line with where that car would have been driven up to the lake. The state crime lab has a crew on the way."

They left breakfast plates as they were, took final gulps of hot coffee, and hurried to the parking lot. Agent Monroe climbed into the sheriff's car and Agent Schuler motioned for Feigen and Bill Skyles to come with him. "The sheriff knows where he's going," Schuler said. "All we have to do is follow."

Feigen got in the back seat. She felt a terrible dread. She had tried to prepare herself for the worst. Once she knew that the car pulled from Cherokee Lake was his, she realized that the odds against Guy Saillot being found unharmed were overwhelming. But until some trace of him turned up and indicated otherwise, she was determined to hold out hope. She watched out the window of the FBI sedan as they drove and soon recognized that this was the same route she'd taken in her search for the hickory bluffs.

Agent Anton Schuler stayed close behind the sheriff's car. After less than an hour's drive they rounded a sharp bend and saw a deputy standing on the side of the road, behind his parked vehicle. He waved as if signaling a halt and the sheriff and then Schuler pulled their cars over onto the dirt shoulder, barely off the pavement. Schuler and Bill Skyles climbed out of the front seat and Skyles was about to open the rear door for Feigen but she pushed it open before he could.

The deputy reported to Sheriff Carter that the grave site was nearly a mile walk into the woods. The terrain was rugged, he said.

"Are you up to this, Rachel?" Bill Skyles asked.

"I was up there before. I can make it."

"I'm not talking about just the walk. Are you up to what you may see when we get there?"

Feigen wanted to be irritated by her boss's chauvinism, but she couldn't. There wasn't a doubt in her mind that he respected her, and there wasn't a doubt in her mind that he cared about her well-being. "Thanks for your concern," she said, "but I can manage."

The five men and Feigen walked in single file, the deputy leading the way. There was no path like the one Feigen had found on her earlier trek to the lake. The deputy followed his own trail, carefully seeking signs of scuffed earth and disturbances in the carpet of fallen leaves that he'd left when he walked this way before. At one point he seemed uncertain and paused for a moment before deciding exactly where to go. He led them up a number of steep inclines as the elevation increased. It was slow going.

Except for the noise of their walking and the hushed conversation, the woods were eerily silent. The sounds Feigen had heard, squirrels chattering in the trees and birds calling their own kind across the distances, were missing. The rustle of footsteps in the mat of dry leaves was magnified by the quiet and seemed as if it might be heard for miles. The fresh odor of dying leaves overhead was overwhelming.

Once again, Feigen was struck by the simple beauty of these surroundings. She'd never been the outdoors type, but it was easy to understand why people relished the tranquility of this striking natural environment.

"There they are," called the deputy leading the group.

On the opposite side of a narrow draw, three other deputies stood informal guard while two men who turned out to be the crime lab technicians squatted beside an area where the ground clearly had been disturbed. A sheet of canvas covered a spot in the middle where the dry leaves had been raked away. A spade, driven deeply into the dirt, stood at the end of the canvas like a marker.

As she walked closer, Feigen suddenly caught a whiff of the terrible, sickening stench of decaying flesh. The others apparently caught it, too. Bill Skyles and Agent Schuler pulled handkerchiefs from their pockets and covered the lower parts of their faces.

Feigen gagged. She leaned against a tree, both hands on the trunk, fingers up, her palms hard against the rough bark. She began to vomit. After two violent bursts the heaving stopped. Skyles and Agent Charlie Monroe stepped to her side, Skyles putting a gentle hand on her shoulder.

"Take this, please, Miss Feigen," Charlie Monroe urged, holding out to her a white handkerchief. "No matter how many times you smell it, it never gets any easier."

She took the handkerchief and wiped at her nose and mouth. Then she began to retch.

Skyles patted her shoulder. "Are you sure you want to go on with this?" he asked.

"Yes." And then more retching.

Agent Anton Schuler, meanwhile, had made his way ahead, crossing the draw and stepping up to the spot where the canvas sheet covered the ground. He spoke briefly with the crime lab men then pulled back the canvas sheet and exposed a shallow grave. A decomposing body, barely recognizable as human remains except for the clothing, lay crumpled in a mixture of dirt and leaves. The deputy who had led them from the road joined Schuler and knelt beside the shallow pit.

Disregarding Bill Skyles' protests, Feigen forced herself to move close. She hated to look, yet she wanted to see—indeed, had to see—what they all believed was the body of Guy Saillot.

Agent Charlie Monroe moved close also, followed by Bill Skyles.

Feigen stared down at the body. One hand had been mutilated, probably by animals, and was infested with squirming maggots. There was no way to make out features because the corpse lay face down. But there was an unmistakable clump of black hair. Guy Saillot's description included black hair and green eyes. Just like his mother, she thought, remembering Marie Saillot and the pain in her eyes as they talked.

That this hideous shallow grave could be sited here in the beautiful woods where children came to run and play and gather nuts struck her as deceitful, an ugly and dishonorable paradox. Marie Saillot's son might have run and played here, too, had he been still a child. And she knew instinctively that if these were the remains of Guy Saillot, Marie would never find true peace of mind again.

"Was there any identification," Charlie Monroe asked, speaking quietly as if out of respect for the dead.

"Only this," one of the lab men said, handing Agent Monroe a scrap of paper encased in a transparent plastic evidence bag. "Our guess is that the victim managed to slip this into a pocket after the killer or killers had disposed of everything else."

Agent Monroe took the bag gingerly and turned it so that the limited sunlight filtering through the trees shone directly on the paper. He studied the scrap for a moment, then handed it to Agent Anton Schuler. "What do you make of this?" he said.

Schuler squinted at the small, irregular piece of paper, holding it close and examining it carefully. "Studebaker," he said. "It says 'Studebaker.'"

Charlie Monroe turned to Bill Skyles. "You may remember that the bulletin on Barney Vidone said he probably was driving a Studebaker pickup," he said. "When we find out for sure who this is, if we can place him at the Tennessee Bend Motel that little bit of paper might turn out to be as good as a noose around Vidone's neck."

Bill Skyles started to answer, but Feigen spoke first. "Maybe it's not Guy Saillot," she said, almost hopefully. "There was no sign that he ever stayed at the Tennessee Bend. Effie Catlin checked the registrations for about two weeks, and like she said 'Saillot' isn't the kind of name she would have overlooked."

"Whoever the poor guy lying there is, Barney Vidone just became a suspect in a murder case," Agent Schuler said. "I hope you get him back in Tennessee quick, Charlie."

Charlie Monroe nodded. "If he's back now it's none too soon."

Agents Schuler and Monroe conferred briefly, and agreed that Monroe would stay and continue to work with the crime lab technicians and Schuler would go to the Tennessee Bend Motel and bring some heat to the investigation there. Feigen and Bill Skyles decided to split up as well, Feigen going with Schuler and Skyles staying at the scene with Agent Monroe.

Anton Schuler's anger was evident in his driving. He drove too fast, bordering on recklessness, and Feigen was worried that they would have an accident. He had little to say—or in any event little that he cared to say. They arrived at the Tennessee Bend Motel in hardly more than half the time it might have taken. Schuler raced up the driveway and into the motel parking lot as if he were in hot pursuit. He got out of the car and walked fast toward the entrance without waiting for Feigen.

By the time she caught up to him, Agent Schuler was standing at the check-in counter face-to-face with Effie Catlin. Effie was visibly upset.

"Let's go through them again," Schuler was saying.

"Yes, sir, I'll look again," Effie said, "but I don't think there's any way I could have missed a name like that. I just don't believe he was ever registered here."

Effie turned back to the filing cabinet where past registrations were kept and pulled out a drawer. Schuler went around the end of the counter and joined her. It seemed to Feigen that he had calmed down some, and he was polite when he asked Effie to stand aside and let him look at the registration forms.

"Is this everything?" he asked.

Effie assured him it was. They were in order by date, she said, and he had all the forms covering four weeks of guest registrations. Schuler began to go through the files and Effie came back to the counter where Feigen stood. Her hands were shaking and she was on the verge of tears.

"Are you going to be okay?" Feigen asked.

"This is all so awful," Effie replied. "They say Barney's locked up in Georgia and they're going down to pick him up. Miss Feigen, Barney would never hurt anybody. I know he wouldn't."

"I'm sorry, but why did he run away then?"

"I don't know. Maybe he was just scared. I just don't know."

Feigen felt great sympathy for Effie Catlin. But how could this woman have worked alongside Barney Vidone for two years and not know him better? Was it a matter of seeing only what she wanted to see, Feigen wondered, or was Barney Vidone simply a different man in different circumstances? After what she had endured in Room 10, Feigen herself found it very difficult to believe there could be a decent side to Effie's boss.

Agent Schuler soon finished his search of the files and moved to where Feigen and Effie were talking. "Miss Catlin, are you positive that all the registrations for that period of time are in that file?" he asked. "No place else one might be?"

"That's all there are," Effie said emphatically. "The man you're looking for just didn't stay at the Tennessee Bend."

"Who takes care of that filing?"

"I do. Every morning when I come in, I take all the registration forms that are finished and move them to that filing cabinet."

"What, exactly, do you mean by 'finished'?"

"I mean that the guests have checked out. The registrations stay over here as long as somebody's still in the motel. After they check out, they go over there," Effie said.

"Who checks people out, usually?"

"I do. I'm here early."

"And who checks them in? Who registers them to begin with?"

"It depends on what time they get here. If it's before I leave, I check them in. If they get here later, Barney checks them in."

"Miss Catlin," Agent Anton Schuler said, speaking very deliberately, "this is important. It is possible, is it not, that Guy Saillot could have registered at this motel after you left for the day and you never saw his registration form?"

Effie acted confused for a moment, but when she responded to Schuler's question her voice was firm. "Yes, sir, I'd have to say it is possible—but not likely. Barney leaves the registration forms for me to file, even if somebody comes in late and leaves real early. If that man had checked in, I would have filed his form."

Feigen could read the frustration on Agent Schuler's face. It was clear that he believed Guy Saillot had stayed at the Tennessee Bend. It was equally clear that, to this point, there was no firm evidence beyond the postcard Guy had sent home to his mother. Why, she wondered, wasn't that enough?

Effie Catlin looked past Feigen to someone coming up from behind. Feigen turned to see who it was, and George was already within reach. He touched her arm and motioned for her to follow, then started back toward the motel entrance. Feigen followed, and Agent Schuler came behind her.

Chapter 25

George walked fast and the two of them had to hurry to keep up. He took them through the parking area in front of Room 10 and on to the rose garden. He motioned for them to stop, then went to the middle of the garden and got down on hands and knees. While they watched, he rolled a small boulder to the side and began to dig at the spot where it had lain. He used his bare hands to scrape away a thick layer of pine straw and leaf mulch that covered the soil around the rose bushes. Soon he was digging into the moist earth, furiously, as if afraid something might happen before he was finished. After a minute or so of digging he lifted a bundle from the ground, stood and brought it to Feigen, held it out with both hands, his eyes pleading that she understand its importance. Schuler nodded that she should take it.

The bundle proved to be a square of red-checked oil cloth, wrapped around something flat. Feigen held it carefully while Schuler looked it over.

"Put it down and let's see what it is," he said.

She put the bundle on the ground. Agent Anton Schuler pulled a seemingly ever-present pair of white rubber surgical gloves from his pocket and worked them onto his large hands. He squatted and carefully began to fold back the edges of the oil cloth to reveal the contents.

"Can he talk at all?" Schuler asked, motioning toward George.

"I don't think so."

If George knew they were talking about him, he gave no indication. He stood by and watched anxiously while the FBI man opened the bundle. Feigen tried to read his face. His eyes showed emotion, but what was it? Anticipation, yes, but also fear. What had he brought to them?

"This is what we need," Agent Schuler said. "Look." He held out to her the first of two small green sheets. It was a registration form from the Tennessee Bend Motel. It showed that on August 25, 1955, Guy Saillot had checked in. There was no entry indicating that he had checked out.

Feigen's eyes filled with tears. "He was here, like he wrote on the postcard," she said quietly. "And somebody tried to conceal that fact." She turned to George. "Thank you, George, for what you did. That took a lot of courage."

This time the emotion in his eyes was clear. He was proud of what he'd done.

"And here's another one," Agent Schuler said. "This one will hit pretty close to home." It was a registration form, also. It was hers. "Whoever tried to get rid of his tried to get rid of yours," Schuler said. "Somebody wanted to erase any record of either of you ever having been here."

Still lying in the oil cloth, face down, was a spiral bound notebook, the kind commonly used by students. Schuler grasped the edges cautiously and turned it over. On the front cover was a neatly lettered label, "Guy Saillot—His Journal."

Schuler lifted it cautiously and began turning pages. "Good," he said. "He dated all his entries. This will help us establish a timeline."

"Will his mother get that at some point?" Feigen asked.

"At some point, yes. But not for a good while. It will be kept in the evidence collection as long as there's a need."

"It would be difficult for her, anyway, knowing this is the last thing Guy wrote."

Agent Schuler stopped turning pages and gingerly held the notebook open flat. "Here's where he left Baltimore, dated August twenty-fifth. He says he's looking forward to seeing Mark Kinder in Knoxville."

"But we know he never got there."

"Here. Dated August twenty-fifth, again. 'Ha ha ha ha. We signed in at this cheap motel and at midnight I had to call the manager because our toilet was stopped up. He wasn't too happy about it.

But here's the killer. He let us move from a really dump of a room to this beautiful, bright, clean room with all white walls—'"

Feigen gasped. "Room Ten! He was in Room Ten. You don't think there's any other room with all white walls, do you?"

"Let's see where this goes. Listen: 'Danny is such a lovely boy. When I saw him standing beside the road somewhere in Virginia, carrying his heavy backpack and his guitar he looked like a little lost lamb.' He picked up a hitchhiker! Could you make anything else out of that?"

"That could mean—"

Schuler finished the sentence for her: "That we've been missing a big piece of the puzzle. He says, 'I've never met anyone like Danny before. I'm both very happy and a little ashamed, dear journal. I'm happy because Danny is with me and ashamed because I never intended to be promiscuous. But Danny is so sweet and innocent and needy.' Are you sure you want to hear any more of this, Feigen?"

"I can take it," she said. "But this kind of personal stuff could be very embarrassing for Guy's family."

"None of it will be used in a trial, unless absolutely essential to the case. And I'm sorry, Miss Feigen, none of it will be released to the press."

Rachel Feigen flared. "Who the hell asked for it? I have no more interest in Guy Saillot's personal life than you do. I want to find him, and if that's his body out there in the woods I want to see whoever did that to him get what they deserve."

Agent Schuler held up a hand as a signal to stop, like a policeman directing traffic. "I'm sorry," he said. "I didn't mean that the way it came out. If I didn't know you well enough by now to know I can trust you with information we wouldn't be standing here having this conversation."

"Then we understand each other. Want to go on with Guy's journal?"

"Yes. 'Danny is in the shower right now. This was the first time either of us had ever had sex. He is so sweet and gentle. I know we will do it again when he comes out.' That's the end of this entry. Let's see what's on the next page. Okay, it's dated August twenty-sixth. 'Danny and I had lunch and dinner at a place called Big John's, which is better than it sounds. The food was actually very good. Danny eats like a Spartan. We came back and made love again. I could get to like this, I'm afraid.' That's the end of that entry."

Feigen shook her head. "I feel like a voyeur, myself," she said. "I have no business knowing this, Agent Schuler. I didn't want to know this."

For the first time since they'd met, Agent Anton Schuler actually seemed to sympathize. "Yes, I feel the same way. It isn't something I want to know. Would we feel different if it wasn't two men, though? I'm sorry, this just sounds vulgar to me."

"I know. And that's not fair. We knew Guy was homosexual."

"Yes, we did. I can't let it make any difference. Whether I like what he did in the Tennessee Bend Motel or not, he didn't deserve to be murdered. Sorry. We don't know for sure yet."

"But you don't have much doubt that that's Guy Saillot's body, do you?"

Agent Schuler sighed. "No, not really," he said, total resignation in his tone. "So let's finish up here and see where it takes us. He wrote on August twenty-seventh—hey, this is important. Listen to this. 'Danny left during the night. He slipped out while I slept. His backpack and his guitar are gone too. He said he could always get a ride and he wanted to get to Knoxville and on to the mountains. Dear God, I miss him so much already.' And that looks like the last thing he wrote."

Schuler was about to put the notebook down, but stopped short. "Look at this," he said, tilting it so that Feigen could see. A corner of a page had been torn off.

"I'll bet a month's salary this edge matches the scrap of paper found on the body," Schuler said. "That little note is on paper ripped from Guy Saillot's journal, and I think we'll find that it's in his hand-writing. The poor man knew what was coming and did his best to help us catch whoever he was afraid of."

"Yes," Feigen said, "and if the hitchhiker is out of the picture I think we know who that is."

Early in the afternoon, Barney Vidone was returned from Georgia and placed in the custody of Sheriff Asa Carter. The officers who brought him said he had been polite and cooperative. When one of the sheriff's deputies informed him that he was to be charged with murder, Barney smiled wanly and said, "Yes, I know." Nothing more.

The sheriff and Agent Charlie Monroe rejoined Anton Schuler at the Tennessee Bend Motel to try and tie up loose ends. They had no doubt that the body the children had stumbled over while hunting nuts up on the hickory bluffs was that of Guy Saillot. Autopsy results and reports from the state crime lab would be back tomorrow, Charlie Monroe said, and formal charges would be lodged against Barney Vidone.

Once all the evidence was in, he added, someone would decide whether to bring him to trial first on state charges—meaning the murder of Guy Saillot—or federal charges of kidnapping. Sooner or later he would face both.

There was still a lot of work to be done. The FBI men wanted no stones left unturned in building their case, determined to see Barney Vidone, Bishop Collins, and Harlan MacElroy all convicted of kidnapping. Sheriff Carter felt the same way about his murder case.

Recognizing that Barney couldn't have managed by himself to get Guy Saillot's body up to the hickory bluffs and drive his car into Cherokee Lake and then get home again, the sheriff guessed that either Bishop Collins or Harlan MacElroy, or perhaps both, also were involved. Harlan had been talking freely and Sheriff Carter was confident he'd break down and tell them everything they needed to know. Barney would be tried just down the road in the county courthouse by a jury of his peers. This meant local people, probably including people who knew Barney and viewed the world much like he did.

"I don't want this one to go to trial without being ironclad," Asa Carter said.

"Nine wise men said justice should proceed with deliberate speed," Charlie Monroe said. "Sometimes that means we should not rush things."

"I have mixed feelings about that," Agent Schuler said. "Personally, I won't rest until these slimy characters are put away. Yeah, I know, we'll move on to other things before that happens, but this case has left a vile taste in my mouth and it's going to take a long time to wash it out."

"That's the price we pay for the line of work we're in. My retirement can't get here soon enough."

"Come on, Charlie, you're going to miss it. You know you are."

"The only thing I'll miss," Charlie Monroe said, "is the opportunity to meet and work with charming people like Miss Feigen and Mister Skyles here. And, Miss Feigen, I truly regret what you have been through." He took her hand and held it, and looked her straight in the eyes. "You strike me as a strong young woman, though, and I'm confident you'll bounce back from this and keep on doing what you apparently do very well."

Sheriff Carter also shook Feigen's hand and said he was sorry, too. "But I'd rather we all leave here on a brighter note," he said. "Charlie, you've been here all this time and we haven't heard a Father Fletcher story yet. How do you explain that?"

"Just waiting for you to ask."

"Then I think it's high time we hear one."

"It would be my pleasure, Ace. But I believe that in honor of Miss Feigen I'll tell a Rabbi Rahm story, instead. Miss Feigen, with your permission."

"Please do," Feigen said.

Agent Charlie Monroe cleared his throat. "Well," he said, "it seems that Rabbi Rahm of Rochester takes a trip to Romania, and there he happens onto a rare Roman ruin. In the ruin he finds a ring with a radiant red ruby set in gold and readily realizes the risk of being found with the ring in Romania. So he rushes back to Rochester and, after some reflection, takes the radiant red ruby ring to Ray, the renowned jeweler, who raves over the ravishing ring and offers the rabbi a royal ransom in cash. But the rabbi recants his desire to sell the radiant red ruby ring and rapidly resolves to take it to Rhode Island and recklessly relinquish it to a ragtag home for ruined Rhode Island railroad workers. The moral? Rarely will a rabbi risk a rant from his reigning rabbinate for rewarding himself with riches."

Rachel Feigen laughed, hard. "How do you remember those?" she asked seriously.

"He doesn't. He makes them up on the spot," Sheriff Asa Carter said. "The man is simply a genius with words."

"I admire genius. And thank you for taking time to create a story for me. I'll never forget it."

Agent Charlie Monroe tipped the hat he wasn't wearing.

Bill Skyles scribbled a few last-minute notes. "And now, Miss Feigen," he said, "I suppose it's time for us to head back to Baltimore.

I'd be pleased to ride in your new Chevrolet."

"And I'd be pleased to have you, Mister Skyles."

They walked out of the Tennessee Bend Motel for the last time. The afternoon sun was scorching hot. There was no breeze. Across the narrow valley, beyond the highway, the wooded mountains looked like an oil painting on canvas, a picture too perfect to be real. Feigen paused and looked about. George's carefully tended roses still had the elegance of spring.

"Such a beautiful place for such ugly things to happen," she said. "I'll try, Bill, but I don't believe I can ever forget."

"I hope you can remember the beauty and forget the rest. We'd better get started."

"Yes," Feigen said, "it's a long trip."

Bill Skyles's blue eyes danced. "But it doesn't have to be boring," he said. "We can pass the time counting the 'Impeach Earl Warren' billboards."

As Rachel Feigen's gleaming new cream-colored Chevrolet moved down the sloped driveway toward the highway, George stood in the shadow of the Tennessee Bend Motel, in front of Room 10. He watched until the vehicle turned north and was almost out of sight, then raised his hand and waved in an humble gesture of farewell.

In a small corner bedroom on the second floor of the Saillot house in Baltimore, Marie Saillot sat stiffly on the edge of a bed and clutched a framed photograph to her breast. It was a picture of Guy. This was Guy's room.

The room was exactly as Guy left it that day when he threw together a few things for what was planned as a short trip to Tennessee. The closet door stood open. A pair of shoes, almost new, sat on the carpet at the foot of the bed. Had he planned to take them and forgot? Changed his mind? She would never know.

It was an austere room. Guy had never wanted lavish surroundings. The walls, although repainted three times over the years, still were the restrained brick red color Guy had chosen when the family first moved in. A front window looked down on a busy street. From a second window, on the side, he could see the tiny formal garden that had been his mother's pride. Guy had loved the garden almost as much as she did, especially the roses.

The room was awash in memories—recollections of her son in the stages of life: the young child who loved to bring friends home from school, the energetic boy who wanted to try everything, the teenager challenged by the burden of conflicting identities, the promising young musician, the serious student torn by uncertainty. How many nights had she tucked her baby into this bed? How many times had she sat alongside it through the night when he was sick, worrying, listening to every breath, praying that he'd be well come morning?

Mental images were supplanted by framed pictures of Guy at his high school graduation and Guy with his grandmother in La Havre which gazed back at her from atop a chest of drawers. The line of his jaw, the overhanging brow, those were from Alain. There was a hint of his grandmother's features, too, more subtle, hardly noticeable except when the two faces were side by side.

Lying on the dresser, as if casually cast aside to await proper handling in another season, was Guy's most recently completed journal. She would read it in good time. Today, tomorrow, next week, seeing his words would bring more pain than she could manage. One day she would read it, every word, because they were his words.

But life-stage markers and endless recollections, details of day-to-day existence captured in photographs or even written in his own words, these were not the story of Guy Saillot. The story of Guy Saillot was more complex, yet infinitely simple. Guy was her child, her flesh and blood, the center of her universe. His absence left her torn and empty in heart and mind. His absence was forever.

Marie Saillot studied her own image in the mirror over Guy's dresser. Guy's eyes were her eyes. But her eyes were red and swollen from shedding endless tears, and she would never again see in them the light that always burned in his—the light of excitement, joy, and anticipation, emotions lost to her forever. All prospect of happiness had been drained from her being.

She held Guy's photograph at arm's length. Tears streaming down her face, she began to sing, softly:

Au clair de la lune
Mon ami Pierrot
Prete-moi ta plume
Pour écrire un mot . . .

Bonus: *Equinox,* a short story by Robert Hays

Ebook published by Prairiescape Books,
an imprint of Herndon-Sugarman Press, Savoy, Illinois U.S.A.

Equinox

Trees on the south slope, which stretched away from the front of the house, were ice-coated from the cold overnight drizzle and glistened in the slanted rays of early morning sun as if decked in strands of diamonds. Essie surveyed the scene through the yellowed lace curtains of a living room window. She was grateful for the sunshine. Two weeks of gray and dreary weather had left her more despondent than usual.

Arthur had promised her brilliant winter days like this. He'd built the house on the north side of the valley after painstaking deliberation, calculating that the rewards of catching the January sun would outweigh the penalty of added heat in July and August. For insurance, he'd planted the fast-growing silver maple trees at carefully plotted locations to afford summer shade and, beyond these, the rugged catalpas in measured straight rows to line both sides of the narrow gravel lane that led up the hill from the main road. All this was a lifetime ago, and the trees were mature now—stately reminders of Arthur's intention that home should be a place of permanence.

The maple trees were among Essie's favorite heralds of spring. One day they would be gray and barren and then, virtually overnight, a delicate auburn fringe of buds commencing to burst into blossom would appear and signal a new awakening. And the catalpas called up memories of warm spring days when the children brought her bouquets—clusters of the trees' delicate white and brown flowers spilling over the edge of their water-glass vase. Before their ornamentation by the freezing drizzle, though, Arthur's trees had stood stark and skeletal, like stick figures on a child's slate, leaving her to worry that auburn fringes and clusters of catalpa flowers still lay in the distant future.

"I'm beginning to think spring will never come," she said softly, as if speaking to herself. She actually was addressing Plato, the devoted orange tabby cat who was well into his second decade as her constant companion.

Plato rose and stretched, then surrendered the spot of sunlight on the kitchen floor where he'd been sleeping and walked toward her. Half way there, he stopped and began to bathe. Essie laughed and waved a hand dismissively. "Go back to sleep," she said. "I'm sorry I disturbed you."

The living room window had become Essie's sanctuary. From here she could view the southern Illinois landscape Arthur had so loved, this land between the rivers: a giant wedge of beautiful wooded hill country bordered on the east by the Ohio and on the west by the Mississippi. And from here she could watch the changing of the seasons, the rhythmic cycles of winter dormancy and spring renewal most apparent in Arthur's trees. The seasons afforded markers for life's passing. At times she felt as though nature's changes were the only thing she had to look forward to.

This had not always been so. How many mornings had she stationed herself at this same window and watched anxiously for Arthur's homecoming? And how many times had she felt the immense relief that came with first sight of his tired old Ford pickup, followed inevitably by a sense of guilt as she waited mute and motionless while it turned off the main road and labored up the lane toward the house? Relief because she always knew, deep down, that one day he wouldn't come home, and guilt because Arthur always wanted her not to worry, always promised that he would take care of himself so that she'd never be left to face the world alone, and always insisted that God would see him through any dangers beyond mortal control.

Essie understood that Arthur's vow of well-being was more from concern for her than from honest conviction. Too many times she'd heard him speak with quiet reverence the names of places like Centralia or Herrin or West Frankfort—sites of mine disasters so terrible they were permanently engraved in the lore of this region that God had either blessed or cursed with deep, rich veins of coal.

Arthur was still alive on the dining room wall, in a sober Larry Gelman photograph taken at the end of a night shift one routine day at the mine. Arthur and eight others had just emerged from the mine shaft, stepping out of the cage at the pithead and squinting in the early morning sunlight, their faces smudged with coal dust. They reminded Essie of a troupe of amateur minstrels she'd seen performing in blackface at the little theatre on the town square when she was a girl.

The tragedy struck three weeks after the picture was taken.

Mr. Gelman had humbly presented framed prints to Essie and a half-dozen other new widows as his lasting memorial to the lost miners. She'd heard that the photograph had become famous, published in a national magazine or some such thing, though she never knew if that was true. All this, too, was years in the past, but sometimes the pain still cut like a sharp blade, as if it were new and fresh.

Coal miners' wives learn to live with constant dread as a matter of self-survival. Essie had always known that one of the dark tunnels could become Arthur's tomb. A cave-in, or a spark and explosion, and miners' lives would be snuffed out in the blink of an eye. She had hardened herself against this possibility as best she could. But she had not prepared herself for the finger-pointing and the uncertainties, and closure might have come more easily had it not been for all the lingering questions.

The worst part was the gossip. Because no one could be sure what actually took place hundreds of feet below the surface of the earth that day when the men died, rumors had floated like dust in the wind during the weeks that followed. Blanche Griglione had viciously proclaimed the disaster Arthur's fault. She blamed him for the loss of her Paulo because Arthur had been the crew leader. Arthur surely must have led the men in the wrong direction after the initial explosion, Blanche said, so they were victims of the afterdamp and helpless to escape the subsequent blasts.

Essie felt guilty because she could not prove Blanche wrong. She wanted to fight back and not allow Arthur's good name to be smeared by Blanche's indictment. Arthur was an experienced miner. His men trusted him. He never would have made that kind of mistake. But she had no evidence with which to answer the gossip Blanche had ignited.

The accusations were even more hurtful because Blanche had been Essie's best friend. From that day forward, neither had spoken to the other.

For her own part, Essie had lain awake night after night wondering what really happened. Only in recent years had she finally resigned herself to living the rest of her life without knowing the truth, beyond the fact that Arthur was gone.

Not that life with Arthur had been perfect. Arthur had his faults. He was human, after all, and on occasion did things for which he was sorry. Yet the shame was hers, because she always assumed that her failings as a wife had somehow brought out her husband's darker side.

And she had not been left to face the world alone. There were the children: Marybeth, their firstborn, who had become the most precious treasure in Arthur's whole universe, and Daniel, man-child from the moment he drew his first breath and bedrock of strength and support for his mother at a time when there was little else to cling to. And the grandchildren. Her home had once been filled by people she loved who loved her back.

Essie—her real name was Esme, but she considered that pretentious—understood as well as anyone that her existence could have been much more difficult. She had been fortunate to have friends and family and she had been able to manage financially thanks to the union's contract with Morgan Coal Company.

But like most positives in her life, these had been severely eroded over the passing years. Arthur's life insurance money was exhausted before the children finished school and, with rising costs, the mining company's once-generous widow's pension had been barely enough to survive on for some time now. Most of her friends and family had scattered and disappeared like dry leaves in the sweeping gales of November. Even the grandchildren were grown and gone, so that Arthur's permanent home had long since quieted from the crying and laughter and incoherent babble of innocent and sweet young voices. No sounds, no smells, no sights or touch of other humans. Plato was the only other living being in her house for days at a time.

Essie's principal contact with the outside world was Roland Quidry, the letter carrier who drove his Jeep up the lane every day except Sunday and left her mail in a box fixed securely to a cedar post Arthur had set deep in the ground. Daniel had replaced the original mailbox a decade or more ago, and now the new box had rusted and the hinged lid squeaked when it was pulled open, but it was more than adequate for such meager deposits as Essie could expect. She often sat on the shaded porch on summer days and awaited the mailman's coming. If he was on schedule, or at the very least not running late, he'd sometimes stop and visit and express his concern for her welfare. During the cold winter months he would watch for Essie's appearance at a window then she'd wave and he would wave back and her connection with the rest of the world would be complete for another day.

As she sat and thought about the ways her life had changed, Plato brushed against Essie's legs and gave her a stout head-butt. This most gentle of creatures wanted and expected her to notice his presence and let him know she cared that he was there, that she received and accepted his love. And feed him, of course, when he was hungry. Essie considered this a small price to pay for his companionship.

"Oh, I'm sorry, Mr. Magnificent," she said. "Your breakfast is long overdue. You're going to lose patience with me one of these days and I can't blame you."

Plato continued to rub against her legs as she stood. She might have tripped over him making her way to the cupboard, but she knew his motion and he knew hers. They had shared close space for years and learned to step almost as one as they went about the house. When Essie moved, Plato was nearly certain to move alongside.

"You're always under foot," she complained good naturedly. "One of these days I'm going to step on your tail." Even if he didn't understand her words, Essie believed, the cat recognized her moods. He was made contented by her talk. He rubbed against her legs some more and purred.

She opened a can of his favorite food and spooned half of it into his bowl. She put the rest in a red plastic container which she covered carefully and placed on a top shelf in the refrigerator. After that, with Plato's immediate needs taken care of, she resumed her watch at the window.

Down by the main road, a lone coyote hurried through the frozen grass, watching carefully for any small game that might make a meal. A red-tailed hawk flew circles high above it.

The sun warmed the bare limbs of the trees and the ice began to fall away, first in little nuggets and then in long, shimmering ribbons which shattered into hundreds of pieces when they hit the ground. Some of the remaining seed pods on the catalpa trees dropped with the ice. Across the valley, Essie saw a bright reflection from the metal roof of Albert Johnson's barn as it finally caught a full share of the sun's rays. Come spring, the hills beyond the Johnson place would be blanketed with redbud and dogwood trees that bloomed beneath the canopies of the tall oaks and hickories before they came into leaf and concealed what lay below. She longed for that season, longed for the fringes to appear on Arthur's maple trees.

Essie sat and watched the interplay of sunlight and shadow until midday. She took little satisfaction in such change as she witnessed, the ice-covered world beyond her living room window no brighter once the sun had melted the ice away. The appeal of the scene before her faded with the morning hours, like a movie she'd seen too many times before. Would the bleakness of February ever run its course?

Plato was hungry again. Essie tended to his needs and fixed a sandwich for herself and made fresh coffee and sat at the small kitchen table with Plato at her feet and tried to remember other long winters. There was that terrible January blizzard. Arthur couldn't get through the blowing and drifting snow and stayed at the mine for four days and nights while she was home with the kids and running out of food for the table. But southern Illinois winters were seldom as severe as that and she couldn't think of any others that were particularly hard.

"This hasn't been too bad a winter, it just seems so long," Essie said. Plato paid her no heed.

"If you'd been here in that blizzard you might have learned to be less particular about your food. A few table scraps would have looked pretty good."

Plato looked up at her as if he understood and if she was talking about food maybe he ought to listen. He stood and yawned and came over to where she sat and threw a shoulder into her leg and curled his tail around it the way he did when he wanted to demonstrate his comfort with their togetherness. This is what Essie supposed, anyway.

"When Arthur finally got home, he brought in a big sack of potatoes and some canned goods," she went on. "He wasn't sure when he'd be able to get out again. I know, we didn't have you yet. And I'm glad you didn't have to go through that January. But I do wish you'd known Arthur. He was a good man and you would have liked him. Arthur was the only man I ever loved."

Much to her own surprise and to Plato's obvious puzzlement, Essie suddenly began to weep. She stemmed the flow of tears with a napkin and used it to wipe her nose. Plato watched with an air of honest concern.

"I'm all right," Essie assured him. "But you're such a sweetheart to worry about me. It's just that sometimes when I talk about Arthur . . ."

Plato still looked to be unsure. Essie leaned down and stroked the back of his head. "You wouldn't believe it to see me now," she said, "but I could have been right popular with the young men if Arthur hadn't come along when he did. I was only eighteen. Maybe I should tell you sometime about Mr. Pratt."

In truth, at the time she met Arthur Essie had never had a boyfriend, had rarely been alone with a man who wasn't family. She had been through the emotional turmoil of girlish attraction, though, first with a high school history teacher and later with a man who worked at the post office. She assumed this was love. Her fascination with the history teacher went away during summer vacation. The man at the post office, whose name was Marion Pratt, posed a bigger challenge.

"Mr. Pratt was a good bit older than me and still lived with his mother," Essie said, choosing to go ahead and share the story with Plato now. "I'd seen him around town for years when I was a little girl and never noticed anything special about him. But one day I stopped to pick up the mail for my papa and Mr. Pratt looked at me in a way no man ever had before. It was in the spring, just after I turned sixteen."

Essie did not need to stop and think about that day before going on with her story. She remembered it well. All the way home, she had considered the expression on Mr. Pratt's face. She worried that she had blushed visibly under his gaze, but Marion Pratt had blushed too, and quickly looked away. That night before bed, she'd studied herself in the mirror, hoping to see herself the way Mr. Pratt had, and she was surprised by what she saw. She was developing into a woman. And she was pretty. Still, she might be imagining things about Mr. Pratt that weren't true. She decided to stop by the post office again tomorrow and see what happened.

"All I knew about men was what Aunt Lornie had told me," Essie said, carrying on her one-way conversation with the cat. "Aunt Lornie loved to dress up and go dancing and it seemed like there was always lots of men who wanted to take her. My mother—Aunt Lornie was her younger sister—my mother didn't approve of the way she behaved but I thought she was real cool, as the young people used to say."

Aunt Lornie had been Essie's favorite among all her blood relatives. She'd often talked to her young niece about men, telling about her own experiences, and her message in general was that men weren't much good.

"I wanted to talk to her about Mr. Pratt," Essie went on. "At least give her a hint that a man had found me attractive. But Aunt Lornie was away at the time, traveling in Florida, I think. I couldn't talk to Mama about such a thing so I was pretty much on my own."

Essie thought back to her visit to the post office after school the next day. She'd pretended to look at the patriotic posters on the bulletin board and tried to watch Mr. Pratt, busy waiting on customers at the service window, out of a corner of her eye. He was watching her, too, and hard as she tried not to she began to blush. She felt the heat creeping up her neck and into her cheeks and wanted to turn and run but Mr. Pratt finished with the last person in line and called her to the window. She stepped forward with a quarter in her hand and asked for two stamps. Mr. Pratt carefully separated two stamps from a full sheet and slid them across the counter.

"Here you go," he said. "And happy equinox. It's nice to have more sunshine. Spring's here for sure."

He took her quarter and made change, counting the last pennies carefully into her hand. His fingertips touched her palm and Essie had goose bumps on her arm. She felt as if Mr. Pratt could see right through the flesh and bone that covered her brain and read her girlish thoughts. How foolish she must look. Surely he would laugh.

But Mr. Pratt hadn't laughed at her then, nor at any other time. He kept on looking at her in that way that made her feel like her blood was rushing through her veins and causing the back of her neck to tingle. Essie never mentioned her attraction to him to Aunt Lornie or anyone else. But for years to come she still had seen Mr. Pratt in a way that was unlike her view of other men.

Essie told Plato, "I stopped by the library on the way home and looked up 'equinox' in the dictionary. I'd never heard of it before. I thought Mr. Pratt must have been awful smart. I'm embarrassed to say that for a long while I made up reasons to go to the post office almost every day. And Mr. Pratt always noticed me."

It was late afternoon when Essie heard the unmistakable sound of Roland Quidry's Jeep approaching the house. She went to the window and waved when he stopped at her mailbox and he waved back and in a minute he was gone. A heavy cloud cover had obscured the sun and the day had turned dark and depressing again.

"I think the mail will have to wait," Essie said. "I doubt there's anything out there worth risking a fall on the ice for." She spoke in the general direction of Plato, who lay sprawled on his back in his favorite living room chair sleeping soundly.

Essie went to the kitchen to check his water dish. She took the dish to the sink and rinsed it clean and refilled it. She filled it too full. Water spilled as she carried it back to its usual spot at the end of the kitchen cabinets and left a wet trail across the floor. Angry with herself, she flung the dish across the room, into the sink, with a loud clatter of breaking china. Plato jumped down from his chair and ran behind a couch.

Essie clasped her hands to the sides of her head.

"What's wrong with me?" she said plaintively. "I'm sorry, Plato—come on out, you know I won't hurt you. I'm sorry for being so silly. I'm just not myself today."

She went to the hall closet and dug into a loose mound of linens. There had been a time when she kept the closet neatly organized, with towels and washcloths precisely arranged by color and size and carefully lined up in tidy stacks separate from the sheets and pillow cases, but she no longer bothered with such effort. She picked the towel with the thickest pile. It had a slight musty odor, but it would be fine for cleaning up the mess she'd made.

Back in the kitchen, Essie got down on hands and knees and began to blot up the water. She made wide circles with the towel in hopes that she was cleaning the floor in the process. She and Plato would be the only ones to know whether the floor was scrubbed or not. She threw the towel, now wet and dirty, into a laundry basket in the bathroom.

Plato gave up his safe hiding place and approached the kitchen warily. Essie scooped him up in her arms and hugged him to her and tried to reassure him.

"I'm sorry, kitty, you know I am," she said softly. "It's like I've been in a gray mood, like the weather. Forgive me for being an old grouch, okay? I'll make some supper and we'll both feel better."

She opened a can of chicken noodle soup—the concentrated kind, that needed water to be added—and let it simmer on the stove for several minutes while she got Plato's food and set a place for herself at the table. Plato had regained his composure with her stroking, and his appetite as well. He was nearly finished eating before Essie had ladled herself a bowl of soup and sat down to begin. She wasn't hungry. She ate only about half the soup and dumped the rest down the drain of the kitchen sink.

The house was cold. Arthur had built it strong so that it would last, but it was not well insulated and the old furnace was not efficient. Essie got ready for bed early. She pulled an extra comforter from the closet and laid it across the foot of the bed. Plato would snuggle down beside her and help keep her warm.

As she did every night, Essie said a brief prayer as soon as she was settled under the covers. She believed in God and heaven and took comfort in the notion that Arthur awaited her in eternity. She didn't pretend to know whether they would be together in physical form, as they had been here on earth, or simply meet again in spirit, and if she asked too many questions of herself her faith was harder to sustain—especially now that she no longer went to church.

She'd once found her church to be a place of comfort, a place where her faith was strengthened and she could enjoy the companionship of friends. These friends included Blanche Griglione. And of course there were the hypocrites—people who said the right things to Essie's face after the disaster at the mine and pretended to sympathize over the loss of Arthur but later whispered behind her back, spreading Blanche's nasty rumors. A few weeks after the tragedy she'd vowed never to set foot in the church again.

Arthur had never been a religious man. Even though he professed faith that God would protect him down in the mine, he hadn't been inside a church since their wedding.

Essie prayed for her grandson Cody, serving time in a Missouri prison for making and selling something illegal. She could not remember what it was. Cody was Daniel's child and bore a striking resemblance to Arthur. He'd been only eighteen when he was sentenced to two years, and as far as Essie knew the first year had passed without incident.

Cody had always been something of an enigma. Daniel said his son simply marched to the beat of his own drummer, but Rachel, Cody's mother, was less generous. She'd labeled Cody a problem child from the time he was ten years old and had pretty nearly given up on him by the time he reached his teens.

So far as Essie was concerned, she loved all her grandchildren equally and she had been careful not to interfere. She and Arthur had raised Daniel and Marybeth to be good parents. Anyway, times had changed and who knew anymore what to expect of children? "Kids today are different," Arthur had observed many years past, "and there's just too many ways they can get in trouble." Essie had always relied on Arthur's point-of-view; she supposed things were even worse today.

Her thoughts were interrupted by Plato's loud snoring. She shifted her position so that he moved and the snoring stopped.

"You're even noisier to sleep with than Arthur was," she told him, and stroked his back until he was soundly asleep again.

Still worrying about Cody, she wondered how Arthur would have dealt with this troubled grandson. Arthur had been overly stern with Daniel and tolerant to a fault with Marybeth, never willing to admit to his double standard. There were times when this may have been appropriate, as Daniel was always challenging and rebellious while his older sister was a constant model of good conduct. But Essie had seen how their father's attitude was reflected in the children's behavior. She'd become protective of Daniel and come to resent sharply what she saw as Arthur's outright mistreatment of their son. Arthur, she decided, would have been too hard on Cody.

Arthur's firmness had been his greatest failing, and yet it was his sturdiness Essie missed most of all—the sense that his strong arms would protect her from the terrors of the world. She missed him physically. Purposely overlooking the dreadful nights of abuse, she imagined him lying in bed at her side. The bad nights were infrequent, after all, and not the true measure of this man. It was only when he stopped at the tavern after work, when he had too much to drink and came home angry and demanding, when he wanted things Essie couldn't offer, it was only then that he was ugly and cruel, only on these long nights that she suffered his impossible physical ultimatums and verbal insults and cowered in the darkness concerned for her safety. She supposed all men were that way and counted her blessings that Arthur's anger rarely had led him to strike her. Remembering the good Arthur, she finally drifted into restless sleep.

Dreams come quickly. Essie is in a pitch-black tunnel, struggling for breath in the foul air, surrounded by silence. Then Arthur is beside her. He takes her hand. "I'm a good miner," he says. "I'll lead you out." His safety lamp lights the way. There is a crosscut and to one side of it an airshaft and they are in the sunshine and she lies on the fragrant grass and revels in the beauty of the trees and flowers and a vibrant cloudless sky. He comes to her. But it is Mr. Pratt, not Arthur, who makes love to her and comforts her and brings ease to her tense body.

Essie was in a deep slumber when Plato woke her, hungry and impatient. She felt as though she'd been asleep for no more than a couple of hours, but sunlight saturated the room and she knew it was late.

She got out of bed and stepped into warm slippers. She trudged to the kitchen, where she fed the ravenous cat and commenced to brew herself strong coffee. Plato's appetite was satisfied after a second serving. He curled against her feet as she sat at the table and sipped her coffee, gazing up with an expression of love and appreciation that brought the first crack to the glum mask behind which she'd begun the new day. Essie smiled and Plato purred and made apparent his contentment.

"It's just you and me, Plato, and another winter day," she said.

Essie finished her coffee. Plato was alert, waiting for her next move. She put on a coat and told him, "We'd best get yesterday's mail. Surely the ice is all gone now."

Plato was at her heels as she carefully stepped off the porch and made her way to the mailbox. The metal box was cold to her touch, but not frozen shut as she'd feared, and she took from it a couple of slender envelopes that obviously were not important and turned back toward the house.

Plato had wandered off to one side. He suddenly stopped and sat, as if on guard.

"Come on," Essie said. "It's still too cold for you to play outside."

Plato didn't move.

Essie started to walk ahead, but Plato struck a familiar attitude that meant he wanted her to come. A few steps closer and she saw why. He proudly stood watch over a tiny yellow flower, barely visible among the frozen blades of grass. He looked first at the flower and then at Essie, as if determined for her see.

She stooped and pinched off the tender stem, separating the bloom from the frozen ground. Plato beamed with pleasure.

"Oh, my," she said, studying the delicate blossom in her palm, "the first crocus. Such a pretty little thing to come right through the cold and ice like that."

The cat stood and stretched, arching his back and digging first his front claws and then the back into the frozen turf. Then he rewarded her with a firm shoulder-block and stood purring at her feet.

"You just weren't going to let me miss it, were you!" she said. This was not a question, but a declaration of praise. "I've been so cross, maybe you knew how much I needed a sign of spring."

And surely that's what the hardy little crocuses were—a sign of spring. They were here every year, popping up as if from nowhere, perennial reminders that winter wouldn't last forever. The equinox would come. Balance. Nature's routine, the promise of long days of sunshine to warm the earth. Just like Mr. Pratt had told her. How could she have doubted? It wasn't the seasons that were at fault, but her own impatience. Hadn't she inhabited her little space on earth long enough to know better? Didn't spring always follow winter? And had she not survived the cheerless days of January by looking forward to April?

Essie's outlook brightened. Before we know it, she thought, the maple trees will be showing their red fringe and the weigela and mock orange will be coming into bloom. And we'll be back at work in the garden.

Her senses jumped ahead. It was as if she could feel the soil, warm and moist in her fingers, as she thinned the lily beds to make them more productive. The pink clematis on the backyard trellis had stood the coldest weather well and should bloom in profusion, and in her mind's eye she saw the waves of daisies that would transform the south slope into a sea of white. Nearer the house, the purple coneflowers and black-eyed Susans would brighten their surroundings and she could almost smell the clumps of watermelon-red monarda and hear the hum of the honeybees drawn to the succulent flowers.

Now she felt almost giddy.

"I'd like more trumpet vine on the fence," she said aloud, "and this year I think I'll try a planting of meadowsweet. Yes, I will! Who cares if it's just you and me, Mr. Magnificent? The equinox is right around the corner and we're going to be all right."

Plato rubbed against her legs, then led her home.

About The Author

Robert Hays has been a newspaper reporter, magazine editor. public relations writer, and university professor and administrator. A native of Illinois, he taught in Texas and Missouri and retired in 2008 from a long journalism teaching career at the University of Illinois. He has spent a great deal of time in South Carolina, the home state of his wife, Mary, and was a member of the South Carolina Writers Workshop. His publications include academic journal and popular periodical articles and ten books, including his collaborative work with General Oscar Koch, *G-2: Intelligence for Patton*, and one published in paperback edition under a different title. Robert and Mary live in Champaign, Illinois. They have two sons and a grandson and an extraordinarily handsome and intelligent orange tabby cat named Eddie.

More Books by Robert Hays

Fiction:

The Baby River Angel

The Life and Death of Lizzie Morris

Circles in the Water

Early Stories from the Land (editor)

Nonfiction:

Patton's Oracle

Editorializing 'The Indian Problem'

A Race at Bay

State Science in Illinois

G-2: Intelligence for Patton (with Gen. Oscar Koch)

Country Editor